LEAVING SHADES

A touching saga set in 1920s Cornwall

After a tragic miscarriage, Beth Tresaile returns to Owles House, the place of her miserable childhood, accompanied by her best friend, Kitty Copeland. Beth feels she can no longer go on unless she gets revenge on her estranged mother, Christina, who neglected her and finally abandoned her on a cold winter's night. But there are many shocks (and joys) in store for Beth, as she learns the truth of the past, and there are fresh troubles on the horizon when her married lover, Kitty's brother, wants her back...

Recent Titles by Gloria Cook
from Severn House

The Meryen Series

KEEPING ECHOES
OUT OF SHADOWS
ALL IN A DAY
HOLDING THE LIGHT
DREAM CHASERS

The Harvey Family Series

TOUCH THE SILENCE
MOMENTS OF TIME
FROM A DISTANCE
NEVER JUST A MEMORY
A STRANGER LIGHT
A WHISPER OF LIFE

The Pengarron Series

PENGARRON DYNASTY
PENGARRON RIVALRY

LISTENING TO THE QUIET

LEAVING SHADES

Gloria Cook

Severn House Large Print
London & New York

This first large print edition published 2011
in Great Britain and the USA by
SEVERN HOUSE PUBLISHERS LTD of
9-15 High Street, Sutton, Surrey, SM1 1DF.
First world regular print edition published 2010 by
Severn House Publishers Ltd., London and New York.

British Library Cataloguing in Publication Data

Cook, Gloria.
  Leaving shades.
  1. Mothers and daughters--England--Cornwall (County)--
  Fiction. 2. Family secrets--Fiction. 3. Cornwall (England
  : County)--Social conditions--20th century--Fiction.
  4. Large type books.
  I. Title
  823.9'14-dc22

  ISBN-13: 978-0-7278-7994-3

Severn House Publishers support The Forest Stewardship Council
[FSC], the leading international forest certification organisation. All
our titles that are printed on Greenpeace-approved FSC-certified paper
carry the FSC logo.

MIX
Paper from
responsible sources
FSC
www.fsc.org   FSC® C018575

Printed and bound in Great Britain by the
MPG Books Group, Bodmin, Cornwall.

One

What magic was this? This was not how she remembered it all those years ago, the house and gardens, and the view down to the cliffs and the sea beyond. To her seven-year-old mind it had been always bleak and lonely, sinister even. How could it all now be breathtakingly clear, enticing, an enchanting multiplicity of colours? The magic at work today was an insidious magic, for what other explanation could there be for the banishment of all the cold creeping shadows she had known before? Even on a day as it was now, gloriously hot and in the height of summer, the smallest thing about her old home and its surroundings had seemed cold and disturbing and full of threat.

Beth Tresaile did not want to find Owles House and the waters out in the bay to be an artful seduction of optimism and beauty. The waters, once inky and ominous to her, were a sun-sparkled and inviting greeny-blue, busy with bobbing pleasure boats, a few hardy fishing boats, yachts flaunting gaily coloured sails, and a distant ship or two. The taste of the tangy salt of the sea was on Beth's tongue. She found herself breathing in the evocative scents of the

5

newly mown lawn, of lavender and roses and dozens of other superbly healthy blooms. She was aware of the distant timeless wash of the cresting waves, and the gentle mesmerizing buzzing of insects close by. Altogether it was a dreadful beguiling harmony.

It *should* not be like this! Not now, throwing the purpose of her return into confusion!

She snapped her eyes shut, refusing to be drawn in or to listen to the peaceful sounds. It was foolish to have come back here. To this quiet place. This hated place. But she had really had no choice, for no longer was she able to ignore the memories of what had happened to her here. Memories that haunted her and refused to let her go. So here she was. Unannounced. With a mission. To seek the answers and explanations she deserved. And needed. And would demand. After fifteen years of absence she had returned to her mother's house. To find out why, with such cold indifference, her mother had neglected her and then rejected her.

Chillingly, her self-righteous anger did not count as protection while she was this close to her past and the confrontation she was seeking. In squalid murky glimpses, her mind replayed old frights and anxieties. Her stomach felt it was being dragged down into a bottomless pit and she could hardly swallow past the lump rising in her throat. Another moment and something huge and sinister from her nightmares might come and swallow her up and wipe out

6

the remains of her carefully assembled confidence.

'I don't think I can do think this, Kitty.' Beth kept one hand on the open door of her Ford Sedan – her link to the more comfortable present, her source of indignant withdrawal. Now it might become a hasty retreat.

Kitty got out of the passenger seat and was there beside her. 'You've come a long way, Beth, literally and emotionally. It's what you wanted, remember?'

'I know, but I was wrong.'

'I understand. Yet it's so important to you. Wouldn't it be a pity to leave now?'

'To run away, you mean?'

'It's what you'd be doing, don't you think?'

Beth sighed. 'Yes, you're right.' She squeezed Kitty's arm, thankful for her far-reaching advice, for being such a good friend. Kitty always gave support of exactly the right kind, at just the right moment. They were so in sync that strangers might mistake them for sisters. Both were poised with perfect posture. Both wore fashionable knee-length, tubular, drop-waist, cap-sleeved dresses and cloche-style straw sun hats. Both were good looking, although Kitty was outstandingly so with a graceful long neck, and a gleaming Titian fringe on show and soft waves that caressed her cheeks. Beth's hidden hair was bobbed and the soft colour of butterscotch.

Dredging up her lost determination, Beth's Louis-heeled shoes crunched over the gravelled drive, formerly a small carriageway, until she stopped at the bottom of the three wide stone steps leading up to the front door of Owles House. The house was square and two storeys high. Its wisteria-clad walls were in perfect symmetry and today they seemed to go on and on up into the storybook-blue sky. The outside of the house, like the gardens, had always been kept in perfect order. The same could not be said about the interior.

'I don't suppose you remember much about the house,' Kitty said, beside her.

'Actually I do, even though I've tried to forget all about it. My private tutor, Miss Muriel Oakley – the spinster daughter of the parish vicar – talked about it a lot. Owles House had gone through some colourful history. It's mid-Georgian, originally built for the captain of a packet ship, who was supposedly a shrewd smuggler. My father, when he wasn't staying away for days at a time, worked the local tradesmen hard into keeping everything up to scratch. I had it drummed into me that everything had to be left exactly how I found it. I expect there's some good stuff inside. I'll say one thing for...' She could not bring herself to say 'my mother'. 'For, um, Christina. She always had good taste in fine art.' Good taste that had all too often been reduced to a mess of wall-to-wall smashed ornaments. Christina had quickly replaced them with more of the same – suitable antiques.

Beth glanced back at the motor car. Before

8

today the vehicle she had usually alighted from was the vicarage pony and trap. Miss Oakley, a plain, jolly type, always smelling nicely of roses, had collected and driven her home from her exclusive lessons. On winter days the daily excursion had been freezing cold and bleak. The vicar's lady – very much in the mould of old Queen Victoria, from the pictures Beth had seen of her late Majesty – never spoke to Beth or even looked at her. If she encountered Miss Oakley with her solitary pupil, Mrs Oakley would refer to Beth as 'that child'. Beth had come to bitterly resent what she saw as being treated like an urchin by the 'bogus queen'. In later years Beth surmised that financial necessity in the vicarage had led to Miss Oakley's genteel employment as tutor to the richest child in the area. Beth had tried to forget Muriel Oakley; ebullient she might have been, but the stooped, thin woman's persona was also cloaked by an unfathomable bareness.

At the end of each school day her mother had not been waiting at the door to take her little leather satchel and ask her how her day had been. There had been no hugs, no treats and no promises, nothing tasty for tea. And after a while, there had been no Daddy finally returning home and no mention of him. He had deserted his family. Beth had learned a few years afterwards that Philip Tresaile, known as Phil, had been killed in the Great War. Beth had been denied her daddy for much of the vital years of her young life, and it was all Chris-

9

tina's fault, according to Grandma. Dear, wonderful Grandma, who had willingly taken over the task of raising her. And now Grandma was dead too.

Marion Frobisher had been Beth's maternal grandmother. 'I'm sorry to say, darling Beth, I have no time for your mother, my daughter, my only child,' was Grandma's oft sadly related remark. 'Not after all she's put you through. Running off for days untold, drinking herself to kingdom come, and finally ending up in a ditch for God only knows how long, then having to be thrown into the madhouse because she didn't even know her own name. What kind of mother was that? A rotten, self-serving one is all I can say. She was a bad mother and a bad wife. When I think of how she treated your poor father – it was no wonder he was rarely at home. Well, you're better off now with me. I'll take the greatest care of you and we'll have lots of fun.'

Marion Frobisher had been true to her word. The rest of Beth's childhood had been filled with the best of pleasures. She had been given lavish birthday parties, outings, visits to pantomimes and the theatre and holidays abroad, a lot of them joined in by Kitty; and there had been wonderful stays at Kitty's house. Yet Beth had suffered terrible nightmares and as time went on she had probed her grandmother about why Christina had treated her so badly.

Marion Frobisher had taken off her glasses and clasped Beth's hands before growing very

10

still. 'Christina was born difficult and wayward. I swear your poor grandfather died young worrying about her. Soon after he died I took Christina down to Cornwall to help us both come to terms with the grief. We stayed at a hotel near Mevagissey and took the usual day trips to other parts of the coast. The minute we got to Portcowl she caused me even more trouble and heartbreak, not to mention the shame of it. It was there she met your father. He wasn't in our league – his father owned a public house – but I found Phil to be quite charming. Christina was immediately smitten with him. I fretted about it because she was only sixteen, but I thought if I kept an eye on her then a brief harmless holiday romance might shake her out of her surly disrespectful ways.

'But, of course, that wasn't enough for her. She sneaked out to meet Phil as soon as I had retired for the night. She also flirted with Phil's younger brother, Kenneth. It ended with a violent fist fight. Kenneth's arm was broken. It caused a lifelong rift between the brothers. The parents saw Christina as nothing but trouble and they took Kenneth's side against Phil's. That was why you were never allowed to mix with your other grandparents and your cousins down in the cove and why they never came up to Owles House.

'I was so ashamed but there was more to bear. Christina became pregnant. I had no choice but to give her the money to get married. She insisted on living at Portcowl. I knew her reason

11

was to get far away from me, and her home here in Wiltshire. Your grandfather had left her a sizeable trust fund, and I agreed to let her have access to it to buy Owles House. Phil swore to me that he'd make her a loyal husband and be a good provider. I believe he tried his best but whatever he did was never good enough for Christina. He took a job in insurance. I was proud of him for that. But he often had to stay away from home and that didn't suit your mother. She turned to drink. Why, I could never understand. She had a beautiful home, some standing in the local community despite her fall from grace – the vicar's daughter tried very hard with her – and she had you, darling Beth, the sweetest little girl a mother could ever wish for. Well, your father put up with her rages and her accusations that he was unfaithful to her while he was away until he could bear it no longer. I believe he went off a broken man. I thank God every day that you didn't have to endure your mother and her wicked ways throughout all your childhood.'

I have more family in this area and I don't even know what they look like, Beth thought. There was no point thinking about them. They wouldn't want to know her any more than they did her father.

'I wonder if there's a dog here?' Kitty broke the silence – Beth had stood silent and rigid for too long. 'See over there, beside the summer house? There's a ball and things.'

'There might be. I've told you about the dog I

12

had for company when I lived here.' There had been Cleo, a gentle-looking German Shepherd. Beth had received much-needed affection and warmth from Cleo. If there was a dog here now, and if it was anything like Cleo had been, it would have barked on their arrival, so either it was old and deaf, or it was out somewhere with Christina.

Although the house appeared to be empty Beth found herself praying that Christina was not at home. No, it would be better if she were. It was best to get this over and done with. To begin the process of laying the old ghosts and banishing the demons, which had become so important to her. Over and done with? Yet this could be the beginning of something even more painful. And what if Christina was inside, hiding away from her unexpected visitors? Christina had been expert at hiding away from people, from life, from her responsibilities.

Beth took a couple of steps closer to her old home. A decade and a half had passed since she was last inside Owles House. She had shut out so many terrible memories. What might she re-member? What would her mind dredge up from the past? Nothing too devastating, she hoped with all her heart.

Of course, it was too much to hope for. She had been a bright child, had absorbed every-thing. She had retained it within her subcon-scious, from where it rose at will to taunt her. She had not forgotten, and never would, the raised voices, the violent voices. Or forgotten

13

the swearing, the demands and accusations from both her parents' voices. She had not forgotten the slamming of doors and breaking of glass, or her mother's crying and sobbing and beating of fists against pillows and walls. Or the screaming – how her mother had screamed. Even now Beth couldn't bear to hear the same sort of pandemonium, the same sort of hysteria. And there had been the horrible noises of her mother retching and being sick in the bathroom. The last time Beth had peeped nervously in there the floor had been littered with splinters of glass and broken tiles, the air choked with talcum powder and reeking of spilled cosmetics.

Why was she risking the measure of peace of mind she had worked so hard to attain by coming back here? From dining table conversations between Kitty's older brother Stuart and his university peers that Beth had listened in to, she had gathered that psychiatrists would produce some long name for the sort of thing that haunted her mind and tormented her soul. Such an expert would explain her needs to her after several sessions. Well, she didn't need any sort of counsellor. There had been Grandma. She had lived with Grandma from the age of seven, after the authorities had contacted her. Grandma had been her source of comfort and wisdom. And from the day of starting at her new school up in Wiltshire there had been Kitty, who was full of compassion, energy and fun and who understood her completely. It was why Beth,

14

who had first thought to come alone to Owles House and face her mother, had gratefully accepted Kitty's offer to join her.

Beth mounted the steps. Those three steps had seemed so steep to her young legs but were nothing now to her slender limbs. The steps peaked on to a terrace that carried on round each side of the house. Beth stared at the front door of ancient solid mahogany, with its heavy, highly polished brass knocker that even now figured prominently in her nightmares.

'Are you all right, Beth?' Kitty was worried her friend might crumble and run away, unable to face the begetter of her troubles now she was only a breath away. She was afraid to see Beth shattered once again, but now it would be so much worse. Kitty was ready to align herself to be Beth's strength, to be her last bit of resolve. She pressed a reassuring hand on her shoulder. 'Don't stop now. I'm right beside you.'

Gulping down the sick feeling in her throat, shaking from head to foot, Beth whispered, 'I've done this before, Kitty.'

She had stood at her mother's door many times before. The young Elizabeth Jane Tresaile had waited until Miss Muriel Oakley had left the grounds before she entered the house. The little seven-year-old was afraid to open the front door before then in case her mother stumbled outside drunken and confused and made Miss Oakley throw her hands up in horror.

The last day Elizabeth had found the door

15

shut tight against her. She had tried the handle again and again but it had refused to turn. The heavy old door was locked. She had stretched up on tiptoe and had just managed to get two tiny gloved fingertips to lift up the heavy door knocker. It stuttered down on the old wood, the door now a massive obstacle preventing her from getting safely inside out of the biting winter weather. The back entrance was always locked at this time of day. Anyway, her mother insisted she enter the house by the main door, as a young lady should.

Elizabeth had waited and waited but her mother did not come to open the door to her. Elizabeth thought she had made too little noise with the knocker. Mummy had not heard her. She reached up again ready to use more effort when at the same moment a strong gust of wind howled up from the sea and the cliffs, rode up over the long lawn and struck Elizabeth on the back, and her head and legs. Her wool coat, fur-trimmed hat, scarf, thick tights and fur-lined ankle boots did not provide enough protection from the cruel force. Elizabeth had hugged herself and shivered fiercely. She was scared. The high winds had always terrified her, seeming to hound her even when she was tucked up in her bed, where she would cower under the covers. There was no use in calling for Mummy in the night. Mummy never came. She was always incapable because of the drink and pills she took. The sudden cold rush of air had seemed like a monster to Elizabeth. She had believed it

16

was trying to rip off her hat so it could scream down her ears and freeze her brain, and then it would freeze the rest of her into solid stone. If she didn't get inside quickly to safety the wind would turn her into a being of stone and she would be trapped for ever, never able to move again. Her heart banging inside her chest, Elizabeth had thrust up her hand yet again, made it to the knocker tap, then let the lump of shiny brass fall harder than before. Rap-tap, rap-tap, rap-tap.

And still there had been no answer.

She was locked out. Forgotten. Unwanted.

But perhaps her mother had slipped to the shops to get her something for tea. Elizabeth had known she was fooling herself. *Where was she?* Elizabeth banged on the door with her knuckles. She banged until her knuckles hurt. Up again she had gone on to her tiptoes and reached for the heavy brass knocker, and let it bang down again and again. Desperation had clawed at her tummy. There was no barking. Where was Cleo? Then Elizabeth remembered. In the kennels! Mummy had taken Cleo there yesterday because they were about to go up to London to shop at Harrods for Christmas.

The darkness of the night was creeping down and in and all around her. The outside porch lights had not been lit. Soon it would be as black as the bottom of the well.

Growing ever more panicky, Elizabeth had kicked at the door – too frightened to worry about scuffing her boots. She was so afraid out

17

here in the darkness that was sneaking upon her. She should peek in through the windows and see if Mummy was at home. But she was afraid to, for she might find Mummy 'asleep' on the floor clutching one of those tall, pretty-labelled, strong-smelling bottles, the bottle empty. One time there had been a little brown bottle too. It had been in the morning, and Mrs Reseigh, the daily help, had telephoned for an ambulance. It was the day after that when Daddy had left never to return. Elizabeth was so afraid she'd find Mummy poorly again. Mummy might have been sick again all over the carpet and cushions.

Her desperation growing ever more keenly, Elizabeth had steeled herself to step along the terrace and look into the sitting-room window. The room had been dark with looming shadows and seemed to be empty. She had edged all round the house, moving faster and faster as she left each window. As scared as she was, she had even gone round and tried the back door. It had been locked, as she had expected. She banged on it as hard as she could but had received no answer. Finally she had hurried back to the front door. Mummy was nowhere to be seen or heard.

She must have already left for London, gone without her! She was never coming back! Like Daddy, Mummy was never coming back. Daddy didn't love them any more – Mummy had said so. Every day she had repeated it in tears of anger and rage. Now Mummy was gone

18

too. She had often threatened she would go.

'Mummy! Mummy! Come back!'

It was fully dark. The night had come down. Even if she could get inside, Elizabeth was too frightened to enter the huge dark house on her own. The 'things' of her dreams might be in there, all come real and out to get her. Shapeless 'somethings' that loomed and followed her and cackled noises at her, noises of the like she had never heard before, and there would be the thuds and slithering and the sliding.

She couldn't stay here. Elizabeth knew she had to get away before she was 'got' by the somethings and they did terrible things to her. It was icily cold and the wind was howling louder and Elizabeth was scared by the way the trees were rocking, bending down their long bare branches, their twigs like clawing fingers. The wind was thrashing through the dead fallen leaves and tossing bits of dust and grit about. Elizabeth was so afraid of the dark, afraid of so many things. Things she couldn't put a name to, things she was told didn't exist and were only in her imagination. She just knew they were there, dark mysteries, and all a constant threat. Witches were real. She was a clever girl and she had read about the witches that had been burned at the stake. There might have been witches burnt to death in the local area. Perhaps even close to where she was now. And witches ate children. It said so in many, many stories. There could be witches about to fly out of the darkness at her right now and 'get' her.

19

She started to run down the long drive, just making out the edges of the wide path. The wind was hitting her with force, trying to knock her over. She was old enough to know there was a storm whipping up out at sea. The waves would soon come charging higher and higher inland. They would flood the little private beach way down below the cliff. The water might climb the cliff and sweep up over the wooden steps that Daddy had had built down to it, and climb up and up and over the cliff top and head straight for the house and the drive and she would be washed away, never to be found!

'Mummy! Where are you?'

She had fled. Growing more frightened by the moment, she had dashed out into the lane and, following some survival instinct, had run along the roughly straight narrow thoroughfare for perhaps twenty minutes. She was racing away from the direction of the church and vicarage, the nearest neighbour of Owles House. Mrs Oakley would refuse to take her in, and Elizabeth was too frightened to go near the churchyard in the dark.

Without halting to gain some much-needed breath she had turned off for the steep twisting hill down to the fishing village of Portcowl. There were Tresailes down in the cove but she couldn't go to them, they'd turn her away too. She reached a cottage near the bottom of the hill and banged and banged on the door. What happened next was hazy to her. A woman

20

wearing a pinafore had lifted her inside into the warmth and light of the home. There had been another kind voice, a man's. A warm drink had been held to her lips and she'd received the first hug she'd been given in ages. Children had crowded round her but were quickly ushered away. There had been a young policeman with a soft voice. Then he had left. 'He's gone up to your house, my handsome,' the kind woman had said. 'To see if your mother's all right.' He had returned and whispered with the kind woman and the man who had given her refuge.

That night Elizabeth had slept in the home of the kind strangers. Next day she had been told that her mother wasn't to be found anywhere. Hours later, Grandma, with whom she'd spent nearly all the school holidays up in Wiltshire, had come for her.

'Dear Lord, Beth, you look as if you're about to faint.' Kitty slid an arm round Beth's waist. 'Perhaps we'd better go. Let you get used to being back in Cornwall again first. We could have a meal. There's a fine fish restaurant down in the harbour, according to the holiday brochure. What do you think? Then, later, you could ring Christina. Don't tell her you're here. Just speak to her first. Get used to her voice. Then ask her if she'll meet you somewhere away from this house.'

'She probably won't want to see me.' It was dead certain she wouldn't. Christina had hardly been in touch with Beth over the years, just the usual pretentious this-is-all-you're-getting-out-of-me Christmas and birthday presents. There had been nothing for the last five years.

'On the other hand, she might. Who knows what's been on her mind all these years?' Kitty said. 'I know it's hard but try not to lose heart. Look around, Beth. See how beautiful everything is. It might help lift away some of the bleakness you associate with this place.'

Shaking her head and sighing, Beth looked down over the far-reaching, neatly trimmed lawn then up over the high, ivy-encrusted wall that separated the property from the cliff path. Beyond the wall, breaking off the path, were the steps down to the little private beach. Further up the coast Beth could see Dunn Head and in the near distance in the opposite direction was Coggan Point, the two headlands that sheltered the fishing cove of Portcowl with their overhangs of hard rock. In the direction of Dunn Head the path led towards Portcowl, emerging quite shortly into the lane above the descent to the cove. The way towards Coggan Point meandered off into many long walks, some of which led out into the lanes; one was near the entrance to the vicarage. The first route trailing off the cliff path quickly went into the woods that gave haven to Christina Tresaile's property. It was all quite beautiful but it meant nothing to Beth. 'You do love your happy endings, Kitty. You'd like to see Christina and me somehow make things up, wouldn't you? Well, it isn't going to happen. I didn't come here for that.'

Smiling a sad smile, Kitty shrugged her shoulders. 'My late father used to talk about some of the suffering he saw in his work at the hospital. If anyone can save themselves from more bad times then it's always worth the effort. Well, we just can't stay here. If Christina is at home and peeping out at us she'll be wondering who these two strangers are who are loitering on her doorstep.'

'Yes, and that's exactly what she and I are to each other,' Beth uttered vehemently. 'Strangers. Let's go, Kitty. I didn't think this through properly.' It was the consequence of her most recent inner turmoil, a secret that only Kitty knew about. 'Let's return to the cottage. Never mind a fish lunch. We can make an omelette and tuck into the fresh cottage loaf and butter we bought at Boswarva Farm when we fetched the cottage key. I need to wander along the beach there and sort out my mind.'

Beth reached the car first. She allowed Kitty to follow at a slightly slower pace to admire the scenery. Kitty enjoyed new experiences. She quickly engaged with all things no matter how simple, but Beth knew she was finding the whole place here fascinating. Unlike Beth, she liked lots of company and she would make a friend of any child or beggar. Lovely, amiable, sometimes hearty, Kitty was a magnet to people of all ages. She caught the eye of eager young men and staid old gentlemen, for her grey-green eyes sparkled and she laughed easily. People were drawn to glance at Kitty several moments before they noticed Beth, something that pleased Beth, who preferred to stay quietly in the background. Whatever happened during the next few days, Kitty would discover a lot to be impressed by. Earlier today, after they had finished unpacking at the holiday cottage, Kitty had chattered about the prospect of going out on a pleasure boat to fish for mackerel and then spit roasting it over an open fire on the beach.

The sound of a loud territorial barking just beyond the wall made Beth freeze as if hit by a sheet of ice. There was a high solid gate in the wall and it was being opened. The nose of a dog appeared and then the whole body of a large German Shepherd came scrambling through, and then it was making a mad dash up the lawn at Beth and Kitty, more curious about them than anything. There was no need to be afraid of it. The dog was so like Cleo had been that Beth was overwhelmed with grief knowing her old friend must have died some years ago. So her mother had got another dog, and now she was bringing it back from a walk.

Kitty joined Beth. 'Will you be all right?'

'I'll have to be.' Beth cursed underneath her breath for not leaving earlier.

Holding herself straight and tall she waited for the dog's owner to appear.

Her mother.

Two

'What is it, boy? Chaplin, quiet now.'

Beth's blood slowed in her veins at the sound of the familiar husky voice. The voice sounded older and weaker and slightly gaspy now, but it was the unmistakable voice of Christina Tresaile. Beth fought against the revolting sensation of her heart icing up.

The German Shepherd, a handsome creature with coarse straight hair, bounded up to Beth and Kitty, halting them. The dog sniffed them, paced about them and sniffed them again, and then as if satisfied they were no threat to its mistress it finally allowed Kitty, who had been offering it a coaxing hand, to stroke its back. Beth ignored it. The dog wasn't Cleo and she wanted nothing to do with it.

Christina Tresaile came sideways through the gate. At first glance she looked rather like a movie star, dressed as she was in a long-sleeved tunic top over loose leisure pyjama trousers. Her sun hat was deep-crowned with three separate parts to the wide brim and she wore tinted glasses. The glamorous effect, however, was downsized by her flat lace-up shoes and the ebony-handled walking stick she obviously needed for support. Then it could be seen that the clothes weren't new, were rather well worn in fact. The hat was good but not couture made and was arranged purely for comfort. She pushed the gate shut and drew the high bolt across to lock it securely.

Once facing the house she was startled to see two strangers in her garden. Keeping her sight rooted on them she approached them slowly, with a slight limp in her right leg.

Kitty glanced at Beth. Saw the unnatural brightness burning in her eyes and knew she was incapable of speaking at that moment. Kitty smiled at the woman to convey cordiality. 'Good afternoon. Please forgive the intrusion. Mrs Tresaile?'

'Can I help you?' the woman asked Kitty, wary of both callers, but she was not altogether unfriendly.

Beth had clamped her lips shut. The lump in her throat was too rigid, too sore to get her voice out past it. Could this really be her mother? Where was all the glamour of the times she had not been drunk? The bottle-blonde hair, the glossy dark red lipstick, the armoury of gold jewellery? Why wasn't she red-and-watery-eyed and raddled beyond her years by all the alcohol she must have gulped down her throat for the last fifteen years? She was wearing no make-up and her skin looked slightly milky, as if smothered with cream as a precaution against the hot sun. Damn it, she looked like an ordinary woman, someone you'd see anywhere and

26

take no particular notice of. Women who neglected their children, who turned their back on them, should look harsh and cruel and rotten, shouldn't they? Like wicked stepmothers were portrayed in fairy tales. For many years it was how Beth had thought of this damnable woman.

'Not me, but my friend here,' Kitty replied, keeping up her bright smile. Then she dropped her eyes, leaving things to Beth.

Christina Tresaile had noticed the second young woman's hostile stance and her own bearing had stiffened. She kept her attention on the red-haired woman, the only stranger prepared to communicate with her. She removed the tinted glasses, and there was all the evidence Beth needed to prove who had mothered her, the clear and direct, cornflower-blue, almond-shaped eyes that were exactly like her own. Why hadn't her mother's drinking rendered her eyes rough and permanently bleary?

She thought she had known her mother's face. Simpering, hard and unfeeling, made wretched by the endless complaints of being lonely and abandoned and not understood. In an effort to gain some sort of comfort throughout her later years, Beth had tried to excuse and understand Christina's self-obsessed behaviour. She had considered her mother weak, pathetic and pitiable, but also callous and pitiless and utterly selfish. Yet here was a woman who, at first glance, came across as none of these.

With nothing more forthcoming from the

speaker, Christina's head swerved to the second stranger. She stared and stared at her. Then her eyes widened, she gasped tremendously and her mouth dropped open. She took a clumsy step towards her. 'It can't be ... Elizabeth?'

This was the point, Beth thought, when she should say with drama and sarcasm, 'Hello, Mother. How good it is to see you after all these years. As you can see, I'm fit and healthy and successful in life, no thanks to you.'

Instead she swallowed hard and was only able to return a curt nod.

'Elizabeth!' Christina let out such a long breath she seemed to shrink in size. 'It's been such a long time but I'd have known you any-where. Well ... I ... I don't know what to say.' Visibly shaken, Christina brought a hand up to her face. The nails were filed neatly, not profes-sionally polished as had sometimes been done in the old days, Beth noted.

With the other two women in a state of shock, Kitty broke the uncomfortable silence. 'Do allow me to introduce myself, Mrs Tresaile. I'm Katherine Copeland, although everyone calls me Kitty. I'm Beth's friend. We've come down for a little holiday.' Kitty gazed at Beth, willing her to add something. 'And Beth thought she'd look you up. Didn't you, Beth?'

Beth felt Kitty nudge her. She watched Chris-tina for her reaction to Kitty's explanation, aware that Christina was watching her for the same reason. Again, all Beth could manage was a quick nod.

'So here we are,' Kitty twittered, desperate to ensure that her conviviality kept Christina Tresaile interested. If she became offended by Beth's coldness she might ask them to leave. Then Beth would adamantly refuse to make any more contact with her mother and she would be left even more angry and confused over the beginning of her childhood. There were times her emotions ran into uncompromising bitterness.

Christina glanced uncertainly at Kitty and back to Beth. 'I can't believe you're here, Elizabeth. Oh, do you prefer to be called Beth now you're all grown up?' She copied Kitty's jollity, talking fast and breathlessly. 'You haven't changed much, Beth. You're tall. I never thought you'd grow tall, but then Phil was tall. Well, I ... I suppose you'd both better come in. Would you like to? Why not come in and ... and say a proper hello to Chaplin? He's Chaplin after the movie star, and I've got a cat called Charlie. Cleo, of course, passed away some years ago, of old age, she died peacefully. Chaplin comes from the same breeder. Perhaps you'd both welcome an iced drink on such a warm day ... would you?'

'No drinks. We're not staying.' Beth got the blunt inflexible words out past her raw throat. This was too strange. Unreal. Bizarre. To actually be here, finally facing her mother, to be confronting her past after all the years she had pictured herself doing so, in many different scenarios, all with explosive outcomes, she

29

making sure she turned out the victor, her recriminations echoing down Christina's uncaring ears ... This person she had just met was not the drink-befuddled harpy she had expected and it had put her off her beat. It was as disturbing as it was unforeseen. Frightening too, with all her hurt and anger, which she'd planned to offload immediately, boiling up inside her and threatening to remain barely in check. There was no way she could bring herself to step inside Owles House today.

'Oh...' Christina glanced away. A habit of hers when facing the unpalatable – Beth had seen it many times before. 'Well, never mind. Um, how long are you down for?'

'Not sure.'

'Would you mind if I sit down?' Christina indicated the wooden bench just off the paved pathway behind her visitors. 'I've walked a little too far, I think. My hip's hurting.'

Every muscle in Beth's face tightened. She must, she absolutely must keep up her defence. Her mother was already intent on wringing out sympathy for herself.

'I mean ... you're not going straightaway?'

'No, we're not,' Kitty said, firm and friendly. 'Why don't you both sit down and chat for a minute? I'll take a stroll round the garden. I'd had no idea it was so beautiful here.'

'Very well, we'll do that,' Beth said tightly, displeased that this gave her no choice in the matter. She glanced around to see what she could remember about the grounds. There was

30

the small walled garden. She was surprised to get a warm feeling. The other side of the high red bricks, currently crawling with red, pink and purple clematis, she remembered was one place here where good things had happened to her. She got a clear picture of the beds of beautiful flowers within, a stone bird bath, and a peculiar gardener, a tiny bent-over old man, a kind, chattering, ancient goblin who had taught her how to prepare the earth and put in plants – *teel*, he had called it. It was unlikely Mr Jewell still worked here. He was probably dead. Beth turned her head away, stricken. Pleasant memories could be her undoing.

Squaring herself, upping her determination, she waited for Christina to limp to the bench and settle herself down on it. Chaplin, the German Shepherd, followed her and sat at her side, a quiet, loyal, watchful companion. And then Beth moved, in long strides with her head up, but choosing a spot on the edge of the lawn where she could look down directly on Christina. Where she could submit her to a steady stream of cold stares – and unspoken accusations. It would do for now, until she picked the right time to let rip with exactly what was on her mind concerning all the years of terrible memories and taunting nightmares this woman was responsible for.

There were moments of heavy, thought-filled silence.

Christina wetted her bottom lip. 'Well. Where do we start? Are ... I ... are you still living in

Wiltshire, Beth? I was disappointed when you were taken out of the county all that time ago.'

'Yes.'

'And are you still with your grandmother?'

'Not for a while now.'

'So you've struck out on your own? Good for you. I see you're not wearing a wedding ring. Is there anyone special in your life?'

'I didn't come here to tell you things like that.' Beth's voice rose with acrimony. It was she who should be asking the questions. She should not have allowed Christina to dominate the situation. She must remember at all costs to fight. Fight for her rights. Keep on top. 'Why be interested in me now?'

Christina dropped her gaze but immediately looked back at Beth, with an uncertain smile. 'I've never lost interest in you, Beth. I guess you don't believe me and I don't blame you. Look, I ... I mean this is difficult for both of us, you more so than me, of course. You obviously have a particular reason for coming here today. Perhaps you're curious about your old home. Perhaps you're curious about me. I hope you are, oh I do hope you are, Beth. Please, ask me anything you like. I'll answer any questions you put to me with total honesty, no matter how hard they might be.'

Such a sweet, soothing voice you have now, Beth thought, irritated, suspicious, sickened. Questions? She had a thousand of them. She felt perspiration breaking out down her back and was grateful for the relief offered by the

32

gentle breeze. This was suddenly like being invited to climb a hill which you knew, in truth, was a mountain, while knowing it must be scaled and conquered if you were to find peace of mind and a clear way forward. While knowing failure would mean being stuck for ever in the bloody awful past. Where to start? It was only after Grandma's death, six months ago of cancer, that she had realized just how little she actually knew about the first seven years of her life. While Grandma had not covered up the weaknesses of her son-in-law, Beth's father – irritability and some impatience on his part – she had sheltered Beth a little too well. A war had gone on in this place of conflicting interests and emotions, and she had been its innocent victim. Her wounds had not healed but had darkly festered. Now that she had come back, those lesions were rent wide open and she felt horribly exposed.

She felt sick. It was a revolting writhing sensation of something clammy, juddering, energy-sapping and dizzy-making. It brought with it pain and anguish from a different source, of the tragedy she had recently undergone, of her unplanned pregnancy coming to a sudden end. She had been preparing to move from Wiltshire so no one would know her child was illegitimate, and she had been looking forward to doing the motherhood thing right by using all her resources. Her aching loss was the focal reason for her being here. She knew she must find the courage to face her past or she would

33

never be able to cope with the future.

But she was reeling with renewed pain and shock. She couldn't make a start on that mountain yet. 'This house must mean a lot to you. You haven't left it despite the break-up with my father. Or your time incarcerated in a mental institution – Grandma told me about that. You've even stayed here since your subsequent marriage. You're actually Mrs Vyvyan. I know that much about you and I want to know a great deal more, but not now. I'm leaving.'

Christina blinked, as if she had received numerous little slaps across the face. She leaned forward, as if eagerly, sagely. 'I understand your ill feelings towards me, Beth. It must have taken a lot of courage for you to come here today. I want you to know that whenever you're ready you'll be more than welcome to come back, at any time. You have the telephone number of course.' Christina rose to walk Beth to the car. She gasped and shot a hand to her hip.

Beth stared at her. 'What is it?'

'Oh, it's only common old arthritis.' Christina gave a self-deprecating little smile. After a moment's hesitation, she dropped her eyes. 'I suppose you'd expected to find me suffering from something else by now, like liver disease. I've been dry since I left the institution, Beth.'

'Are you proud of that?' The question emerged steeped in more bitterness than Beth had intended. She wouldn't get anywhere if she put Christina on the defensive.

'Yes, actually I am, Beth. I hope you'll

34

believe that, and also believe I have a great many regrets about the past and especially how you suffered. I'd do absolutely anything to – well, never mind about what I want. I know this isn't about me. I'll leave you to make up your mind what you want to do next.' Christina raised a hand as if to emphasize something she was about to say, changed her mind and dropped it, and hung her head a little. 'I really hope you keep in touch, Beth. There's something I'd like you to know.'

'Really?' Beth shrugged coolly. 'Don't bother to see me off. If you're in pain why not go inside?'

'Yes, I think I will. Thank you for coming, Beth. Please return, it's meant so much to me to see you again after so long apart.' Christina gave a smile that was a little watery and then limped away, favouring her bad leg.

Kitty rejoined a motionless Beth. 'Where's she gone?'

Beth explained.

'All in all it seemed to be a good first meeting. She didn't seem to be trying to put any pressure on you.'

'Oh, yes she was. She's clever. Grandma used to say she was a cunning piece and that it was something I should never forget.'

Beth sniffed the air. Could she pick up some sort of vibration from the past? She concentrated. Was there a feeling, an atmosphere she could absorb? She took in all she could see in a sweep of her eyes. The fountain, the greenhouse, the many steps and paths all leading off to interesting nooks or dead ends; places where she used to take refuge when the atmosphere was hostile. The summer house had been another of her former sanctuaries, the time spent exclusively with Cleo for she had never had other children to play with. The summer house peeped out now like a familiar face from its shelter of beech trees. Everything seemed more or less the same. She supposed that round the back of the house the kitchen garden, the former stable block and dovecote remained unaltered.

'What is it?' Kitty prodded her.

'It's not this actual place I need fear, Kitty, only that while I'm here I get hurt again and end up feeling worse than before. Of being taken in by that woman, my mother, that clever woman who failed me.' She took another quick look round. 'But something is different here. Something is out of place.'

'It's been years since you've been here. There's bound to have been changes.'

'No, it's not that. It's ... Something more is here.'

Kitty glanced here and there and then shrugged. 'Could be your imagination.'

'Perhaps. But I didn't imagine the neglect I suffered here, Kitty. Both of us must keep that firmly in mind. I was right to come back. I know that more than anything. If I have the chance to have more children one day I need to learn everything about my past life here to be able to give them my best.'

'To learn everything about Christina, you mean? The reason for her drinking?'

'Yes. Certainly that. But also why she and my father hated each other so much.'

Beth's whole body jerked as Christina called out to her. 'Beth, I don't suppose you'll tell me where you're staying?'

'Not for now, I'll ring you,' Beth shot over her shoulder. 'See, Kitty? She's insistent already.'

'Beth, when?'

Beth went to the car before answering. She had come here partly for revenge. Some revenge, like keeping Christina hanging on, would be damned wonderful, although it might prove unproductive and perhaps it was even childish to play mind games with a woman who she recalled was an expert at the very thing. Beth mouthed to her mother, 'Didn't you hear me? I said I'll ring.'

Three

A taxicab pulled up in the back yard of Owles House. A child got out.

Christina hurried out of the kitchen, followed by Chaplin, to wave a thank you to the driver and to embrace the young passenger. 'How did everything go at athletics club, darling?' She smoothed the boy's close-cropped dark hair, still damp from his exertions, which he endured with a patient smile. 'I'm preparing your favourites. Grilled prawns, ham and apricot skewers, and hot buttered corn. I thought we could eat it out by the summer house.'

'That's great, Mum, but you shouldn't go to so much trouble. You're shuffling. Don't tell me you've taken Chaplin for a really long walk.' Joseph Vyvyan was sturdy in limbs and had the stride of a confident young man. Although it was towards the beginning of the long summer school holiday he was wearing the sports kit of the athletics club at his St Austell private school, and he was trailing his sports bag. He gently disentangled himself from his mother's clutches then dropped to his knees to hug Chaplin and receive in return an enthusiastic licking. 'I hope you haven't dragged the

38

things out of the summer house. I'll do that.'

'I've managed fine, and I've been sensible and left the lifting for you to do. You don't have to worry about me, Joe.' A shadow clouded Christina's indulgent expression as her thoughts shot back to the abrupt appearance and leave-taking of her other child, just hours ago. 'You do know, darling, that I'd take and collect you from school and your club if this hip allowed me to drive. I'd love to watch you run but I know Mr Matthews only allows parents to main events.'

'Of course, Mum. Anyway, I'd look an absolute dope if you were hanging round the sports field. I managed two whole seconds off the eight hundred metres today.' Joe grinned up at her. 'Richard said I flew along the track like I had a torpedo up my backside.'

'Richard Opie would.' Christina would have gushed something to express again her pride in Joe, but Beth's sudden presence had hewn off a large chunk of her confidence. Besides, Joe preferred quiet encouragement. 'Well, Mr Matthews says you're the best boy he's ever had at the athletics club, and that you should easily win everything this season for the inter-school under-thirteens. But never mind the school's expectations, Joe, you do it for yourself.'

'I will, Mum, but most of all I'll do it for you.'

'Bless you, Joe.' Her son often said such touching things and each time warm tears of pride gathered in Christina's eyes, but today those tears were tinged with sadness. If only

Phil Tresaile had been like Joe's father, Francis Vyvyan, then perhaps she would not have let Elizabeth down so horribly. Beth had known about her second marriage but she didn't, apparently, know that Christina was a widow, that Francis, the man she had adored, who had helped her to turn her life around after years of terrible guilt and loneliness, had died three years ago, tragically drowned out in the bay after a boating accident. A Portcowl man, Francis had known the full facts about the daughter taken away from Christina. Christina had told Joe, as soon as he'd been old enough to understand, that he had a half-sister, had explained why she did not live at Owles House. But he'd shrugged it off and had never asked about her. Now Christina would have to tell him that Beth had been here and planned to return.

Leaving Chaplin, Joe glanced to see if the plump, pure white cat Charlie was dozing in his usual spot on the low wall there. Then, linking his arm through Christina's, Joe walked her back inside. 'Are you sure you're all right, Mum?'

Christina returned to the food she was skewering for the grill. 'Why do you say that, darling?'

Joe helped himself to fresh lemonade from the cold cupboard. 'You seem a little jumpy. Has the pain been getting you down?'

The edginess in Christina's smile had nothing to do with her reply. 'Yes, I admit, it's a little sharp today. If it doesn't ease off in a couple of

40

days I'll pop along and see Dr Powell.'

Joe leaned his head to the side in the endearing way that was his. 'You're not worrying about me, are you?'

'Course not.' She playfully tossed a dish towel at him. 'Why should I worry about a big boy like you? You're already as tall as the cliff. Time you went up and changed. Be a dear and put your kit in the laundry basket. Poor Mrs Reseigh keeps remarking that it's like she has to clear up after a dozen messy boys. Food will be ready to start cooking in ten minutes.'

Joe took a swig of lemonade, pounced on the model aeroplane he had abandoned before going to athletics practice then pounded up the stairs, making loud engine and stuttering dog-fight noises.

Christina shook her head over the forgotten kitbag. It amused her how Joe became mysteriously forgetful the instant his attention turned to something entertaining. Her hands were clumsy while grilling the food and getting the trays ready to be carried outside, for her mind wasn't on the task.

She never took Joe's presence in her life for granted. She never grumbled about his behaviour, as was the inclination of many a parent, and Joe could be every bit as wilful, stubborn, noisy, messy and downright disobedient as any other child. Instead she felt it a privilege to have given birth to him, to be raising him. Joe was a blessing to her in every way. He was fun loving, caring and conscientious in his lessons. He was popular at school and in the village. Just like his father had been. Francis had given Christina everything a woman could desire. He had been a wonderful loving husband and father. His brave war record and dedication as a parish councillor had seen him much admired and respected and his untimely death had been greatly mourned. After the first couple of years of their marriage many people had gradually forgotten Christina's sordid past and had begun to show her the same consideration.

'I didn't deserve you, Francis.' Her hollow tone was seamed with tears and sounded like a mournful lap of waves on some unreachable distant shore. Francis was on some distant shore now. She tried every day to see where his tragic death had taken him – a fantastic place, a golden paradise, where one day she would, God willing, be worthy to join him. 'Nor did I deserve you, Joe.'

Oh God, I should have asked Elizabeth to write to me.

What if Joe answered the telephone before she could reach it and Beth was on the line and asked to speak to her mother?

But I couldn't just send you away, Beth. I wanted you to know how wonderful it was to see you again after such a long separation, how important it is to me that we keep in touch. You were taken away from me. There was no other choice at the time. I don't want you to keep on hating me.

Christina relaxed her tense shoulders. 'Stop

42

panicking. Take deep breaths. Beth is bound to be cautious, a little overwhelmed at first, and she wouldn't have come all this way just to cause trouble, surely?' She prayed that Beth, remote and confrontational, with so much understandable hurt, bewilderment and anger entrenched inside her, would allow her to explain about *all* that had happened. The universal opinion was that a mother was the most important influence in a person's life, one of life's strongest, most enduring links to love, nurture and stability. If only it had been so for Beth. It might have been like that for Beth if certain people hadn't kept interfering in her marriage, had not been so cruel!

Christina's mind drifted back to her meeting with Beth in the garden. But she imagined a different scene, her desperate wish for how it should have been, with Beth presenting a soft, interested expression on her lovely bold face, eager to reach out to her mother and to be reached out to.

'I hope you don't hate me too much, Beth. It's probably too late for us to be mother and daughter, for you to allow me to be the mother to you that I should have been, but we could be friends. We could try...'

'Mum, why are you talking to yourself?'

Flames of old guilt coupled with new guilt flooded all the way up Christina's neck to her hairline. She was forced to draw on her hard-won awareness of self-worth and determination to stay on top of things. 'Was I, Joe?'

'It's one of those times when you've got something important to tell me, isn't it?'

'I can't fool you, can I? You go ahead with the drinks tray, darling, and get the things out of the summer house, and I'll bring out the food. Then while we're eating we'll have a serious chat.'

As always, when faced with a difficult situation, Christina's confidence roller-coasted in gut-wrenching waves. She needed the heat of the sun to thaw her chilled bones, the air to clear the confusion from her mind, and the sight of the brilliant waters of the bay to inspire her, if she was even to begin to tell Joe his half-sister had suddenly turned up today.

Looking at him now, as they sat outside the summer house, Joe piling his plate with food, Christina regretted not sending Elizabeth away, telling her to get out of her life and never come back. She couldn't bear to see even a little of the shine wiped out of her son's trusting smile. To have his noble need to protect her undermined; he saw himself as the man of the house now.

She regretted it, but only for a moment. Once more came the joyful leap in her heart at seeing Beth, her Elizabeth, her little girl, again. Joe had a right to know Beth had been here, to know all about her. As all those years ago, Christina had had the right to a normal life with her daughter. Of all the things that had played havoc in her life throughout the years this was what she regretted most. She regretted it with anger and bitterness. And the aching need to put matters right, as a loving mother does.

44

Four

The little girl on the beach was happy. The happiest she had been in ages. She had a new pink bathing costume, a new beach bucket with brightly coloured fishes painted on it, and a large matching spade. Mummy had said the spade was too big for her but she let her have it anyway. Elizabeth was going to build a sandcastle. A really big sandcastle, so big that the tide wouldn't be able to wash it away, and Mummy would see how clever she was. When Elizabeth told Daddy about it he might be proud of her and say, 'Well done,' instead of his usual, 'So what?' Or even, 'Chrissie, get this brat away from me!'

Elizabeth liked it when Mummy made a fuss of her. When Mummy's eyes weren't huge and staring and she wasn't stumbling about and crying. After she had finished her enormous sandcastle Elizabeth would throw sticks for Cleo. Cleo was running in and out of the waves, barking with the fun of it. It was making Mummy laugh. It was lovely when Mummy laughed, it sounded like tinkling bells. There were no shops and no ice-cream seller near the beach. Mummy explained that the little length of cliff-sheltered sand and shingle here at Mor Penty, a fairly long walk from home, was only a small beach. But Mummy had promised that as soon as they got home she'd take her down to Port-cowl and buy her a big ice cream with raspberry sauce on it. All wonderful treats! But best of all was Mummy being with her. Mummy wasn't usually well enough to take her anywhere.

After a minute of digging in the soft pale sand, Elizabeth looked across to the rug. Mummy was still there, beside the picnic hamper, smoking a cigarette, watching her. Elizabeth liked it when Mummy watched her. It made her feel safe.

'Elizabeth, come here, darling,' Mummy waved to her. 'The sun is very hot today. I think you should have your sun hat on.'

More memories of being here at Mor Penty as a child came seeping back to Beth, lost memories ignited only the morning after her short visit to Owles House when she had walked on to the tiny beach below the holiday cottage. Christina had brought her here only once to this little secluded cove, roughly a mile down the coast from her childhood home. Back then the cottage had been a tumbledown affair owned by a lobster and crab fisherman, now long since dead. Hard granite rock shot up at each end of the beach and behind it, giving kindly shelter from wind and wash. There was the spot in front of a rock pool where Christina had laid out the rug. After finishing her cigarette, she

46

had helped Beth build her sandcastle. It had been a big one, lopsided and not very round, but it hadn't mattered. Then Christina had suggested they comb the shore for little pieces of driftwood to make doors and windows and a drawbridge. They had gathered shells, pebbles and gull feathers to decorate the castle. Finally Christina had produced a tiny packet of flags she had bought at some time from a gift shop. Beth had been so proud of those flags, and she had loved her mother so very much on that day long ago.

She visualized Cleo bounding about, forgetting her explorations to rush up to the edge of the rug to beg for treats when Christina had opened the food hamper. Beth suddenly missed Cleo so much. She'd not had a dog since. Grandma had not cared for them.

Turning her back on these few good childhood memories, Beth gazed out to sea. The tide had turned its back too. It had ebbed away and left wet flotsam strewn on the shoreline. The company Beth had today was stranded seaweed, scraps of rotten timber and a small tangle of fisherman's net. A lonely neglected scene, which suited her mood. She did not welcome poignant thoughts of Christina. It might put her off guard. And one happy occasion didn't cancel out all the frightening wretched ones. As a child, it hadn't occurred to Beth that her sandcastle would be sucked down and destroyed in short hours by the approaching grabbing waves, but that of course was what had happened.

Nothing good stayed with her for long. The innocence of her childhood had been wrenched from her. She had lost her parents' love. And just weeks ago she had lost the man whom she had thought of as the love of her life, a man who had made a fool out of her. Then she had lost their baby, *her baby*. That ache, that void, that tragedy was a thousand times worse than the hurt from her childhood. Sadly, she couldn't share with Kitty all the facts about her miscarriage. It involved a secret Kitty must never learn. Grandma had died before the dreadful event, so Beth had been denied her consoling presence – although Grandma would have urged her to have the baby secretly and give it away for adoption, and Beth would have refused to do that. But she still had Kitty and would do anything to keep her friendship.

Since leaving Owles House yesterday, Beth had regretted the wisdom of getting in touch with Christina, before changing her mind and changing it again. 'Turn and turn about will get you nowhere,' Grandma used to say when Beth was in a dither. 'Slow down and think it all through. Lay out all the issues. It will help you make the right decision.'

Beth made mental notes. There was no need to mull over all the negatives. She had them written on her heart. Christina had seemed co-operative, eager to come clean, in fact. In the end Beth might come away with everything she wanted to know and having said all that she wanted to say. Able to put the past in the past, which was what she needed most to do.

There was the awful possibility that Christina might follow her to her home – Christina's old home, inherited from Grandma – and upset her future as much as she had her past. Might. Might. Might. The only way she was going to find out what *might* happen was to face Christina again and get on with it. She had come down to Cornwall, been to Owles House, and gone through the first meeting with Christina. It had been a hugely emotional occasion, it couldn't be anything else, but she had kept her emotions in check, then and since. It hadn't been difficult; she was feeling kind of numb. It was all rather unreal to her.

The meeting could have been so much worse. Christina could have been drunk, a haggard, diminishing husk of a being, and she could have demanded that Beth leave her property and never return. Beth would have hated that but she would have been justified in loathing Christina even more. The pleasant, lucid, motherly version of her mother she had met yesterday was an enormous surprise and hard to comprehend. There was only one thing for it. She must make that phone call to Christina.

Kitty was watching the small distant figure of Beth from the somewhat neglected, but otherwise charming, garden of the holiday cottage. At last Beth was on her way back. Kitty slipped away to the kitchen to start cooking the breakfast, hoping to tempt Beth to eat her first substantial meal in two days. She hoped the fresh farmhouse bacon and eggs and thickly toasted home-made bread would relieve Beth of some of her terrible pallor. She needed building up. The miscarriage had robbed her of her usual vitality, she had ended her association with her mystery lover, and now she was in the throes of an emotional make-or-break mission.

Earlier, while Beth had wandered the beach, Kitty had laid the kitchen table for breakfast and spread slabs of the farmhouse bread with delicious creamy yellow butter, before setting the bacon and eggs out ready to be cooked. She had cut a bunch of rock roses and put them in two vases to give the cottage a homely feel. The cottage had been left pristine by the farmer who owned it. The linen had been aired. Kindling wood and rolled-up newspaper were laid in the little sitting-room grate, and there was a full basket of logs at the hearth in case warmth was needed. Mor Penty. Kitty liked the name of the cottage and the beach. The rooms were furnished with post-war items and lots of plump cushions. Unvarnished wooden mirror frames were embellished with seashells. There were pictures of boats, sea and coast and old salts and the like, and ships in bottles. A scrap of fishing net with green glass floats was strung up from the low ceiling beams in the sitting room. A bookshelf held titles like *Moby Dick*, *Great Sea Adventures* and *Foes from the Deep* as well as lighter holiday reading. In recent times an extension had been added to give a third bedroom and a bathroom and a sweet basic conservatory. It seemed a pity no one actually lived here, Kitty thought, that it was just a holiday let.

Her tummy grumbling for food, her appetite stirred by the fresh tangy salt air, Kitty glanced out of a window and wished Beth would make faster progress coming in. Beth was dawdling so slowly, with still plenty of beach to cover before the short steep rocky climb up to the little back garden gate. She was a lonely figure in trousers, a short-sleeved blouse, dangling her sandals from her fingertips. Kitty tuned into Beth's loneliness. She wanted to rush to her but Beth needed to make her inner journey alone. The decisions she came to would affect the rest of her life. Was she thinking about the father of her baby? The mysterious man she'd had a brief fling with? Kitty had known nothing about the love affair until the onset of Beth's miscarriage, which had started with great distress for her friend while the pair had been sharing an evening at Beth's home. The doctors had praised Kitty's quick actions in getting her friend to the hospital; it had been obvious her predicament had required more than the services of the GP. It had also been obvious that Beth's lover was unattainable, the reason for her secrecy, even towards her best friend.

While recovering in the hospital bed, Beth had miserably confided to Kitty, 'I was about to tell you I was planning to go away and start a new life. Of course you would have been invited to come and stay with me whenever you liked.'

Poor dear Beth, she had so wanted her baby, in order to keep a part of the man she obviously still desperately loved.

'I wish I knew who the man was,' Kitty muttered on the breeze. He obviously wasn't free and he should never have allowed the affair to happen. Kitty longed to challenge the selfish swine. 'See what your philandering has done? Beth didn't deserve to have you messing up her life.' Kitty acknowledged it was better she didn't know the man's identity. If she tore into him it would distress Beth even more.

Kitty wondered if Beth would like to eat outside, but decided she had probably had enough fresh air for the time being.

Something caught Kitty's eye. Someone was at the side of the cottage, on the path. A boy. He was astride a bicycle, one foot taking the balance, leaning forward over the handlebars. And he was staring at her.

He kept staring. Kitty got the impression he was trying to make out if he knew her. 'I deliver newspapers.' His tone was gruff. 'Do you want any?'

Kitty kept quiet. She wasn't going to reply to such insolent behaviour. Cheeky brat. Didn't mothers teach their children manners hereabouts? He had a smug air about him and the usual tousled hair, scraped legs, shorts and drooping socks and scuffed sandals. He was staring past her now, searching the garden and the beach beyond. He looked at the beach for

52

some time, his expression unreadable. He was staring at Beth. Then he turned back to Kitty and smiled. It was a handsome smile. A smile that was totally disarming and easy to respond to. He was a handsome boy. Dark and well built. A future heartbreaker, if ever there was one, Kitty decided.

'Are you enjoying your holiday? Everyone who stays at Mor Penty enjoys the stay. My name's Joe.'

Kitty was struck at how well spoken he was, and after his initial brusqueness he was full of charm too. He was barely an adolescent but she fancied he already looked over girls. 'I'm here for a few days with a friend. I'm Miss Copeland,' she answered. 'Thank you for the offer of a newspaper. If we want any we'll fetch our own.'

'As you please. So you're Miss Copeland?'

It was more a statement than a question, but there had been a probing edge to it. The searching stare was back in his eyes. This boy was sharp and not entirely friendly. 'That is what I said. Look, Joe, can I do something for you?'

'No, thank you, Miss Copeland. I've got the right place. That's all I wanted to know.'

'What does that mean?' Kitty demanded.

'I'll be seeing you again, perhaps,' Joe said, taking a long stab again at Beth on the beach. Then he turned his bicycle round and pedalled away.

'Wait a minute!' Kitty called, but it was to empty air.

53

Joe had found it easy to discover where his half-sister was staying. His mother's daily help, Mrs Reseigh, had met up with Farmer Read's wife, and this morning Mrs Reseigh had prattled to his mother about how two young ladies from 'up country' were now staying at Mor Penty. These young ladies were dead certain to be Elizabeth Tresaile and Katherine Copeland, and Miss Copeland had just confirmed it.

So his half-sister was the woman loitering on the beach. The fact that his mother had another child, an older daughter, had not bothered him before. His mother had kept nearly all her thoughts about Elizabeth Tresaile to herself. She had once said, 'I forfeited Elizabeth through my own bad behaviour and I'll always regret it.' Joe had never been interested in his half-sister. She lived far away, had never got in touch, until now, and he had never expected to meet her. His mother had photographs of her as a young girl but Joe had never looked at them. His mother was the best mother a boy could get. He adored her and cherished her, and his only concern now was whether this stranger was a threat to her peace and health.

Keeping his rear up off the saddle, his strong feet and legs pumping madly to scale the bumpy slope from Mor Penty to the ribbon of coast road, he stopped in a passing place where there was a good view of the cottage.

'You had better be careful what you do and say to my mum,' he told the tall figure on the sand. 'I won't let you hurt her, not one little bit.'

'Food smells good.' Beth flopped down wearily at the pine kitchen table. 'Are you all right, Kitty? You're rather quiet.'

'I hope you've worked up an appetite,' Kitty said, sounding jolly, moving sizzling rashers of bacon about in the frying pan on top of the stove. 'Bread's ready and there's fresh tea in the pot. There was someone here just now.'

'Oh?' Beth got up and washed her hands. She wasn't hungry but she'd make an effort to please Kitty, the dear old thing.

'It was a boy, aged about twelve I think.'

'What did he want?'

'I don't know really. He said he was a paper boy and asked if we wanted a delivery. I think he was lying. He might have been just plain nosy, I suppose, but there was something more than that. The way he stared at me, and down at you, it was, well, unsettling. He said his name was Joe and when I introduced myself he seemed to have heard about me already. I think that must go for you too. What could it all be about?'

'Goodness, Kitty.' Beth patted her arm before resuming her seat. She poured out two cups of tea. 'I thought I was the one with the fanciful imagination. I booked the cottage under your name, so he probably got hold of your name easily enough. His mother probably sent him snooping here so she can spread gossip.'

'He seemed very surly. Just before he left he said, "I'll be seeing you again, perhaps." I didn't like it, Beth,' Kitty said, adding eggs to fry with the bacon.

'Well,' Beth shrugged. 'It doesn't really matter if people discover I'm Christina's daughter. I've decided to see her again. As soon as we've eaten, I'll phone her. I'll ask to see her again today.'

Kitty brought the two plates of food to the table. 'I'm glad about that. I'm sure it will be for the best in the end. Want me to come with you again?'

'Yes I do, but I think I should go alone this time. Christina might be too much on the defensive if she feels she's faced with a committee. You don't mind, do you Kitty?'

'Not in the least. I'll come along but get out of the car at the drive then pop down to the harbour. Call in at the local shops. See who's about. If I happen to meet any of your relatives I'll see what they're like, but I won't mention you, of course. I need a good stretch of the legs. I'll walk back here on the coast path. Are you nervous? Do you know what you'll say to Christina?'

'I'm too damned angry to be nervous. I want to know why she was a stinking drunk. I loved my baby even though I'd never seen it or knew if it was a girl or a boy. I'll ask her why she was such a rotten mother to me, why she didn't love me.'

A while later, up in her bedroom, Beth

changed out of her casual clothes into a stylish chevron-patterned slip-on dress with beaded detail and a scalloped hem, and put on high heels. She would carry her crocodile-skin clutch. She applied a little enhancing make-up. She wanted to look polished, successful and reaming with confidence, to show Christina that her life with Grandma had been the best thing that could have happened to her. One moment Beth felt like that, the next she felt her insides curl up and she longed only to drive all the way home and try to forget her mother even existed. Christina was expecting her at eleven o'clock. Beth would be half an hour late, with the intention of making Christina feel jumpy. She might get a taste then of exactly how horrid it felt to be on the lookout for someone who should turn up and not run out on her.

A little while before, having driven to the next village to use the public telephone, Beth had bristled at the sound of her mother's voice answering her call by speaking the telephone number of Owles House. Christina had sounded cautious.

'It's Beth. I want to come and see you. Shortly. Is it convenient?'

'Oh, Beth, it's good to hear from you so soon. I've been worried that you wouldn't want to see me again. Come as soon as you can. You're very, very welcome. Will Miss Copeland be joining you?'

'No.'

'I see. I – I think you should know that I won't

be alone. There's someone here I'd like you to meet.'

'Your husband will be with you?'

'No. I'm sorry, I didn't realize you hadn't heard. But he died three years ago.'

There had been a choked note in Christina's tone, but Beth couldn't respond to it with sympathy. 'No. How on earth could I have known?'

'Oh, it doesn't matter. I'll explain who's with me when you arrive. It's not right to tell you over the telephone.'

Beth was furious. She assumed Christina had called her solicitor in to advise her. Was she afraid Beth wanted her money? Damn the woman. Beth was well off. Grandma had left her the significant sum of money that would have gone to Christina, if she had deserved it. And Beth wouldn't accept a farthing off Christina if she were struck down by poverty. 'Very well.' Beth had placed the receiver down.

Beth went to the window, which faced the sea and was hung with freshly laundered cotton curtains; dark blue in colour and with white wavy lines depicting the sea, they were quite faded now. She stood quietly. Then, as she did every day, she spread her hands over her stomach. The flatness of it, the emptiness of it, flooded her with grief and numbness. The baby had brought an end to her love affair with Stuart Copeland, Kitty's married brother. The scandal of fathering an illegitimate child, of betraying his good-natured wife and two young children, would have cost Stuart everything. His marriage, his son and daughter, his home, and his position as a college principal. Beth couldn't do that to him, but Stuart had panicked anyway and begged her not to let their affair become public. The last thing Beth had wanted was to bring heartbreak to Stuart's wife and children. Beth prayed Kitty would never find out her shameful secret. Kitty believed in Stuart, she looked up to him, and she loved her sister-in-law and nephew and niece.

Her vision blurred as tears started to burn her eyes. She had so wanted her baby. She had looked forward to the sleepless nights, the nappy changing, the teething, the toddler tantrums, every last jot of child rearing. She had been sure Grandma would have been delighted about the baby once she had seen it. Grandma would have loved the babysitting and family outings. But fate had forced its cruel way in and denied the baby any life at all. Then the guilt and doubt reared in Beth, over the reality that she would have gladly given birth to a child that would have one day asked who its father was. Her idea to pretend to be a widow was bound to have been exposed at some point, and how her child would have suffered from the scorn and isolation of not having a legitimate name. *No!* Beth screamed inside her head, then she talked quietly and painfully and lovingly to her lost baby. *I would have taken you abroad, to the ends of the earth, to protect you. You would have been the most precious thing in my whole life.*

Drying her eyes, Beth heaved a tense sigh. She was glad she was going to Owles House. Her loss was threatening to overwhelm her. Putting Christina in her place, confronting her over the injustices she had made Beth suffer, was just what she needed to temporarily help her to forget her more recent pain.

Beth couldn't help smirking. If the nosy locals could send a boy to cycle to this secluded holiday cottage just to see its latest holiday-makers, what would they make of it when they knew about her true identity and that she was making visits to the mother who had so sorely neglected her?

Five

Kitty was lounging on a long backless bench set against the whitewashed front wall of the Sailor's Rest pub. She was nibbling an ice-cream cone, despite feeling full and satisfied after earlier wading through a large fruit-packed saffron bun with a pot of tea, in a nearby tea shop called simply The Teashop. She had eagerly trawled her way in and out of several shops, indulging in chit-chat with every shopkeeper and assistant, but careful not to reveal where she was staying and that she had company in case she was talking to a Tresaile. Beside her on the bench were her bags of shopping, lots of fruit and a few light groceries, and summer-wear from a dear little clothes shop she had discovered in a side street. The baker's, which smelled like food paradise, had yielded her a slab-shaped yeast cake, half a dozen splits, and two enormous steak pasties that would make the perfect teatime meal. She had entered every little gift shop and bought scenic postcards and lots of trinkets, tiny Cornish piskies set on top of china thimbles, teaspoon handles, toadstools and wishing wells. And small models of Cornish fishing boats, roughly accurate to the luggers currently moored up in Portcowl's charming stone harbour. She had bought rubber quoits, and curling lollipop-shaped rock for her nephew and niece, and tea towels printed with the Cornish coastline and place names for her sister-in-law, and a hiking stick with the Cornish badge on it for her brother, Stuart. For Beth she had got a pretty, delicately made seashell necklace. She had bought enough to happily burden herself for the walk back to Mor Penty.

So here she was sitting outside the pub, hoping to spy a Tresaile or two. She was nearly as curious about them as she was Christina Vyvyan. What were the precise reasons for Christina to have become an emotional raving drunk and then to have successfully rehabilitated herself? Why hadn't she gone under again when her second husband died? She must have certain strengths to have stayed living in the same house where her first marriage had plunged to such destructive depths and from where she had lost her young daughter. Kitty hoped Beth would give her mother a chance. She hoped she'd get another chance herself to see Christina, and to see inside Owles House.

She was keeping on the outlook for the boy, Joe, hoping to find out exactly who he was, whether he liked it or not. She wasn't going to be intimidated by some cheeky brat. There were several happy-go-lucky local kids playing on the quay, and numerous seaside-dressed, bright-eyed holidaymakers' offspring, but not a peep of the enigmatic Joe. There was the inevitable squawking of scavenging, beady-eyed gulls. Holidaymakers were idly passing by and browsing the shops. Others were picnicking and frolicking in the sea and older folk were relaxing on striped deck chairs on the two small beaches situated either side of the industrial heart of the harbour. Around the curve of the quay, sitting on a bench outside their terraced, slate-roofed homes on the quay front, were an elderly woman and two young housewives, all knitting swiftly, probably fishermen's jerseys to supplement their men's earnings. Behind them, row after row of similar housing, quaint and weather-strong, climbed with the rise of the land. On top of the cliff sat two impressive-looking small hotels. One was the Grand Sea View Hotel; the other the Dunn Head Hotel, where Beth's mother and grandmother had holidayed all those years ago.

Near where Kitty sat there was a chandlery and a sail-making loft. There were other lofts where the fishermen repaired their nets and made up their lines. Kitty had learned this from an old whiskery, weather-hewn, tobacco-chewing local who, with a newspaper tucked under his arm, had paused to chat and gladly answer her questions about the fishermen's working practices. 'Fleet'll be out in a few days pilchard driving down off the Wolf Light, that's a lighthouse, some way off from here, I can tell 'ee. The Wolf itself is a great tower of rock, some dangerous it is, many a vessel been lost there down the years. Used to have great big holes in 'un, and the winds and tides used to send out the most terrible weird howling. Was God's warning to ships, till evil wreckers blocked up the holes. Well, Miss, wish I was going with 'em but age gets the better off of all. The men are making the boats ready. So the sight you see now of them luggers out in the outer harbour will be missing till nearly autumn, then it'll be time for the dogging season. Enjoy your holiday, Miss.' The old gent had doffed his cap to Kitty before going on his way.

Once she got back to Mor Penty, she'd off-load the shopping then make a quick excursion to Boswarva Farm for fresh milk, clotted cream and lots of vegetables. She and Beth would eat well for the next day or two, unless Beth wanted to leave after her visit to Christina. Kitty hoped for the chance to stay in Portcowl for several days, to get Beth to eat in the fish restaurant, from which the whiffs of cooking were divine. She found the whole area beautiful and fascinating. Every time she gazed out to sea she felt a strange little tug in her heart, as if the waters were calling to her. Nothing and no one had done that to her before.

Her back, pressed against the pub wall, was getting numb and she shifted to bring relief. Then, to her mild embarrassment, she realized the ice cream was melting down over her hand and dripping on to her skirt. She was getting like a mucky child. She delved into her canvas shoulder bag and found her handkerchief. She

64

wiped her hand but it stayed sticky. Hoping she wasn't making a spectacle of herself she quickly devoured the ice cream before licking off her hand and wiping it dry.

Well, it didn't matter. All that mattered was Beth. How was she getting on at Owles House? Then her thoughts turned to Stuart, the older brother she was devoted to, and his family. Her thoughts tended to be spontaneous, numerous, fleeting, deep, searching and sometimes unstoppable, as was her constancy in gaining knowledge. It was a gift to her and sometimes a torture. Sorting out her scrambled thoughts and findings she usually saw things clearly for others, which would be followed by her ruminations on the best way to tell them her solution; sometimes, of course, she decided she should keep her counsel.

She rarely found herself in a quandary concerning her own life. Kitty was content with her life, she accepted each moment as it came and she was philosophical. A hefty trust fund from both sets of her grandparents meant she was self-supporting. She had no hankering for a profession or to achieve something profound and she was thankful for it. It meant she enjoyed all the opportunities and occurrences that came her way, using the time to absorb their every single aspect, from the remarkable and the bizarre to the serene and the baffling. Kitty loved a mystery. She kept a nightly journal. Perhaps one day her experiences might make an interesting book, perhaps on the ironies of life or something. If not, it didn't matter. If love found its way to her doorstep, so be it, otherwise she'd find something useful to do to benefit the wider world until she slipped out of her mortal flesh. It didn't matter if she was soon forgotten. It was enough for Kitty if Stuart and his family were well and happy, and Beth too. Although how she could help Beth become really happy by putting her heartaches behind her wasn't an easy matter. Unlike Kitty, Beth had really suffered. Kitty looked up at the calm blue sky and sent up a quick prayer that all was presently going well for her friend.

In Kitty's bag was her camera and she had taken snaps of the luggers before drifting off on her cogitations again. One lugger was named *Our Lily*, perhaps after a beloved woman. Another boat was *Morenwyn*, softly romantic; from a mythical Cornish character? *Pilgrim*, a religious owner? *Sea Days*, really nice. Kitty roused herself. She glanced at her wristwatch. Almost midday. It was time to get her last purchases and leave. She wanted to be settled back at Mor Penty before Beth returned, but she was reluctant to go. She gathered up her shopping. She shivered unexpectedly as a chilly breeze hit her bare arms. Suddenly the gentle south coast wasn't as gentle as it had been a minute ago. There was quite a chop to the wavelets now racing in to fill up the basin of the inner harbour where rowing boats and punts lolled high and dry on their sides on the pale sand. Soon these small craft would be floating upright, gently tugging on their mooring ropes.

'Sure you can manage that lot all by yourself?' An amused male voice startled her. There was male laughter, male banter, and Kitty looked up at what seemed to be a whole crew of fishermen crowded before her. The men and boys, including a pair of twins, were obviously from one family, such was the similarity of their thick dark hair, high cheekbones and friendly dove-grey eyes. The man who had spoken was carrying engine parts, the others were hauling other equipment, and all were showing off their trophies of hard graft, oil-stained faded overalls and blackened, greasy hands.

'Of course I can,' Kitty laughed with them all. Being whipped out of the realms of her own concerns was diverting, and being so used to Stuart's cheerful antics with his friends from their university days she wasn't easily embarrassed by men.

'Got far to go?' the same fisherman asked.

'Not really.' Kitty couldn't help smiling back into his confident eyes, which were set in a pleasingly weather-milled, thirtyish face. She stood up. 'If you'll all excuse me...'

The fishermen spread back to give her plenty of room, chuntering to each other. The confident one spoke again. 'The name's Rob. I'll be in the pub tonight. Come and have a drink with me.'

'He's in there every night when he's not at sea,' one twin guffawed. 'And watch out for he, Miss. He don't let the waves grow high under

67

him where the ladies are concerned.'

'Just being friendly,' Rob said, now feigning bashfulness with jocular sideways looks.

Jauntily raising her brows, with her bags in both hands, Kitty set off on her way, knowing the men were watching her back and the way she walked. She liked this local family. It was obvious they always had a lot of fun. She smiled impishly to herself, wording in her head how she would tell Beth about her comical encounter, and how one of the local fishermen was rather enticingly handsome.

'Maybe I'll find out where you're staying and pop along for a mug of tea and a hot buttered scone,' Rob called after her.

Kitty gasped at the blatantly suggestive remark.

She heard the men's feet carrying on their way to the working boats. Would Rob turn round and look at her? He did. Smiling broadly he passed his burden into one strong arm and waved to her. Kitty didn't return the wave but she allowed him a friendly smile.

Six

Beth had driven Kitty past Owles House and nearly all the way down Portcowl Hill. She had stayed in the motor car while Kitty walked away from her down to the harbour, striding energetically and turning her head in all directions to take in the views. Beth had pulled up just below a cottage near the bottom of the hill. She stayed put to take the time to still her churning emotions before turning round and driving up to Owles House. Now Kitty was gone she was on her own and felt a thousand times alone.

She wished she had the belief and courage of the biblical Daniel when he had been dropped into the lions' den. He'd had faith because right had been on his side. Right was on hers too, but she felt God wasn't. If she asked him for his opinion he would say, 'Elizabeth Tresaile, I would rather have you come seeking peace and reconciliation with your mother, not revenge. I'm the One who decides when and where vengeance is due.' Then there was the part in the best-loved prayer about forgiving others' trespasses. But it wasn't a simple matter to forgive someone out of hand, especially the one person who should have made you the centre of her life, instead of treating you as if you were valueless, a nuisance. When her selfish actions had caused you to be wrenched from your home and she had virtually forgotten about you, even if your loving grandmother had taken you in and afterwards given you a wonderful life.

Over the years Beth had not thought much about the way her father had treated her. As far as she remembered he hadn't been at home much and when he was there he'd had very little to do with her. 'Hello Elizabeth' had been his usual greeting. Then he, a tall shadowy figure, would place a hand on top of her head. A heavy pressing weight, Beth recalled it now, remembering too that the only words he'd said to Cleo were things like, 'Out of my way, dog!'

If Christina was there she would give him a report of Beth's behaviour. Always good ones, Beth thought now, to prove she was an interested mother. Once she had remarked, 'Elizabeth is doing very well at her lessons, so Miss Oakley said.'

'I should think so too, with the money we spend on her for that vicar's dried-up daughter,' Philip Tresaile had barked back.

Another time, Beth had overheard her parents from the sofa where she'd been snuggled up to Cleo, a cold flannel across her brow. 'Elizabeth fell over in the garden today. She's got a bad bruise and a large bump on her head.'

'Where were you? You should have been watching her! Is it too much to ask that you take

70

care of the child?'

One of Beth's hands flew from the steering wheel of the car to press on her middle. She was squirming inside with the same sickening trembles she'd suffered in her girlhood. Her careless trip over Cleo's legs in the garden that day had led to another shouting and screaming quarrel between her parents. Beth shuddered fiercely and felt the same miserable panicky tears well up inside her.

No! She wouldn't allow herself to take the blame. Little children fell over every day of the week. It was all part of growing up. Grandma used to say on such occasions, 'Well, if you didn't fall over, darling, you'd never learn to pull yourself up again.' And she had added kisses and cuddles. Beth drew in a deep determined breath. Well, she was up and she wasn't going to allow herself to be beaten down again in any way. She saw one thing clearly now. Her father had not particularly cared about her. It seemed his mission in life had been to keep up the battle he and Christina had embarked on of scoring points off each other.

To help her with this second visit to Owles House, Beth tried to recall the better memories of her life at her childhood home. She had run to Mrs Reseigh, the kindly daily help, after frightening or painful incidents if her mother had been incapable through her drinking and depression. She had wished her mother was more like Mrs Reseigh, a proper mother, slightly chubby, wearing a shapeless dress, a full wrap-around apron and cardigan, thick stockings and chunky shoes, her arms always ready to give cuddles, and a loud tinkling laugh to cheer her up. Mrs Reseigh had worn her chocolate-coloured hair in a scraped-up bun, rather like a teatime treat. Mrs Reseigh had been brilliant at baking. Beth had never tasted lighter scones since then.

Beth lit a cigarette. She drove a little further down the hill to the space on the verge that was wide enough for vehicles to turn round. On the way back up the hill she looked down the path that led to the cottage she had run to for help as a terrified abandoned seven-year-old. She glimpsed its name burnt into the porch top. Wildflower Cottage. An apt name and a lovely gentle old name, Beth thought, feeling a little soothed. It was one of the few properties in Portcowl that stood alone and had a large garden. Way up beyond the back garden wall she could see the cove's allotments. To her recollections it appeared that an ordinary, hard-working, happy family had lived here. From time to time over the years she had wondered about the family who had so readily and comfortingly taken her in. She remembered the man's voice, 'Aw, the poor little cheeil. Have we got any sweets in the house, Posy? Don't be frightened, my handsome. You're safe and sound in here with us.' The man had been a proper father, someone a little girl would feel safe with. Posy had been the mother. If only her own mother had been like Posy, who had sat Beth on her lap near the kitchen range, having first wrapped her up in a blanket, and held a cup of warm sugary milk to her lips.

Grandma had found out who the family were – Beth had forgotten their name – and had sent them a large box of chocolates with a beautiful summer cottage scene on the lid, and a thank-you letter. 'That will make their Christmas,' Grandma had said. 'I doubt they've ever received anything of the like before.'

If the same people still lived in Wildflower Cottage they would know a lot about Christina and Phil Tresaile, about the rift between Phil and his family. The same could be said for all the locals. Beth had the urge to stop the car and get out and knock on Wildflower Cottage's door, to personally thank her rescuers, if they were still there. She wanted to meet them and get to know them. Some of the children who had been there that night would be round about Beth's own age. What did they do now? And she recalled Mr Jewell, the gardener at Owles House. It was a pity that he was unlikely still to be alive. How wonderful it would be to see her aged friend again. She could pick his brains about the disturbing goings-on up at the property. And Beth wanted to seek out Mrs Reseigh, she must have witnessed so much at first hand.

If she really wanted to learn the full facts about Christina Tresaile-Vyvyan, these people, and other locals – including the other Tresailes – were the best resource. They could help fit together the pieces of her emotional jigsaw. She might even gain a complete picture, and that could be the biggest help of all to her getting her life properly on track. If she didn't attempt to get to know Christina without hostility, she might come away with false conceptions and plunge off her high horse, ending up with self-inflicted pains.

'Do give Christina a chance, Beth,' Kitty had implored her on the drive here. 'She's given up the evil brew. Wouldn't you like to know why?'

Beth did want to know why as she closed in on the entrance to Owles House. She felt a little ashamed about her dismissive remark to Christina over the death of her second husband. That had been mean. Christina must have felt hurt, she might be angry with Beth now. Beth would apologize to her first thing. She must steel herself to try to build an amiable relationship with Christina. When she had learned all she could about her, then she would know how to leave Christina behind for good.

From his bedroom window, Joe looked all the way down to the bottom of the drive at the wide, open gateway in the laurel and rhododendron hedging, waiting for Elizabeth Tresaile's Ford Sedan to appear. Either the woman was disrespectfully late or she had changed her mind and wasn't coming at all. If she did deign to present herself here, Joe would dash downstairs and out of the house, with Chaplin, in time to reach Elizabeth Tresaile before she got out of her car. He had a speech all ready for her.

74

'You're not welcome here! You're a horrid woman for coming here yesterday full of indignation with my mother. She told me about it and I believe you've only come to punish her. I won't have you upsetting her. My mother is a wonderful and good-natured person, and she is not well. I listened in on the upstairs phone to the call you made to her. You were rude and cruel to her when she told you that her husband, my father, had died. You've been very disrespectful arriving so late and making my mother more anxious. You're beastly and nasty. My mother told me as soon as I was old enough to understand that she used to drink, and that she had a daughter, but got too ill to bring her up. She's always regretted it. She tried to keep in touch with you but she gave up when you didn't seem to want to know. You're obviously here for petty revenge or to try to get your hands on this house. Well, you've got no right to it. My mother has left it to me in her will. You've got no right to me. My father was an honest, well-respected man. Yours was a truly rotten swine. You can ask your uncle the pub owner, the only Tresaile left down in the cove, about him. It's well known he only has bad memories of him. And as for your grandmother, I believe she was nothing but beastly to my mother. My mother owes you nothing. Now clear off or I'll set my dog on you.'

Joe had his speech ready for Elizabeth Tresaile and he would shout it right into her face. He ached to open up his lungs and blast her, but he wasn't going to as much as whisper a harsh word to her – if she bothered to show up, and he prayed to God she would not. He'd keep his mouth firmly shut because first he needed to know exactly why his half-sister had appeared. Then he'd know the best way to deal with her. He wasn't top of his class for nothing. He was clever and he could be artful, like his father had been, the father he still looked up to more than anyone in the world, the father he still missed three years after his death with silent tears during the night.

Also, hurling wrath at Elizabeth Tresaile would distress his mother too much. She was on the edge of her nerves, flurrying about getting everything ready for her daughter as if it was royalty she was expecting. In a wavering voice she'd asked Mrs Reseigh to do an extra polish in the sitting room and told her she could go home early today. 'Now you leave everything to me, Mrs Vyvyan, and to Joe too, you know he'll help out, the dear of him. We'll make sure everything is ship-shape for your visitor.' Mrs Reseigh, reassuringly motherly and now heading out of middle age, had cleaned at Owles House from the day his mother had moved in as a young bride, and she was as loyal to his mother as a batman was to his officer. She had found out where his mother had been committed after the mental breakdown and had written to her long cheery letters which, his mother often remarked to Joe, had helped her get through her recovery, to dry out from the years of alcohol abuse. Although his mother had asked Mrs Reseigh to call her Christina, Mrs Reseigh was old-fashioned and preferred formality. But that had not stopped her from slipping her arm round his mother's waist and leading her to the kitchen. 'Now off you go and bake that cake and biscuits that you want to. I'll clear up after you. You're not to worry at all, you hear me?'

While Mrs Reseigh had been busy, singing her heart out with a medley of war favourites and hymns, and making the house smell of lavender, his mother had baked a Victoria sponge and butterscotch biscuits. 'I know you're not happy about this visit. But you will be polite to Elizabeth – to Beth – won't you, Joe?'

Joe had stayed with her to help her curb her anxieties, and fetched things for her and put the used cookware into the sink of hot soapy water. 'I'll be polite, Mum, course I will, but I won't let her upset you.'

'I don't think it will come to that, darling. I mean, Beth's bound to have a few hard questions for me about the past. She's bound to be distressed. I let her down terribly. I've told you how she came home from school that last day to an empty house, how scared she got. No child should have to go through that sort of thing. I'm willing to face up to my misdeeds, her understandable anger. I've always wanted the chance to put things right with Beth. You understand that, don't you, Joe? You'll always be the most important person in my life.'

'I'll be on my best behaviour, don't worry, Mum.'

'Thanks Joe.' She had smiled through her flushed floury face. 'You're my rock, my reason for living.'

However nervous his mother was, Joe was sure he matched it for her sake. Aside from her arthritis she wasn't physically strong. The years of alcohol abuse had left her with a poor digestive system, her vital organs having taken the brunt. Her mental health was good most of the time but she could be forgetful and jittery. Simple difficulties could turn into massive problems to her if she wasn't quickly reassured.

'What should I wear, I wonder.' This question had swiftly brought his mother to shaky agitation. Joe had gone up to her room with her. He wasn't going to see her tossing half her wardrobe on to the bed and lamenting about the right shoes. 'Your burnt orange dress is my favourite. You look gorgeous in it. It'll be perfect, and a long string of pearls. A pair of black shoes will go well.'

Twenty minutes later she had appeared on the landing, where he was waiting for her, and she was looking incredible in the embroidered dress, pale coloured stockings, low-heeled ankle-barred shoes, and the necklace, a gold slave bangle and dangling gold earrings. She had put on a little make-up including a touch of pale blue eye shadow. Her shingled hair had turned grey years ago, was almost white, and suited her. Mrs Reseigh, who had come upstairs to say goodbye, had approved of the outfit. 'Your lady mother is a very handsome woman, young Joe,' she'd said, clearly full of admiration. 'Looks ten years younger than her age, she does. I'm glad to see you're so proud of her. I wish you both luck with Miss Elizabeth.' (Mrs Reseigh had pledged her silence as to the visitor's identity.) Right then Joe had been bursting with pride. His mother was like a girl, shy and oh-so-hopeful. God help this Elizabeth Tresaile if she reduced his beautiful mother to tears today.

'I'll go downstairs and wait for Beth,' his mother had said, swallowing nervously. 'Hopefully she won't be long now.'

But time had gone on and on and the visitor, the *scourge*, was despicably late.

Finally a motor car pulled into the drive, the right car yet the wrong car. 'Right, Chaplin,' Joe squared his wide shoulders, 'we're on guard duty. Shield and protect. If this damned woman isn't careful she'll get her arse kicked all the way out of Portcowl.'

'I see she's here, Mum. We're on our way down!' Joe and Chaplin went down the stairs in a thunder of feet and paws.

Her tummy trembling with nerves, Christina shot back from the sitting-room window, the sudden movement hurting her bad hip. She was anxious to avoid annoying Beth by staring out at her. She ran her damp hands down over her dress. Using her walking stick she went out into

79

the hall and patted fretfully at her hair. Had she remembered to get the tea tray ready? She thought hard, grimacing in the effort to remember. She was sure she had. She wouldn't have left the kitchen if she had not, and Mrs Reseigh would have mentioned it anyway if she'd forgotten it. Yes, she had done the task, and she had put out the sponge cake and the best of the biscuits, which thankfully had emerged perfectly from the oven.

Joe was there and he took her arm and tucked it through his. 'You look brilliant, Mum. Let's go to the steps and wait for her.' Chaplin went round to Christina's other side, and Christina was taken outside within this protective escort.

With only yards left to drive Beth saw them waiting to meet her. Who was the stranger with Christina? Obviously not her solicitor. The boy was too well dressed to be a village boy. A relative of her late husband perhaps. She stopped the car where it would give her a clean sweep to turn around and leave smartly if she wanted to. She turned off the engine. Took a deep steadying breath. Picked up her clutch bag and got out of the car. And faced the welcoming committee.

Beth strode forward then halted. The boy. She was in no doubt who he was. It was Joe, the 'paper boy' who had turned up at Mor Penty. To look her over, see what made her tick. See what she was up to and, if he'd felt it necessary, warn her off; the overriding seriousness marked on him at this moment made that fully apparent. If only he'd stayed until she had come up off the

80

beach. She might have found out exactly who he was. Had Christina sent him to find out where she was staying? It was more likely, Beth felt somehow, that he'd done it without telling her of his intention and his discovery. Christina was smiling down at her, wavering smiles that she needed to keep reissuing.

Christina raised a hand. 'Welcome, Beth.' Then her mind shut down on her. She didn't know what to say or do next. Her old enemy Panic, in numbing sickening waves, was surging through her. She couldn't do this. She was going to faint and make a scene, make the sort of drama that would make Elizabeth resent her more.

Joe felt her trembling and heard her gasping for breath. He squeezed her arm. 'It's all right, Mum. I'm here. If you can't speak, I will. And if she doesn't like it she can leave us in peace.'

Calling on all her acquired techniques to bring calm, while breathing deeply, Christina put herself into her 'happy place'. It was enough for her to summon back her smile. 'Wel-welcome, Beth. Would you like to come inside?' She got out her oft-rehearsed invitation. 'I'd like you to meet my son, Joseph Vyvyan. He likes to be called Joe. Joe, this is Beth, my daughter, who I've told you about.'

Beth had reached the top step. Again she was brought stock-still. This boy was Christina's *son*? Before the full implications of this news sank into Beth's brain, Joe said stridently, 'Good morning, Beth. Welcome to Owles

81

House. Do come inside. My mum has baked a cake for you.'

Beth glanced at him, then at Christina and then down to the dog. She felt she had been invited into the lions' den. You've got right on your side, she reminded herself. Their jaws can't hurt you. You'll emerge unscathed. Well, physically she would, but spiritually and emotionally she might end up devastated.

She proffered her gloved hand. 'How do you do, Joe?' She wasn't going to say, 'It's nice to meet you, Joe.' There was wariness and hardness at the edges of his startlingly piercing eyes. His hand seemed to come at hers and her hand was taken in a firm shake then quickly released. It was then she realized that this boy, grown-up beyond his twelve or so years, was her half-brother. Her mother had gone on to have another child – one, the facts were loud and clear, whom her mother cherished and who in turn adored her. To Beth it was like receiving a double slap across the face. She felt she was being mocked on her old doorstep.

Joe saw her confusion. Well, she wasn't totally a superior bitch, she had that in her favour, but she had better not bring out any self-righteous claptrap. He said politely, 'Would you like to follow us?' It was designed to make her feel she was very much an outsider and would stay that way.

Christina disengaged herself from Joe. From the time of Beth's telephone call, she had vowed she'd do all that was possible to make Beth feel comfortable, and hopefully want to be here. 'You go on ahead with Chaplin, Joe.' She was careful not to give him any endearments that might irk Beth. 'I'll walk Beth in.'

Joe did so, with Chaplin trotting dutifully beside him. Boy and dog were on such a par they did everything together by instinct. Joe looked back over his shoulder and shot Beth more of his solemnity.

She returned a wide smile designed to convey that she was simply a friendly soul looking up her relatives. What a thing though, to discover she had another flesh-and-blood relative in Portcowl, and one as close as a half-brother. It would take time to sink in. She could imagine Kitty's response to the news, 'But that's rather wonderful really, isn't it?' Dear Kitty, ever the optimist and blissfully lacking experience of anything that might have shaken her life to an almost unbearable pitch.

Her mother was wearing the same familiar warm perfume that smelled of heavenly orange blossom and creamy jasmine. It was a young, sensuous scent. Beth had loved that smell when her mother had let her sit on her lap or kissed her goodnight in bed. It was the smell she had craved on the days her mother had failed to wash or groom herself. She was well groomed now. It was a shock to realize Christina's once peroxided hair was now actually grey. She had given up another bottle and allowed her true colour, now she was nearly forty years old, to be on show.

83

Beth realized that she hadn't yet said a word. 'Thank you for agreeing to allow me to see you again.'

'I couldn't have been more delighted to get your call,' Christina said enthusiastically, pleased to hear the lightness in Beth's tone. She limped along ushering Beth into the hall. 'I think you'll see quite a few changes, but many things are still the same. May I enquire where Miss Copeland is?'

'She's gone down to the cove.'

'I thought she might have. She seemed to enjoy the view of the sea yesterday.'

'Mrs Vyvyan, before we go on, there is something I'd like to say.'

'Yes Beth, what is it?' Christina asked nervously. It was a timid, anxious question, and Joe turned and frowned darkly at Beth.

Beth saw his warning. It made her feel small but in this instance she deserved it. It had been spiteful of her to belittle Christina over her husband's – *Joe's father's* – death. 'I want to apologize for my remark about your husband. I didn't realize he had passed on. What I said was inappropriate and unkind. My apology extends to you too, Joe.'

'You weren't to know,' Christina said, giving her an understanding smile.

Beth couldn't tell by Joe's blank expression if he was placated or not. She said, 'Nevertheless, it was unnecessary of me.'

'Thank you, Beth.' Christina's thin shoulders heaved with relief. The remark had been hurtful

84

to her but Beth's sincere apology gave her hope that Beth was prepared to give her a chance to atone. 'Well, this is the hall. What do you think?'

Beth had planned to take no notice of the house, this place of so many bad memories and the warped and terrifying images in her nightmares, yet she couldn't help herself. She looked all around and up and down. The general effect was toned down, lighter and roomier than before. Christina's decision to put the past behind her and start anew? The stairs straight ahead, with a second flight overhead turning back on itself, had formerly been bare mahogany but were now painted a gentle cream; a crime to the purist but not unpleasing. The constant and beautifully elaborate Georgian and Victorian furniture had been replaced by Arts and Crafts items of squarer lines. Carpets and curtains had, of course, been changed with the wear and tear of the passage of time. There were few patterns and opulent splashes now. The paintings of fully rigged sailing ships remained but the late-Victorian penchant for rural scenes had gone in favour of Stanhope Forbes Cornish harbour scenes. There was a lot of studio pottery and bronze dancing figures. In a tall cabinet a collection of eighteenth and nineteenth century Chinese snuff bottles blended in well.

At last she said, 'I recognize some things but it's mainly quite different.'

'Do you like it?'

85

'Yes,' she replied truthfully to Christina's anxious question seeking her approval. It wasn't what she would choose for herself but it was nice. 'It's soothing.'

'I'm so pleased you think so. That was what we had aimed for, Francis and I, Joe's father. Shall we go into the sitting room? Would you like some tea, Beth, and cake?'

Beth suddenly became aware of how fast her heart was beating, how her blood was whooshing through the whole network of her veins at just being inside Owles House again. Her throat was as dry as ashes. 'That would be nice.' It would be interesting to discover how well her mother could bake. 'But if you'd like, we could all go into the kitchen and sit round the table. It would save you trotting about on your bad leg.' Beth wasn't exactly being thoughtful. She just did not relish being alone temporarily with the boy, the snotty young thing. His eyes were on her relentlessly. He was waiting his chance to bait her, to give cause for her to be sent packing and for his mother to be glad of it. Beth wouldn't allow that. She was Christina's first child, and Christina owed Beth for what she had done to her – or rather for what she had not done, been a good, loving, nurturing mother.

'Oh, yes, that's very good of you, Beth.' Christina beamed her a warm smile. This seemed to be going better than she'd imagined, beyond all that she had hoped for.

The company trailed on through the hall then forked off to the left-hand side of the staircase to the short passage that led into the spacious kitchen. Joe made a production of pulling out the nearest chair for Beth at the long linen-covered table. 'Do take a seat. We'll have the things ready in a jiffy.'

Beth couldn't help being impressed by the boy's aptitude about the kitchen. It was practically unheard of for a male of any age to lift a finger in the house, especially in the kitchen. Helping Christina wasn't a ruse to give him an air of superiority for the occasion. Joe did it to make things easier for her and he actually seemed to enjoy it. They were a team, moving as one as the tea was made in a Royal Worcester teapot and placed on the table. Joe went to the refrigerator and poured himself a tumbler of milk. Devouring their every action and natural interaction from the table, Beth felt like a child again abandoned in the night, left out. Another passion surged through her, jealousy. Why hadn't her young life been like Joe's was? Why hadn't her wretched mother done little every-day things like this with her? She had not been important to Christina. The only company she'd had in this kitchen, refurnished on crisp modern lines, was with Mrs Reseigh.

Beth felt the eyes of a guard on her. The German Shepherd had settled its big sleek body between her and the Vyvyans. Tears hung heavy behind Beth's eyes. *I'm not the bad one here, the uncaring monster.* It was all so damned unfair. But she had to behave like an interested visitor or she would be sent away, rather than being the one choosing to leave again, this time for ever. 'Does Mrs Reseigh still work here?'

'Oh yes,' Christina said, looking avidly at Beth while lifting the protective net covers off the sponge cake and plate of biscuits. 'I couldn't manage without her. She's been a treasure. She kept in touch with me and even visited me throughout my drying-out treatment. She took Cleo in until I returned home and was well enough to cope with her. She even stayed here with me during my first week home.' Christina gave a sort of grim smile and then glanced at Joe. They joined Beth at the table.

Christina went on, 'I've kept nothing from Joe so you can speak freely, Beth. He knows all about how I left you alone that winter's day. How I'd left the house in a drink-fuddled haze and ended up unconscious in the woods after wandering off the cliff path. It was Joe's father Francis, helping in the search, who found me. Eventually, I wrote to thank him. When I was well, love grew between us and we got married.' At the last word she looked down, a little bewildered, not sure what to say or do next.

'Why don't you pour the tea, Mum?' Joe said softly.

His encouraging words were enough. Christina rallied. 'Yes! Let's have tea. How do you like yours, Beth? Please help yourself to a slice of cake or biscuits, whichever you prefer. Or both, of course.' It was a jolly, nervy invitation.

'I like my tea medium strong with milk, thank you. The cake looks delicious.' It truly did,

88

yellow and plump and oozing with raspberry preserve and cream, the top dusted with icing sugar. Beth wanted to regain the upper hand. 'Shall I serve you first, Joe? I bet you're looking forward to the cake, and a second helping.'

'Absolutely.' Joe smiled, his grin wider than necessary. Chaplin was edging into his side and he was automatically stroking the dog's broad neck. 'I helped to make it, you know.'

'Really? How clever.' Using the silver cake slice Beth lifted a pre-cut wedge of the feast on to a bone china plate and handed it to Joe. He took it with a polite 'Thank you.' A typically ravenous boy, however, he was already clutching his cake fork.

She turned to her mother. 'Shall I do the same for you, Mrs Vyvyan?'

'Oh, would you mind cutting off a half slice for me, please?' Christina replied, looking pleased at Beth's friendliness.

'Mum's got a rather delicate tummy,' Joe interjected, adding pointedly, 'She needs a bit of looking after.'

'Don't make me sound like an old lady, Joe.' Christina pinked with embarrassment. 'Would you like sugar in your tea, Beth?'

Using the tiny silver tongs – Beth remembered these with their ornate arms – she took one sugar lump from the matching bowl and dropped it into her tea. 'Thank you.'

She had just taken her first bite of cake when Joe asked, 'What do you think of what Mum told you just now?' *Brat!* Beth thought. She couldn't answer until she had chewed and swallowed the cake and she would seem rudely quiet.

She had barely consumed the mouthful when she gave a small shriek. Something had been thrown on to her lap. What had the wretched boy done to her? Her first reaction was to rail at him but she would have to laugh off his prank. It would work in her favour if Christina sent him from the room. She was getting nowhere with him here.

'What is it?' Christina clattered down her cake fork in alarm.

'I don't know.' Beth gritted her teeth, trying to smile. She would have pushed out her chair but the thing on her lap was quite heavy and it was moving. She felt sharp needles digging through her dress and into her legs. She screamed. Chaplin was up on his feet and barking loudly. 'What are you doing to me?' Beth cried at Joe, who to her mind was feigning bewilderment.

Joe leapt up and lifted the linen tablecloth from Beth's side of the table. His hands reached down for the source of the disturbance, his sturdy young face brimming with amusement. 'It's Charlie. It's only my cat. Sorry, Beth.' He was grinning and then he was laughing; it was outrageously funny to see this disdainful, vengeful woman red-faced and fit to burst and getting her 'bloomers in a twist', as he planned to tell Richard Opie later in the day, when he joined him from down in the cove. 'Charlie's a devil. He wants to sit there and it's his way of telling you to get off the chair.'

'Joe, take the cat off Beth at once,' Christina ordered, horrified for Beth.

'I'm about to,' he said, ready to scoop up the slant-eyed culprit.

'It's all right.' Beth pushed Joe's hands away. 'I love cats. Charlie can stay. I'll just unhook his claws. I've had two of my own, a tabby called Tufty and a black one called Velvet.'

While Joe looked nonplussed, Christina said, 'Are you sure, Beth?'

'Absolutely.' Beth smiled very sweetly at Joe. He shrugged his shoulders and Beth was sure he was re-evaluating her.

Joe flopped back down easily in his seat and attacked his cake. 'Silly names for cats,' he muttered.

Beth smiled. *Got you.*

Christina smiled. *This is going well so far, thank God.*

The company sipped and ate. While Joe, forgetting his manners, gobbled down a butterscotch biscuit, he eyed the rest of the cake. 'Oh no you don't, young man,' Christina said, 'you can take some more cake to share with Richard this afternoon. Richard is his best chum, Beth.'

Beth was tickled as Joe's dark complexion clouded over. He had just been embarrassed, a horror for a boy his age and particularly so for a boy trying to act with the sternness of a grown man.

'Did you and Miss Copeland spend a comfortable night, Beth?' Christina shone her full

91

attention on her.

'I didn't sleep much,' Beth said truthfully, making the point that she had inevitably had a lot on her mind. 'Kitty slept like a log, as she always does. We're staying at Mor Penty.'

'Really?' Christina was thrilled at Beth offering the information. She seemed to be unravelling some of her animosity. 'When I could walk that far I often used to walk the cliff path and cut off for the lane and go down on the beach. The cottage has been beautifully brought up to date. Will you be staying there for a while?' she asked, hope forming in her heart. It had been her dream since her recovery to be reunited with her daughter.

Beth gazed down, deep in thought, then lifted her head and faced Christina directly. 'I've come down here to learn all about my childhood, to find out all the whys and wherefores concerning you during that time. My father too, I know little about him. My grandmother said he was a good man, she always seemed fond of him, but I remember him as always being remote. I spent my earliest years mainly without love. It was pretty dreadful. Then I went through that terrible time of fleeing in fear from here in the dark. Now that I'm here and I've met you again, now I've learned that you have a son, and have met Joe, I don't think I can leave and go forward with my life unless I learn the whole truth.'

'I understand, Beth. Your mind must be in even bigger turmoil,' Christina said quietly.

'Don't speak like that, Mum, like you're ashamed,' Joe blurted out, jumping up and going to her, wrapping his arms round her shoulders. Chaplin went with him. 'None of it was really your fault. And you can't tell her everything anyway. Your illness blocked out a lot of your memory. The doctor says you may never remember it all and it might be detrimental if you do.'

Christina went rigid and pale.

'See?' Joe turned on Beth, who had blinked and gasped at the suddenness of his tirade. 'See what your coming here has done to her? My mother is fragile. There's many things she is nervous about, so many things that she's not up to any more, like facing people. She hardly ever leaves these grounds unless it's for my sake. This house is her refuge from life's ills and cruelty. She's suffered enough. She doesn't need you raking up old scores. She's genuinely sorry that you went through a rotten time but she can't take it back. I'm sorry about it too. You've seen for yourself what a wonderful mother she is to me. Don't you think if she could have been different when you lived here she would have been? What good will it do anyone raking up the past? You might learn things that will make your life even harder. Have you thought of that, Elizabeth Tresaile?'

'Beth...' Christina raised a hand helplessly, her chest rising and falling with the rapid beating of her heart.

Beth had clenched her hands together. She

93

hadn't known what to prepare herself for when first deciding at home in Wiltshire to come here, but she could never have envisaged being thrown into emotional turmoil by a feisty young half-brother. A boy who had succeeded in making her, of all things, feel some guilt about her quest. Easing the cat off her lap she got up and looked at her pale, teary-eyed, quivering mother and her angry, indignant brother. 'I concede that you have a point, Joe. I – I need to go away and think about it. Perhaps I should leave Portcowl.'

Heavy tears of despair funnelled down Christina's face, making streams in her make-up. She shook her head desolately and mouthed soundlessly, 'Please don't go, Beth.'

Beth had to get away or the echoes of the past – of angry voices, shattering ornaments and slamming doors – might break in. She pictured her young self putting her hands over her ears to shut out the terrifying sounds. There was no Cleo to run to now, no Mrs Reseigh or old Mr Jewell to shrink to for comfort. She had never felt so alone and she needed to be with Kitty. And the echoes of Joe's rant were spinning round inside her head.

Beth looked at Joe. He was serious now and seemed so sad. He had taken a lot on his young shoulders, for years it seemed, another child whose formative years were affected by Christina's weaknesses. He was wise beyond his years, wiser than she was, and at that moment he had the courage she lacked. She had leaned on self-righteousness and gone about this wrongly from the start. It was such a profound realization she felt all her energy seep out of her. If she left here now she knew she would never come back and that would be the worst thing she could do. And, she had to admit, it would not be fair to Christina and Joe. They all needed to talk.

'I'm sorry for upsetting you both,' she said quite breathlessly. 'Would you mind if I sat back down?'

Seven

It was such a big empty bed. Lying in the middle of it Christina felt all the debilitating loneliness and abandonment of being cast adrift miles and miles out at sea, a dot of meaningless humanity, just a scrap of flotsam. She moved swiftly to what had been Francis's side of the bed. She felt safe here, where his tall stocky body had lain beside her. Francis had slept the sleep of angels, calm, never restless, and every night she had moved in against his warm strong back or into his arms. Any fears or worries she'd had would instantly disappear, and although sleep never willingly claimed her, she rested in his might and devoted protection.

'Do what you can easily manage each day, darling, and leave the rest to me,' Francis would say, holding her, lovingly caressing her. 'And no worrying ahead, do you hear me? That's my job. You just look after yourself and our precious little boy. Whatever happens, I'll always be here taking care of you both.'

But fate had cruelly stolen his vow. Francis had been the manager of a prestige boat-building yard a little further down the coast. Also a working craftsman, he had been proud of all the finished boats, from punts and fishing luggers to gigs and sailing yachts. Every so often he had liked to take to the waters alone in his own small engine-powered boat, *Firefly.* 'To clear the wood shavings out of my brain,' he had laughed.

Three years ago, in the spring of 1924, Francis had set out on a calm early morning and never returned. The crew of the Portcowl fishing boat *Our Lily* were the last to see him and he had waved happily to them; the lugger had been heading out to long-line for ray down towards the Lizard. Just after midday his boat was found abandoned and drifting, the engine still alive and puttering gently. A week later Francis's body was washed up on shore in between inaccessible rocks near Gorran Haven. With the spot too dangerous to approach by sea, Francis's body had been retrieved and brought up by the coastguard. What was left of Francis's clothes, his wedding ring and St Christopher medal, a present from Christina to keep him safe, had been the means to identify him. It had ended Christina and Joe's desperate hopes that he had been washed up somewhere alive, perhaps not knowing who he was.

The hammering reverberations of her heart-torn howl at the news, brought to her by a gentle committee of a senior coastguard officer, Dr Powell, the Reverend Oakley and Mrs Reseigh, still echoed inside Christina's head almost every day and her grief would be renewed. Strangely the grief didn't thrust her under and threaten to take her back towards the mental institution. Francis had left her with the purpose and the strength to carry on. Joe. Although with many a struggle, she had done so, as Francis would have wanted. Francis was very much part of the woman Christina now was. 'I'll never leave you, Christina,' Francis had promised her. 'If anything ever happens to me I'll always be here for you, my darling, watching over you, loving you. If you look out to sea, I'll be there. If you look up at the sky any time, day or night, I'll be there. I'll be out in the gardens, on the cliffs, and inside this house. You can trust me.'

Christina believed his vow, believed it so strongly she talked to Francis all the time. Right now, she had clasped to her chest the bedside photograph of him, a handsome shot of his head and shoulders. His St Christopher medal was wound round her hand. She lifted the plainly framed photograph above the bedcovers and kissed Francis's smiling image.

She repeated the words she had spoken hours earlier to the image, soon after Beth had left the house. 'She came back, darling. You were right in your belief that Beth would one day seek me out again. She's so lovely but so sad. She has a lot on her mind, much more than wanting to know all she can about her childhood, and me, that's for sure. A mother knows these things. She's not well. I thought she was going to faint. Dear Joe, he's really suspicious of her because he's worried about me, but he was quite understanding when Beth asked if she could sit down

98

again after he had spoken harshly to her.'

Christina gave a little chuckle. 'At least he was impressed that Beth likes Charlie, and Chaplin too. When Joe came down off his high horse with Beth he plied her with more tea, cake and biscuits. "To build yourself up, you are a little thin," he said, bless him. Chaplin nuzzled Beth cautiously and she made a lot of fuss of him. I think Chaplin made her think wistfully about Cleo. Joe said he'd take her to see Cleo's grave, if she liked. That will happen tomorrow. Beth is coming here to spend the whole day, to give her and me plenty of time to talk. I'll tell Beth about the other grave, of course. I hope it won't be too much of a shock for her.

'She said she's looking forward to meeting Mrs Reseigh again; they were so close. I've told Beth that Mrs Reseigh's son took over as gardener here three days a week and Mr Jewell passed away. Mark will be working here tomorrow but Beth said she's not concerned about that. Beth says she'd like to look over the house and grounds. I think she'll have a pleasant surprise or two. I've invited her friend too, if she wants to join us. Katherine Copeland seems very nice.

'Joe's promised to make the effort not to get ratty, as he calls it, with Beth, if she does happen to get a bit angry with me. Joe's so brave, so grown up, bless him. I think he's taken it on board that it's understandable that she has a lot of problems to come to terms with. I am her mother. I was responsible for her and I let her

99

down terribly. It would be so wonderful if it ends with her forgiving me and allowing me to build up a relationship, on whatever terms that suits her. Pray for me, darling, that this will happen. I love you for always. I hope I dream about you tonight.'

Christina put the photograph back on the bedside table and draped the St Christopher medal over it. Snuggling up like a child, she closed her eyes and began to make plans for the next day, the meals she'd make for Beth, the flowers she'd give her from the garden ... and more, until she fell asleep.

Christina dreamed, but about the wrong husband. Phil Tresaile was stretched across the bed, his slim arms and legs swollen into heavy weights and so long they were hooked under the bedstead, his enormous bulk crushing her and pinning her down. She gasped to breathe and every breath was hard won, agony. His rugged, arrogant face was the same, his blacker-than-black hair and the trimmed moustache he wore to give him more swagger. Christina couldn't speak, only plead inside her head to him to get off her, to stop tormenting her and leave her alone. 'Please Phil, go away, don't hurt me any more.'

'I sent her.' Tresaile blew stale breath into her mouth and eyes and up her nostrils. He was poisoning her. 'She'll never love you. She hates you, just like I did. And she's a slut and a whore just like you are. Take her to that little grave, tell her what you put in the ground.'

'It wasn't my fault,' she wailed in her tortured mind. 'I wasn't strong enough.'

'You killed him. No one else did it. Murderer!' Phil Tresaile head-butted her in the chest and this time the pain was so intense she was able to scream. She screamed and yelled and shrieked and struggled.

She woke with a sickening force, gulping for air and groping to sit up straight, quivering in fear and revulsion. Somehow she managed to push in the switch on the bedside lamp and thankfully this brought her eyes straight to stare into Francis's gentle loving perpetual gaze. 'O-oh, my God, darling, it was terrible.'

Clutching the photograph to her body she edged herself up until she was solidly propped against the pillows and headboard. She cried, frantic tears of humiliation, but quietly so as not to disturb Joe. Thank God she didn't scream aloud, or he would have run to her. She felt tainted. She didn't want Joe looking at her and seeing her shame. She had felt tainted with Phil from their second secret meeting, when he had raped her. She had cried in pain and horror, and he had begged her to forgive him. 'I'll never hurt you again, Christina, I promise. I got carried away. I couldn't help it. It was your fault. You can't really blame me. You're so beautiful and you flaunt your desirability.'

So she had taken the blame. She shouldn't have gone off somewhere alone with Phil. His brother Ken had tried to warn her. 'You want to be careful of Phil,' he'd whispered, taking her

101

aside in the pub's back yard; his father had been the landlord back then. 'Phil flatters all the women. He's only after what he can get from them. The minute you go back home he'll forget all about you. He got someone in trouble back-along, told the poor unfortunate girl to get lost, only they weren't the words he used. She ended up marrying someone else, an old bachelor, for security, and Phil put it all round the cove that the baby was her husband's. Which is ridiculous, she's the image of Phil, a Tresaile to the core.'

'What the hell's going on here?' Phil had stormed outside to them.

'I've told Christina you're no good,' Ken had hurled back. 'And about your illegitimate child that you've refused to acknowledge and support. You should leave this girl alone, she's very young and far too good for you.'

'Bastard!' Phil had seethed. 'You've always been jealous of me. Being the old man's favourite son isn't good enough for you. You want what I've got but you'll never have her. That's what you're out to get.' He'd sniggered, laughed uproariously and made a lewd gesture. 'You're too bleddy late anyway. I've already dipped my wick in her.'

Roaring with fury Ken had lashed out at his younger brother. There had been a vicious, prolonged fist fight, and on Phil's part, kicks and spitting and dirty blows. The patio furniture and plant pots in the yard had been wrecked, and windows smashed. Phil had ended up battered

102

and bruised. Ken had suffered a broken arm, broken ankle and cuts across his face. Christina's mother had blamed her for the ugly incident, accusing her publicly of flirting with both brothers and playing them off against each other. Phil had brought so much strife and trouble to his parents' door they had banished him from the family. Marion Frobisher, however, had felt sorry for him and had given him the money for a room in a lodging house, for the rest of the summer.

'You're a disgrace to me, Christina Frobisher,' her mother had yelled at her at the scene and slapped her heavily across both cheeks. 'You've always been a disappointment to me. You're not clever or accomplished in anything. All you have is good looks and you're using them to bring me down. I don't know what I've done to deserve a child like you. Why can't you be like your brother was, my darling Leslie? Why did he have to be the one to die? Just a dear little boy of three years, he was, when you passed on the whooping cough to him. He would have grown up to be a successful young man and made me very proud.'

After her mother's rants, Phil got it into his head that Christina had actually been flirting with Ken. He had never trusted her again, and once they were married and living at Owles House, he had forbidden Christina to go down to the cove without him.

'I loved this old house the moment I stepped inside it,' Christina had confided in Francis, at the beginning of their tentative romance, two months after she had finally been discharged from the hospital. 'I didn't care that my mother had sullied my name in Portcowl, that everyone thought I was a loose woman. I was content to make a home for Phil and our coming child. Things weren't too bad. Then I gave birth. Elizabeth was born a healthy baby, then events took a tragic turn. I had been carrying two babies and didn't know it. My little boy, Philip junior, only lived an hour. His lungs hadn't formed properly. Phil blamed me, he said I should have known I was expecting twins and should have taken better care of myself. Everything went quickly from bad to worse. I couldn't cope ... I started to drink ... the rest, well you know the rest.'

Lifting Francis's photograph, Christina kissed his image with trembling lips. 'If it wasn't for you, my darling, I would have died that night I wandered off in a drunken stupor and left poor Beth alone and terrified. That monster made me weak. He'd crushed me and tormented me. He won't leave me alone even now, but I won't allow him to haunt me. Beth's come back to me, and I'll make everything right. I'll show her that it will be good for her to be part of my and Joe's family. Watch over us, Francis. Help me with the strength to tell Beth the whole truth. Why her grandmother delighted in causing trouble for me over Phil. And how she had a twin brother who tragically only lived for such a short time.'

104

Eight

'I'm so proud of you, Beth,' Kitty said gaily, driving in her carefree way to Owles House. A moment earlier she had been singing 'Baby Face'. She had her window down and the breeze, so welcome on an already hot dry day, fluttered her fringe and pushed at her hat. 'You're a heroine, giving Christina this chance with goodwill and making such an effort. I can't wait to meet Joe again, properly this time. What a young character he seems to be. Has it sunk in yet that you have a brother?'

'I suppose so. I've thought a lot about Joe,' Beth replied, yawning. Having turned over in her mind, almost throughout the night, every moment spent at her old home the day before, she was tired and drained. 'He'd make any mother happy to have him. Christina's a good mother to him.'

'Well done.'

'What for?'

'For saying that without a trace of envy or bitterness. The hurt is still just as raw for you though. You can't hide that. Hopefully, some of it will soon be soothed away.'

'We'll see. It's strange, but after all that time

nursing my resentments and feeling the pain of rejection, I'm almost resigned to accept the outcome of my next meetings with Christina. I suppose Joe has levelled things out. After he harangued me, I saw things from a different perspective. I've learned that it's better I reserve my final judgements until I've found out all I possibly can. Joe was quite nice to me soon after being so angry. I have to remember that it must have been hard for him to be suddenly faced with the sister he'd known about but never thought he'd actually meet, and although he's very grown up he's still a child.'

'Well, if at the end you feel it's not possible for you to be reconciled with Christina, but you come away accepting the situation, that'll be really good.'

Stifling another yawn, Beth stretched her arms up as far as the Ford Sedan's roof allowed, then she eyed Kitty with affection. Kitty's smile was as bright as the sun and her green eyes sparkled like the sea. 'You'll certainly enjoy some of the day, you old optimist, you. But don't expect to come across any handsome fishermen.'

'I'm not expecting to,' Kitty laughed. 'And what would I have in common with one anyway?'

The women found Joe sitting with Chaplin on the bottom doorstep, a quietly serious reception team. Joe stood up as they got out of the motor car. Chaplin fell in beside him. 'Good morning,' he called down to them. He was wearing an immaculate short-sleeved white shirt and long shorts, smart socks and white plimsolls. His dark hair was combed neatly.

'Hello Joe,' Beth called back, glad she had also made an effort with her appearance. Her dress was one worn only once before, with handkerchief points.

Kitty waved to him cheerily. She was in a blouse and leisure trousers.

'Would you ladies follow us round this way.' Joe spread his long arm to indicate the side of the house. 'Mum is out by the summer house waiting for you both. I'll bring some drinks. Would you like something hot or cold?'

'Cold please,' Beth and Kitty said in unison.

He quickly disappeared inside and the women followed his instruction. 'I agree with what you said, he really is so grown up,' Kitty commented.

'Yes, and a little awe-inspiring and strong-willed and no sufferer of fools, I'd say. He is determined to protect Christina at all costs. Admirable, of course, but I'm not going to get very far with her if he doesn't allow me to spend time with her alone.'

'It's a good thing I'm here. I'll try my best to get him away somewhere. I'm quite prepared to take a long walk with him and the gorgeous Chaplin. I'll try a spot of probing and hopefully I'll glean something about the current situation from him, and later you and I will be able to compare notes.'

* * *

'What do you want to know exactly?'

'I beg your pardon?'

Joe's blunt question brought Kitty's long easy strides to an abrupt halt a few hundred yards along the cliff path and tore her eyes away from the sea thirty feet below. It was the second such breath-stopper he had given out today. He had carried out the drinks tray and placed it on the picnic table, poured out four tumblers of iced lemonade, his head held high. He had seated himself fluidly next to his mother, who was shaded by a large parasol, on a firm cushioned patio sofa, and then he had looked straight at Beth. 'After this, I shall invite Miss Copeland to join me to take a walk somewhere of her choice, and we'll take our time, to give you and Mum plenty of time for a heart-to-heart. I'm sure none of us want an emotional, drawn-out time while past events are brought to light. Mum couldn't stand it and I won't allow it.'

Christina had choked on a swallow of lemonade and patted her chest to help get the liquid down. Clearing her throat, she had shot a worried glance at Beth. 'Joe, you're sounding rude.'

'I'm only being sensible, Mum.'

You're sensible and intuitive but confrontational, and you always throw in a warning, Kitty thought now. Joe might be young but he was already a force to be reckoned with. Joe, the man, was going to be dynamic. Kitty knew from information given to her by Beth yesterday that Francis Vyvyan had been a parish

108

councillor. Joe seemed to have the intelligence and drive to reach endless heights, and the way he loved and protected his fragile mother made him compassionate, bold and steadfast. 'OK Joe, I'm glad you've got straight to the point. I'm sure Beth would be interested to learn about the spot where your father found your mother after she disappeared that night. Do you know where it was?'

'I do. Follow me. You'll see precisely how hard it was for Mum to be found quickly. And how if it wasn't for my father she might not have been found until it was too late and would have died.'

'What would you like to do first, Beth?' Christina smiled shyly. *Please, please, let this go right.* Her insides were being gradually raided of stability. She was frightened that the slightest thing, a single wrong word, a sudden bad memory would reopen the wounds in Beth and she'd rail against her and leave for good, vowing never to get in touch again. Christina chewed a thumbnail. 'You can ask me anything you like. I'm sure you have a long list of questions. You're welcome to look anywhere over the house and grounds. Mrs Reseigh is here. She's really excited to know you're here today. I was going to cook a special lunch but she's insisted on doing it for us.'

Beth was struck by how childlike and vulnerable Christina seemed. Her mother had looked something like this on that enjoyable day long ago when she had taken Beth to Mor Penty's little beach.

'I'm looking forward to seeing Mrs Reseigh again too,' Beth said, surprised she was actually feeling relaxed but remembering the summer house had been a haven to her in the old days, where she'd played make-believe, and dolls and teddy-bear tea parties, with dear Cleo. 'How old was Cleo when she died? Was she buried in the grounds?'

Christina's eyes misted over as she was visited by fond memories. 'Cleo had a long life. She inevitably slowed up and got a bit achy. The last few weeks she grew wearier and wearier and wanted only to sleep. Francis and I sensed when she was reaching the end. We were both with her when she passed away in her sleep. Cleo used to lie down on the summer-house veranda for ages or wander about as if she was searching for something.' Christina bit hard on her lip. 'I think she was looking for you, Beth. Anyway, Francis buried her in another of her favourite spots, one she used to share with you. Shall I take you there now?'

'Yes please, I'd like that.' Beth passed Christina her walking stick and reached out to help her up, the act of care coming naturally to her. Grandma had weakened rapidly as the cancer had done its worst and Beth had helped to nurse her at home right to the end. The doctor and district nurse had said she would make a good nurse. Not me, Beth had thought at the time, but Kitty would. I don't have a calling to care for the sick or the frail or champion the underdog. Yet she was doing it right now. Christina was frail, and even though Beth didn't really want to acknowledge it, her mother had been an underdog all her time on this property until Francis Vyvyan had saved her and loved her. There was a strength and purpose in Christina that had been missing when she had first been a wife and mother. Could Beth go so far as to see her as a victim, as she herself had been?

'Thank you, Beth,' Christina said, when she was firmly up on her feet. 'It's very kind of you.'

I'm not a particularly kind person, Beth reflected as a simple statement and with conviction. I'm not a sacrificing sort. I'm quite selfish. She had arrived at that conclusion after much soul-searching following her miscarriage. From the time she had gone to live with her grandmother, while loving her, and establishing a devoted friendship with Kitty, she had mostly cared about her own needs. Survival instinct perhaps, but she maintained she was selfish nonetheless. She could have and should have walked away from her attraction to Stuart Copeland instead of blatantly acting upon it. She had fallen deeply in love with him. Stuart had been content with his wife and family, his job and his home. He had been an active member of the local church. Beth's subtle flirting, followed by deliberate acts of playing the helpless female and getting Stuart too often alone with her, had been a selfish, shallow operation.

She had not given a thought to Stuart's undeserving wife and two young children, how if the affair became known it would devastate their lives. Stuart himself would have lost his job and the respect of his colleagues and the church. Losing her baby had been Beth's just punishment. She also knew the uncomfortable truth that it had been something of a relief to Stuart that there would be no baby. He may have loved her but he hadn't really wanted to leave his family and lose everything else. Dear, wonderful Kitty might have ended up hating the two people she said she trusted with her life, her brother and her best friend.

What and who had made Beth do such a wanton, potentially destructive thing? She had always blamed her faults and weaknesses on her mother's neglect, but as her astute young stepbrother had pointed out, it wasn't as easy as that. And one should always take responsibility for what one chose to do once an adult.

'I don't think you'll find me a kind person,' Beth said flatly.

Christina's hand hovered to touch Beth's arm but she was afraid it would be shrugged off. She had not earned the right, at least not yet, to comfort her daughter. 'If you really believe that, Beth, then it's not your fault.'

'And perhaps it's not all yours.'

Coupled with the fight to keep in control and stay clear of doing or saying anything offensive, this lifting away of some of Beth's resentment towards her made Christina burst into tears, while using a hand to hide her quivering lips.

'Do you want to sit back down?' Beth asked. She felt genuinely concerned for Christina.

'No.' Christina's answer was watery and emotional. 'Thank you for saying that, Beth, thank you so much. It shows that you do have kindness to openly admit that to me, not to blame all your miseries on me. I let you down so badly. I shouldn't have let things go on for so long like they did. I should have got help. I'm so sorry. I'm so sorry.' She sobbed wretchedly for a moment then with a supreme effort she stopped and smiled through her saturated face. 'It's so wonderful having you here. I promise I'll be totally honest with you.'

'I'm glad too,' Beth said, while Christina mopped up.

The mother took the daughter to the dog's resting place. It was round at the back of the house, past the far side of the kitchen garden, under the low branches of a giant willow tree. The women ducked their heads carefully to enter the quiet spot. 'It's where you and Cleo used to come and curl up together and sleep. You used to bring out a little crochet blanket and biscuits for you both to nibble on.'

'How did you know all that?' Beth said in astonishment, crouching down to touch the small grey memorial stone with the name *Cleo* and the words *Faithful Friend* inscribed in it.

'I used to watch you play, quite a lot actually, even when I was more or less unattached to life.

113

Mr Jewell told me about this little place. Sometimes I'd peep in here to make sure you were safe. Cleo always heard me but she'd just stay snuggled up to you. You always seemed so comfy and happy fast asleep with your companion. I'd feel so ashamed because you felt safer with Cleo than you did with me and she could give you more than I could. I think Cleo understood somehow that I was often incapable through the drink of responding physically to you.'

Beth ran her hand along the top of the little smooth headstone. 'Dearest Cleo, I missed you for ages. Grandma got me some kittens and she bought herself a sweet Pekinese, but the dog wasn't the same to me as you were.'

Leaving the peaceful grave the women made to enter the house by the back door. 'So you weren't as neglectful to me as I'd thought?' Beth said.

Christina nodded. 'I hope you believe me, Beth.'

She had sounded forlorn and quite pathetic, and Beth got the notion that Christina had slipped back in time in her mind to when she might have pleaded often to be believed, to be taken seriously by Phil Tresaile. Beth could imagine her hard, aloof father treating Christina as if she were a worthless hysteric. And Christina was probably somewhat at a loss without Joe and Chaplin at hand. 'I believe you're being honest with me. It was good to see Cleo's grave.'

Thrilled that Beth was not taking her for a liar

114

– one of Phil and her mother's most constant accusations – Christina took Beth's arm this time. 'Beth, there is another grave you should know about. It's in the churchyard.'

'Oh? I take it you're not talking about your husband's grave.' Beth's heart speeded up uncomfortably. What was she about to be told? Christina was very nervous.

'No,' replied Christina, with a painful lump in her throat. 'It's a baby's grave. You had a twin brother, Beth. He was named Philip after your father. He was born twenty minutes after you. It was a shock to me to go into labour again. I'm afraid he didn't live very long. He was so tiny and his lungs hadn't formed well enough for him to survive.'

'I've got – had – another brother?' Beth whispered in shock. 'Why was I not told before?'

Nine

'You did see what I meant?' Joe stared at Kitty. They were walking back through the woods to the cliff path, the firm ground under their feet dancing in light and dark patterns where the bright sunlight daringly bypassed the high leaf-heavy branches. 'And you will tell Beth?'

'Of course I will.' Kitty met his stern gaze. 'Beth has come down here to learn the whole truth. It's what she needs. And it's what I want for her. I want to see an end to all her inner torment so she's able to move on with her life.'

'If my mother could have got back to her that day she would have done. But as you've just seen it was totally impossible after she'd wandered off in a daze and fallen down that steep slope. She was virtually out of sight. My father was helping with the search. The whole village scoured the area, even those that Beth's father had turned against my mother, including the Tresailes. Most people thought she had jumped or fallen off the cliff into the sea. It was my father's idea to get Cleo out of the kennels to help find Mum. Cleo led him this way and she scrambled straight down the slope. Dad climbed down on his rear after her. It was very tricky

116

for Dad to carry Mum up but Cleo picked a way for him to follow. Dad wrote to her at the hospital. He really never left her side until the boat accident.'

'I'm so sorry about the loss of your father, Joe. I admire you for the way you've stepped into his place. Have you got someone to go to when you need advice and some comfort?'

'I do all right,' Joe replied, offhand, but he was impressed at his companion's thoughtfulness. He stole several sideways looks at her. Miss Copeland was really something to tell Richard Opie about. She was gorgeous, a bit like a movie screen siren but without all the powder and paint, and she didn't know just how luscious she was. Best of all, she wasn't prissy or twee. She was easy to get along with, a bit of a grown-up tomboy.

'I'm on the outside looking in on the situation, Joe. Beth is as close to me as a sister could be, and I've witnessed how she's been affected by her earliest years, but I want you to know, Joe, that unless I learn to the contrary, I have sympathy for your mother. She seems to be a very pleasant lady.'

Joe nodded, pleased with Kitty's last outlook. 'You knew Marion Frobisher. What did you think of her? Did you see her as a good woman? Mrs Reseigh says there were two sides to her. I think she wants to tell me more but is waiting until I'm older.'

'You're hoping I'll say that Mrs Frobisher had a harsh side.' Kitty gazed frankly at Joe. 'If she

117

did, I didn't see it. She adored Beth, gave her the best of everything, introduced her to the arts, the theatre, took her to foreign countries, but she was also a typical adult in not wanting Beth to grow up spoiled and ungrateful. I found her a fascinating woman and she was a lot of fun.'

'Did she send Beth to a boarding school?'

'No, Beth attended the same private girls' day school as I did.'

'She packed my mother off to boarding school from the age of six, when her son died aged three. Before that there was a nanny. Mum was rarely allowed to go home in the holidays. She usually spent them at various other boarders' homes. She must have felt very unloved.'

'It sounds as if your mother must have had a very lonely childhood.' Kitty thought sadly that perhaps Christina had found it hard to relate to her own daughter. Marion Frobisher had made it plain that she had no time for Christina, but she had spoken a lot about her cherished dead Leslie. Now Kitty had met Christina she had to admit there was conflict in Marion Frobisher's attitude towards her daughter and granddaughter.

Chaplin was running on ahead sniffing out the familiar territory. He left the woods well ahead of the others but suddenly he was running back to them. He stopped yards away from them and barked, tossing his broad neck. 'Chaplin's found something,' Joe cried like the boy in him. 'He wants us to follow him.'

Grabbing hold of Kitty for a moment he hurried her along. 'Keep up!'

She laughed, happy to go along with the order. It seemed Joe had accepted her as an older playmate. He must trust her and that was brilliant. Chaplin barked again and shot off, making sure all the way that he was being followed.

Kitty blinked as they emerged into full sunlight, at the beginning of the short scrubby path that meandered down to the narrow cliff path. It wasn't near the hottest part of the day yet but already the sun was beaming down relentlessly, its intense heat bouncing off the granite rock. As she went along, matching her longer legs to Joe's swift pace, Kitty slipped her arms into her cardigan to avoid getting sunburned.

They reached a stretch of scrubby ground heaped with gorse bushes, brambles and wild foliage. Swathes of pink and purple heather and pink thrift and white and yellow wildflowers gave lots of pretty colour.

Chaplin leapt in among the shrubbery and soon lowered his head to the ground, his long tail up and wagging. 'He's licking something, something living I'd say, perhaps hurt. Stay back, Miss Copeland. Leave this to me.'

'I'm not a helpless female,' Kitty protested, but obeyed anyway, slowing down considerably, which was wise anyway because of the prickly growth. 'What is it, an injured bird?' She was going to add, 'Be careful,' but it wasn't really necessary. Joe wasn't a fool.

119

Joe went down on his knees, nudging Chaplin aside. 'Hello there, little one. You're in a sorry state, aren't you?'

'What is it?' Kitty was dying to know. She could hear whimpering. Joe had his back to her and she could not see.

Joe gathered up something seemingly tiny in his arms. He turned round to Kitty. 'It's a puppy. Abandoned and ill-treated.'

Rounding a last gorse bush, Kitty saw Joe's pathetic trembling little burden. The scrap of puppy had a long tangled coat, light brown and white with a bit of black. A pair of pinprick, watery dark eyes gazed at Kitty partly in apprehension and partly in hope. 'Oh, the poor little thing, it's starved. How do you think it got here?'

'It was dumped.' Joe rolled his eyes as if she was stupid. 'Probably tossed in the woods but somehow it made its way here.' He turned the puppy's lower half over a little then held it firmly. 'It's a girl. She's a cross-breed. See her pointed ears and tapering snout? She's got long-haired collie in her.'

Bending close to the puppy, Kitty gently smoothed its head. It had curled up into a tight ball in Joe's arms. 'She's so sweet. Well, we mustn't stay here. She urgently needs food and water.'

'That's obvious,' Joe sighed.

Kitty ignored his impatience. 'Can I take her?'

'She'll make your clothes dirty.' Joe moved

past her. 'Good boy, Chaplin, you've done well.'

Kitty followed the boy and dog procession until they were all clear of the foliage. 'I'm not concerned about my clothes.' She reached over Joe's arm and touched the puppy again. 'I'd like to carry her. Please give her to me, Joe.'

'She's got blood on her paws, and has fleas and probably worms,' Joe said doubtfully.

'That doesn't matter.'

'Good for you,' Joe said, with an approving smile. Carefully he passed the trembling puppy into Kitty's arms.

Kitty used the side of her cardigan to shield the puppy from the sun, now it had been taken away from the shade of the bushes. 'Oh, you're such a little darling,' she cooed.

Joe led the way back to the house fast. 'After she's been fed and watered we'll give her a gentle bath then make up a little bed for her.'

Delighted that he had included her in the puppy's care, Kitty asked, 'Will your mother let you keep her?'

'She can't stay with us, I'm afraid. Chaplin protects Mum. She easily copes with him but another dog would be too much for her. Any puppy is demanding until it's trained and a dog with collie in it will need a lot of exercise. I'm sure someone local will take her in.'

'Have you got any idea who might have abandoned her?'

'I have actually. The puppy is lucky to be away from there.' Joe would get Richard Opie

121

to join him soon in paying a certain individual a visit.

Kitty carefully lifted the puppy up on to her chest. It gazed up winsomely at her and whimpered. 'It's going to be all right, you little darling. You're safe now. No nasty person is going to hurt you again.' The puppy snuggled in under her neck, trusting her. Kitty cuddled it protectively. In those moments she bonded with the hapless little parcel she was carrying. 'There won't be any need to look for a home for her, Joe. I'm going to keep her.'

'You might want to think again about that,' Joe said. They had reached the garden gate, and he opened it and ushered Kitty through.

'There's no need. I love her already. She's beautiful, adorable. She's so tiny I'm going to call her Tiddler.'

'Don't be silly! She won't stay small. Look at the size of her paws. A name like Tiddler would embarrass her.' Joe locked the gate.

'OK, I take your point. Don't be disparaging,' Kitty chided.

'Well...'

'Well nothing, young man.'

'Don't call me that. I hate it!'

Kitty laughed.

They both laughed.

Ten

Beth put her hand on the door handle of her childhood bedroom. She was almost afraid to go inside. Dreadful memories might wrap themselves around, pull her back to all the insecurity and trauma of old and imprison her in it. It would make her despise Christina all over again. After what had been revealed to her so far, and how Christina was now, or seemed to be, Beth was feeling herself thawing towards her mother. Christina had, apparently, always loved her and never stopped. She had lost a baby. Beth knew the tragedy and aching loss of that. There were matters Beth still needed to resolve, but she certainly didn't want to be plunged back into the role of accuser, didn't want to become more vulnerable than Christina was. As well as learning she had had a twin brother there had been another shock. Beth also now had to come to terms with having an older half-sister, an illegitimate forsaken child of her father's who lived down in the cove, her name Evie Vage. 'This is all too much right now,' Beth had said to Christina, who had looked at her with such concern. 'Tell me all about her another time.'

'Would you like to look over the house, Beth?' Christina had offered some moments ago, after they had downed a pot of Mrs Reseigh's well-brewed tea, around the kitchen room. Beth had liked this room the best during her first years, ensconced in here with Cleo and the cheerful, motherly, cuddle-giving, high-busted, slightly chubby Mrs Reseigh. Mrs Reseigh had seemingly not aged at all. Fashion had passed her by. Her hair was still the colour of chocolate and in a fat bun at the nape of her neck. Her dress was dark and shapeless, her full pinafore was a dark blue print, and a saggy cardigan was worn on top. This had been the same however hot the weather. Today she had on soft lace-up shoes. In the winter she had donned brown calf-high boots.

'I'd like to very much,' Beth had replied, eager for it yet afraid she would lose the peace and wonderful familiarity gained from Mrs Reseigh's wholehearted reunion.

'I can't tell you how wonderful it is to see you again after all these years, Miss Elizabeth.' Mrs Reseigh had smiled her habitual cheery smile. 'You were a handsome little maid then and you've growed up to be a lovely young lady. You're so like your mother. Do you remember my son Mark? He's a few years older than you. He used to fetch up shopping and run errands for your mother. He married and made me a proud granny. Sadly he lost his wife, but little Rowella is the delight of our lives.'

'Congratulations on becoming a grandmother,' Beth had replied cheerily. Mrs Reseigh had the knack of lifting up others' spirits. Beth could only recall Mark Reseigh as a tall, skinny boy, reluctant to speak, who was soon off when his task was over.

'He's still as quiet as a church mouse. You probably won't see him today. He comes no nearer than the back yard to fetch his mug of tea. Well, this is lovely having you here, Miss Elizabeth. Mrs Vyvyan is over the moon you've come back.'

Christina had given Beth a smile, which Beth saw as being frantic with hope that she would understand this, know it, and be truly pleased about it.

'I'm glad I've made the journey.' Beth's tone had been calm and light.

The obvious first choice was her old bedroom, where she had spent so much time alone with Cleo. She had climbed the stairs and walked down the long landing without taking notice of anything else. There was no point in being interested in other things if she was about to discover something hateful and hard to bear.

And now she stood before the bedroom door, trembling as she wondered what effect the excursion inside would have on her. Then she thrust up her head. 'Don't be silly. Christina is not a monster, and even if she was, I've survived my childhood, and she can't hurt me now.'

One look in the room and it was confirmed to Beth that Christina was anything but a monster.

Christina had kept her bedroom exactly the same as the day Beth's grandmother had brought Beth back into it to pack a trunk of clothes and her favourite toys to take away for her new life. A doll that Beth had not played with much was lying on the bed alongside an array of stuffed and knitted toys that had also been left behind. There were the same nursery friezes of fairies and pixies on the walls, and the same matching pink and beige curtains, carpet and bedspread and quilt. Her dolls' house was in the same corner. Her dappled rocking horse with a full mane of hair was in the same spot, and there was her pull-along waddling duck, and the box of bath-time toys. Her little pink-painted wooden table and chair, fashioned in the manner depicted in old fairy-tale books, had also been kept. She had sat there and played schoolmistress with Cleo and her toys as pupils.

'I was very strict and bossy,' Beth whispered, grinning to herself. She had copied Miss Muriel Oakley's habit of looking down over her round-rimmed spectacles, using her thumbs and forefingers to form a pair of glasses. Miss Oakley had not been bossy. She had been softly spoken and quietly encouraging. She had always smelled nicely of roses. According to Mrs Reseigh, she was still languishing in the dark shabby old vicarage with her father. Beth remembered Miss Oakley's parents as being rather 'barmy'. The Reverend Oakley had flapped about in his black robe, sometimes topped by a long cloak, and had frequently talked aloud and thrown up his stretchy arms as if he was acting. Beth had wondered in her young mind if he had elastic bones. He'd worn a gold crucifix so big and heavy that during his antics it had thumped against the full length of his chest. Miss Oakley had hurried Beth away on these occasions. 'Come along, Miss Elizabeth. Dear Papa is in full flight again. His sermon, you know. We mustn't disturb him.'

The vicar's wife had seemed much like the old Queen Victoria, young Beth had thought. In her high piping voice she had referred to Beth as 'the little Miss. Well, we must suffer her, I suppose.' Thinking about it now, Beth realized Mrs Oakley had been embarrassed that her husband's stipend did not stretch to all their needs and Miss Oakley had taken on private lessons to help out. Mrs Reseigh had said that Mrs Oakley had become bed-bound due to a stroke and Miss Oakley had dutifully nursed her until her death.

Beth turned round and round in the room, taking everything in with delight. Crying softly and hugging herself she lowered herself down on the little bed. 'You didn't want to shut me out of your life, Mother. You never forgot me.'

So why had her grandmother given her the impression that the woman downstairs, who had welcomed her return so openly and with such gratitude, had been a totally uncaring, rotten mother?

Beth continued weeping for a short while, then she dried away her tears and went to the

127

high window to see how different the view down over the lawn, the cliff and the sea would be to her now, as an adult. She saw Kitty – who appeared to be carrying something – and Joe. The pair were involved in an animated conversation. Chaplin kept glancing up at whatever was in Kitty's arms.

Beth ran out the bedroom, heading for the stairs. She had to see Christina before her friend and young brother came inside.

At the foot of the stairs, leaning on her walking stick and looking up worriedly, was Christina. Again Beth saw her mother was steeped in that hope that was like a stranglehold on her.

'You're not about to run away are you, Beth?' she pleaded.

'No, no!' Beth called down to her, thundering down the stairs.

She made the bottom then, mindful of Christina's frailty, she slowed down and smiled the biggest smile of her life. Then her arms were out at full stretch and she was sobbing with every emotion she possessed. 'Mother, Mum...'

She took her mother into her arms and laid her head on Christina's shoulder. Christina sobbed, 'Oh, Beth, my darling Elizabeth...'

Eleven

'Scruffles would be a good name for her,' Joe declared in an authoritative tone. He was in the scullery, carefully washing the forlorn foundling puppy in a large white enamel bowl placed inside the deep stone sink.

'I don't like Scruffles.' Kitty made a face. 'I certainly won't be calling her that.' She and Mrs Reseigh, Christina and Beth surrounded Joe, all wanting to help him. Kitty was particularly anxious to take a major role in the clean-up of *her* puppy.

Joe was stubbornly ignoring her advice and that of the other three women. 'Oh, do stop all that silly cooing over her,' he had ordered the four of them from the start. 'You'll frighten her all the more.'

'Don't be rude, Joe,' Christina had scolded him, but not seriously. Joe was being his usual I'll-take-charge-of-this self. And she was too happy to be annoyed with him, or with anyone or anything else. She was wonderfully happy. She and Beth had just become reconciled, the outcome beyond all her cherished dreams. There were still events to be chewed over, explanations and apologies to give, doubtless

129

some uncomfortable moments for them both, but the fact that Beth had called her Mum and grasped her so firmly in the hall surely meant the reconciliation was unbreakable. Christina had glanced at Beth, and her heart leapt in delight at witnessing Kitty mouth to Beth, 'Is everything all right?' And Beth had smiled and nodded, before taking an avid interest in the poor tiny bedraggled puppy.

'I'm sure you'll find something the poor little mite can have to eat and drink, Mrs Reseigh,' Beth had said when Joe and Kitty had brought their pathetic little find inside. Then she'd turned to Joe. 'The puppy first has to be shown it can trust us. You're doing a great job, Joe.'

'Absolutely,' Joe had replied.

Christina knew that despite his preoccupation with the puppy, Joe had taken in the new terms between her and Beth, and Christina's heart had soared to hear her children relating so well to each other. It touched her deeply that Beth was automatically allowing Joe the leadership of the situation.

'Some water to drink and some warm milky sops to begin with, eh, Mrs Reseigh? And is there some meat paste?' Joe had said. 'When she's full I'll clean her up.'

'I can do that,' Kitty had cut in.

'It's best left to me.' And Joe would not be swayed otherwise.

Thinking the puppy was a soulful-eyed adorable creature, and that it was typical of Kitty to immediately decide to give it a home, Beth had relaxed and watched engrossed throughout the proceedings. The discovery and arrival at the house of the puppy had been timely. Its plight and rescue had mopped up a lot of the pain of her emotional reconciliation with Christina and placed their particular situation on an even keel. It had cut through any need to mention what had taken place between the two of them. Their ease with each other was apparent to all.

Lifting up the saturated shivering puppy from the bowl, Joe deftly tipped out the dirty soapy water then gently rinsed the puppy's coat with warm water from the pitcher Mrs Reseigh had put on the draining board. Finally it was over and the puppy was a woeful dripping scrap, trembling in Joe's hands. The women oohed and aahed.

Kitty had ready one of the old towels kept to dry off Chaplin when it was necessary. 'I'll take her now, thank you,' she told Joe in a tone that permitted no room for argument. 'She is to be my dog.'

'I was going to suggest that.' Joe handed the puppy over to Kitty and helped her to wrap the towel round it.

'There you are, my poor darling, finished at last.' Kitty caressingly dried off her new little friend and kissed the top of its damp head. 'You'll soon be warm and dry and no one will ever hurt you again.'

While Mrs Reseigh slipped away to check on lunch, the rest of the company went along to the sitting room. Kitty took a quiet fireside chair with the puppy, now snuggled into a small soft blanket in her arms. With Chaplin close at his side, Joe pulled up a chair next to her and talked about what food was suitable for the puppy, cautioning that it might require a trip to the garden soon to relieve itself. 'If you haven't got any oatmeal or ham in the cottage then get some. Chop the ham into tiny pieces. You can have the first sleeping basket we bought for Chaplin.' He proceeded with tips for training.

Beth and Christina sat on the same sofa. Neither knew quite what to say for now and they were content to focus on the endearing drama in their midst, the first thing they had shared together for many long years.

Kitty had not taken her eyes off her bundle for a moment. 'I'll call her Duchess.'

'You certainly will not,' Joe snorted.

'What's wrong with Duchess?'

'It's ridiculous for her.'

'Well ... um ... Lady.'

'Too soft.'

'Daisy.'

'Hardly.'

There was a thoughtful pause from Kitty. 'Ah. She was found huddled amidst some ferns. Fern, I'll call her Fern. It's perfect.'

'Daft.' Impatient sigh.

'For goodness sake, Joe, she's my puppy.'

Beth and Christina exchanged amused glances.

Kitty stroked the puppy's damp forehead, the love she already felt for it clear on her lovely face. The puppy stirred and opened its eyes, and lifted its head to lick Kitty's fingers. 'You're mine. You're beginning to feel safe with me, aren't you?'

'She's bonding with you, Kitty,' Beth said. 'You're going to have to forgo some of the sightseeing you hoped to do by looking after her. I'll be glad to help, of course.'

'It's good that we're not leaving yet awhile,' Kitty replied meaningfully.

'There is a lot of getting to know one another to do. Will that be all right with you, Joe?' Beth asked him.

'As long as things stay the way they are now; amiable, with no resentfulness or digs.

'I know,' Joe said. 'You could name her after a famous movie star. Bebe, after Bebe Daniels.'

'I don't think so!'

'Greta or Garbo. Or Clara, after Clara Bow.'

'Never. I don't believe you'd even contemplate those names, Joe, if you weren't a moving picture devotee. I am too, by the way. The very name for the puppy has jumped into my mind. She's going to be called Grace, after a favourite old aunt of mine. She's Grace and that's an end to it.'

'Grace is perfect for her,' Beth said, just as the puppy's tiny face again popped out from the confines of the blanket. Its big sad eyes sought Kitty's face, searching for approval and reassurance, a place where it was wanted and where it belonged. Kitty lowered her face to the puppy and laughed when Grace licked her chin. Kitty

133

clucked to her and kissed her several times. 'Oh, just look at her. She loves you already, Kitty.'

Beth was also sending admiring looks at Joe, occasionally catching his eye. He returned a steady gaze each time. Her half-brother was clever and capable – and a little domineering with a budding arrogance – and he was totally comfortable in the company of women. Although she had not taken in all the implications of her emotional discovery that Christina had never stopped loving her, that it seemed that circumstances outside of Christina's will had led to her mother's neglect of her, Beth now had different questions on her mind. If she got fully involved with Christina, if she bonded with her and came to fully care for her, wanting to share Joe's role in taking care of their fragile mother, how would Joe react to that? He was at ease with Kitty, in a way he was even flirting with her, but while he seemed to have accepted the new understanding Beth had with Christina, would he ever want a brother-and-sister relationship with Beth? He had taken practically no notice of her throughout the ministrations to the puppy. Would Joe ever trust or accept her?

Christina said nothing but smiled hopefully. Finding the puppy at this time was such a helpful distraction, a way to dissipate the unease of the day. It seemed to be a sign that all would be and stay well.

Joe shrugged his sturdy shoulders. 'Grace will do, I suppose. We've kept all the things we used

134

when Chaplin was a puppy. I'll dig them out of the old stable for you.'

'Thank you, Joe,' Kitty said. 'I shall be glad of any advice you can give me.'

Joe gazed at his mother and then at Beth. He was happy to take Kitty Copeland as he found her, a thoroughly pleasant, undemanding individual, and fortunate, he felt, not to have undergone any life-shattering experiences. As for Beth, he accepted she'd had a rocky start culminating in an incident of harrowing proportions. He understood why she had held years of antipathy towards his mother. He was pleased Beth had enough of an open mind to realize quickly that his mother had not been utterly streaked with badness. Phil Tresaile and his grandmother, between them, had nearly succeeded in destroying his mother. Phil Tresaile had been an amoral heartless swine but the full reasons for his grandmother's malice must be uncovered. Beth had come here wanting to learn the whole truth. Joe was not going to allow her to leave until she had got all of it. Only then would she become who she really was, and if she had inherited those same rotten traits as her father and grandmother, he, boy that he was, would send Beth Tresaile packing for good.

Joe suddenly put an end to his mother's and Beth's wishful musings, and it caused shock all round. 'Mum, Beth, obviously there's going to be a lot of soul-searching ahead. Why not bite the bullet and get on with it? It won't be as

135

difficult if you're under the same roof. Mum, I'd like to suggest that Beth and Miss Copeland move out of Mor Penty and spend the rest of their stay in Cornwall here, with us.'

Twelve

Rob Praed, the fisherman who had spoken to Kitty on the quayside, pushed his way into the Sailor's Rest and in his usual manner swaggered up to the bar. With him was his father Linford, known to all as Lofty for obvious reasons. Rob dropped some coins down on the bar towel.

'The usual, gents?' Ken Tresaile was already reaching behind him for the men's personal pottery tankards kept permanently on a shelf.

There was no need for either Praed to answer Ken. The pint would be the first of two that Lofty would drink this evening, before leaving at nine o'clock for Wildflower Cottage for a bite of supper. Rob would down as much beer as took his fancy and he'd go home when it suited him. He was to play euchre with Lofty, the skipper of the lugger *Our Lily*, and two fishermen from *Morenwyn*, until Lofty left for home. Then he might continue with cards, or play darts or skittles, or simply hang about chatting to other local patrons. He also enjoyed banter with holidaymakers. His soft grey eyes conveyed an easy-going nature but his well-set stubbly jaw suggested some hardness. Rob might call in at one of the other two pubs in Portcowl. It wasn't many nights he went home before closing time.

Often he sought some female company before finally going home to his quayside cottage where he lived with his two younger sisters. Judy, the elder, kept the house and made pin money by knitting fishermen's jerseys. She was one of the two young women who had watched Rob from round the quay the day he had flirted with a beautiful red-haired lady. Judy had later found out, through customary women's chit-chat, exactly who the young lady was. Alison, his other sister, worked in a sail loft. Rob cared for Judy and Alison with a fatherly eye, but he insisted they did not interfere with his life.

He pulled out a packet of Players Weights and offered it first to Ken, who took a cigarette, and then to Lofty, who put one behind his ear 'to smoke later'. Lofty smoked very little and his wife Posy usually ended up with his free gifts.

'That's a turn-up for the books, eh, Ken?' Lofty said, after savouring the first thirst-quenching draught from his tankard. He pushed back his peaked cloth cap, revealing his receding hairline. His fingers, like all fishermen's, were deft but thick, covered with the scars of his trade from baiting up and hauling in heavy nets and handling scaly fish. 'Phil's daughter returning to Owles House. And she staying at Mor Penty and you not even knowing it. Young Miss Elizabeth Tresaile, the poor, frightened, frozen little maid Posy and me took in that night. I'll never forget her huge desperate eyes, how she clung to Posy. You remember it, don't

138

you, Rob? You was there.'

'I do,' Rob said, listening while slouching against the bar and gazing about, smiling and nodding at the early evening regulars and dressed-up holidaymakers who were drifting in. There were no attractive women in yet.

Burly, seasoned and amenable, landlord Ken sucked in his breath. He had a wealth of greying hair and thick trim black eyebrows that moved about in time with his changing expressions. 'Surprise, you say? You can say that again, Lofty. My niece staying in Portcowl and me not knowing it.'

'How'd you feel about it, Ken?'

Putting his elbow on the polished mahogany bar top, Ken settled his heavy chin in his palm. 'S'pose it'd be something to see young Elizabeth again, not that I caught many glimpses of her as a child, mind. She had such a woeful little face and no wonder. Can't picture her all grown up. Now she's at Owles House and if she's really forgiven Christina after what she done to her, maybe she'll call in here, curious about me. I'll leave it to her.' Ken sighed heavily, still hurt over the irony that he was another victim of his younger brother's wickedness. Ken's wife, Myrna, had left him years ago, taking their three young children with her, after constantly accusing Ken of being secretly in love with Christina and thinking of Myrna as second-best. Myrna had not been far wrong. For a while Ken would have liked to be in Francis Vyvyan's place, but once their son had

139

been born Ken realized that he and Christina had nothing in common.

'I wouldn't mind meeting her friend again. Miss Katherine Copeland,' put in Rob, his eyes shining with possibilities. 'She's very beautiful and I like redheads. She was sitting outside the pub a couple of days ago, Ken. Perhaps she was hoping to catch sight of you to report back to her friend what her uncle seemed like.'

'Maybe. Pay you to keep away from this redhead. No good will come of it.' Ken's words were gruff, with an embarrassed catch in his tone. It was well known that he'd been 'sweet' on the young and naive Christina Frobisher. He moved away to serve another customer.

Lofty looked at Rob. 'Elizabeth Tresaile coming back will dredge up more bad memories. I'm thinking about Evie Vage, Phil's other child. How's she feeling, I wonder, having a rich half-sister practically on her doorstep? Mind you, Evie will take it all in her stride and say little. She's the most reserved person in the cove. Davey might not like it, it'll remind him he's her adoptive father.'

Rob made a dismissive face. Evie Vage had been with Judy the day the Copeland beauty was outside the pub. Judy had said that, as usual, Evie now couldn't be drawn on her thoughts about Elizabeth Tresaile. 'I'm only interested in her friend,' he answered.

'Well, unless this Miss Copeland comes down to the cove this weekend you might miss her altogether,' Lofty said, as he and Rob took their

drinks to the euchre table. 'We're all off pilchard driving come Monday.'

'Yeah,' Ken called out to them as he served a
half pint and a port for an elderly holidaymaker
and his wife. 'For the next few weeks the fleet
will be moored up at Newlyn and you men'll be
home only at the weekends and my takings will
be down. So drink up!'

Rob and Lofty won the first round of euchre;
their opponents, Davey Vage, Rob's next-door
neighbour, the engineer of *Morenwyn*, and one
of the crewmen, a young family man named
Arthur Trenchard, won the second. Rob bought
the next round of drinks. Davey's was lemonade. Rob sat down, passed round his cigarettes
to all except Davey, who preferred his pipe.
Rob lit a smoke himself, and then leaned back
idly in his chair and eyed Davey while the older
fisherman dealt the next hand of cards. 'How do
you feel about Evie's posh sister being back in
the area then, Davey?'

Lofty's annoyed eyes, and fresh-faced
Arthur's stunned ones, shot to Davey and then
to Rob. Lofty was vexed. Rob was a happy-go-
lucky bloke, but when the mood took him he
got mean; he would bait someone, anyone,
deliberately provoking hurt. It was always
unexpected. Lofty said tartly, 'It's none of our
business, Rob. Let's just get on with the game.'

'I'm only curious,' Rob said smoothly – too
smoothly for Lofty's liking – while keeping his
gaze fixed on Davey.

Davey Vage calmly shifted his well-loved

141

ancient pipe to the other side of his bristly bottom lip then picked up his cards. He gave Rob a quick shrewd look, conveying that he was not going to answer him. Not now, not ever. It was Davey's way. He had once rattled a bully, a slovenly mannish woman, as it happened, by his refusal to rise to the bait and he had received a beating, started deviously, for it in this very pub. People respected Davey for not backing down, and because he was a hard-working and fearless fisherman.

Lofty smirked to himself. Rob was dogged in all his intentions, but this would teach him a lesson for being such a big-head. In his sixty-three years Davey Vage had never left the cove unless he was away from it working. He was a man of simple tastes, content with his allotment near the cliff top and his radio. He attended the Methodist chapel, situated two narrow streets up behind the quayside homes, but only in the evening accompanied by his adopted daughter Evie. Evie, like Judy, kept house and earned money by knitting. Evie also made lace. Davey did not use bad language, as far as everyone knew, and he never raised his voice. He avoided being drawn into an argument and never offered an opinion about others' lives, shunning topics like religion and politics. He spoke little, and Evie was just the same.

The Vages seemed to eat well but otherwise they lived frugally. People considered Davey to be tight-fisted with money towards Evie, who at twenty-five had not for some years put on a

142

new item of clothing. She did not have her hair cut short in the current style but wore hers longer, resting on her shoulders. She was slim and darkly pretty, as her mother Iris had been, but she also resembled Phil Tresaile. She was apt to keep her head down when approached until spoken to. She would be polite and smile pleasantly but offer scant conversation. Male interest in her had never been reciprocated. No one was aware of Davey chasing off would-be suitors to her, but people considered him responsible for her lack of a social life.

It had been assumed that Davey, who had lived a long time alone after his parents' deaths, would never marry, and the cove had been shocked when he'd made an honest woman of the shamed and four months pregnant Iris Keane, after she was heartlessly abandoned by the loathed parish he-goat Phil Tresaile. Rumour had it that Davey had never consummated his marriage to Iris. Three lots of single bedding used to be pegged out on the Vages' clothes line, and the couple had maintained a passive but kindly relationship. Davey had been quietly delighted when Iris's baby girl was born. He had given the child his surname and always called Evie 'my handsome', an affectionate term to the Cornish. Sadly, nine years later, Iris had died of pneumonia, and Davey had kept Evie almost isolated at home.

Still staring at Davey, Rob pulled his mouth to one side and smiled. It was a smile Lofty did not like.

Thirteen

Philip James Tresaile
Beloved Son
17 May 1905

It was a large grave for a baby who'd been born and died on the same sad day. A three-foot stone angel, kneeling and praying, was at its head, the epitaph engraved deeply into the plinth. The rest of the grave was enclosed by stone kerbing and filled in across the top with marble. It all portrayed the importance of the little soul buried underneath.

This was the second time Beth had visited her twin's resting place. Yesterday she had driven here with Christina. Each had brought a posy of carnations and rosebuds. Beth had picked the flowers from the gardens and Christina had tied them with royal blue ribbon. Christina had worn black, her cloche hat netted at the front, and as the weather had been cool she'd added a crossover light summer coat. Beth had not brought any black clothes with her but she had managed to find something suitable from Christina's wardrobe.

Side by side they had solemnly entered the

churchyard. Beth had carried the posies and a bottle of water. Christina's walking stick had been essential to her safety due to the rough neglected paths. Almost all of the consecrated grounds were sadly overgrown. There was a riot of red clover and primroses, weeds and nettles. Beth had kept a watchful eye on Christina.

The little grave was just beyond the church building, immediately off the path. The grass around it was trimmed, and lily of the valley and violets grew there for religious significance – and, Beth thought, as a living remembrance of love for the lost baby.

'I get Mark Reseigh to cut the grass every other week,' Christina had said in a whisper of a voice. It was obvious to Beth that coming here, even after twenty-two years, was still raw and painful for her. 'The Reverend Oakley is criminally lax at keeping the grounds in order. The same can be said for all his duties. It's the common opinion it's time he retired. Well, Beth, here is where young Philip lies.'

Crouching, Beth had quietly trickled water into the two marble pots, one at the top and one on the middle of the grave, and carefully placed the flowers. She put a gloved fingertip on her twin brother's name. *Philip*, she said softly in her mind. He had grown with her inside her mother's womb. Could she feel an empathy with him? She had always felt something was missing in her life but had thought the cause was the insecurities of her childhood. Perhaps it was also the loss of the companionship of

145

her twin.

She had concentrated to see if she could gain some kind of connection with Philip. She'd felt a growing tugging sensation in her heart, like warm fingers touching it. Was Philip communicating with her? As far as she knew from attending church, the souls of children, like those of the faithful dead, were sleeping in Jesus' care, until the time of the new earth and heaven. Beth was warmed and soothed at the thought of Philip sleeping peacefully and protected. 'Philip,' she mouthed, feeling at one with her brother. She felt suddenly she was complete. The old insecurities were falling off her like sheets of ice. And she was further comforted at wondering if her own lost baby was with Philip.

A sense of deep peace had fallen. The breeze was sharp but Beth couldn't hear a rustle from a yew tree, a holly or a laurel bush, or a long wavering grass. There was none of the usual harsh cawing from the rooks. The stillness washed over Beth. Christina touched her shoulder and Beth was sure her mother had felt it too. They were sharing a haven from all the rigours of life and it was balm to their souls.

'Philip,' she had repeated to herself. 'I hope you can hear me. It's me, Elizabeth, Beth, your sister.' She listened. She concentrated. Nothing came in return to her words but the sense of peace intensified. 'Rest in peace, Philip.'

She straightened up, and as she did so her ears were filled with the sounds of wind-blown

146

greenery and the croaking of big black birds.

'Are you all right, Beth?'

Beth heard the huskiness of emotion in her mother's voice and looked straight into her eyes. 'Yes, I'm fine. How about you?'

Christina nodded, although her cheeks were pale and flushed with pink spots. 'This is all very moving for me. Having my twins re-united.'

Instinctively, Beth had put her hand inside Christina's, and Christina had squeezed her hand gently. 'Did he look like me?'

'Yes he did. He was less than half your weight and a yellowy, poorly colour. I knew he was gravely ill but I willed him to get better. I was only allowed to hold both of you together for a little while. Then the midwife pulled Philip out my arms and took him away to the next bedroom. I wasn't told Philip was going to die. I never saw him again.'

'That must have been awful.' From holding Christina's hand Beth had gathered her in to hug her gently. 'I know there must be a lot more to this sad story. I'd like to hear it all, even if it's painful to me. Will you be able to manage that? It will be very hard for you.'

'I want everything to become absolutely clear to you, Beth. Thanks for thinking of me,' Christina had said, steeped in gratitude and glorying in her daughter's caring embrace.

When the two of them parted they both dabbed at their moist eyes and smiled watery smiles.

147

'Shall we talk back at the house where it will be comfortable and totally private?' Beth said. 'As I remember, the Reverend Oakley had a habit of haunting the churchyard and throwing holy water about. To drive out evil forces brought in by the unsaved, Miss Oakley used to say, although she'd add she didn't believe it was strictly necessary. Mr Oakley could be a scary sight.'

'He hasn't changed,' Christina smiled. Then she was pensive. 'Do you mind if I take a minute to go to Francis?'

It was on that plaintive question that Beth was sure she knew beyond any doubt the sum of her mother's character. Christina was always eager to please. She sought acceptance from Beth even now, and that made Beth sad. Christina was keen not to offend and that made her vulnerable, easy to manipulate and put down. It was how she had always been. *My God*, Beth thought, *if I was suddenly horrible to you now, if I dredged up some new hurt, real or imagined, you would apologize and accept the blame.* Beth felt sick in her stomach. Long before she herself had been a neglected, suffering soul, her poor mother had been the same sort of victim, and her heartbreaks had been so much worse. Beth saw her mother now the way Joe and Mrs Reseigh saw her, the way Francis Vyvyan had seen her. A good, unselfish person not embittered by all the tragedies heaped on her. Beth's heart almost broke for Christina. She felt guilty for having allowed such a torrent

148

of loathing for her mother to build up.

Beth had tucked Christina's arm through hers. 'I'd like to walk you there. If I may I'd like to be with you at Mr Vyvyan's resting place.'

'Oh, Beth,' Christina had quietly wept in delight.

From that point a new relationship between Beth and Christina had been forged in peace and understanding and the bond of blood.

Now Beth had come to Philip's grave alone. Not dressed in black today, she expressed no outward sign of grief. That she kept in her heart. 'Hello Philip, it's me again. Beth. I had to come again. Mother and I had a long talk after we left here yesterday. She's OK. Everything is all right between us now and always will be. I wanted you to know that, just in case you were worried.'

Making sure no one else was about to disturb her, Beth sat down on the firm grass, avoiding the flowers on the ground. She just wanted to be alone with Philip for a while. Soon tears welled up in her. 'Things might have been so different if you'd survived. I've told Mother about my baby. Perhaps he or she is with you now. Next time I come here I'll lay some flowers for my own lost child.' She bit her lip. It didn't stop the tears. She let the cascade fall.

She had cried a lot yesterday, both she and Christina. They had chosen to talk in Beth's old room, sitting side by side on the little bed. The

149

sky had cleared and the sun was shining con-
tentedly by the time they arrived back at the
house. Kitty and Joe had taken the dogs outside,
Grace cradled in Kitty's arms, the haven which
she had barely left since her rescue.

'A-after Philip died,' Christina had begun, as
the two clutched hands, 'Phil blamed me for our
son's death. The doctor and midwife said no
one was to blame. The baby hadn't formed
properly and it was one of those cruel acts of
nature, it had not been God's will he should live
for very long. Phil ordered them to get out,
saying they were useless and should have been
aware I was carrying two babies. He threatened
to make complaints about them, but he never
did. Your grandmother had written that she
couldn't make it here for my confinement, so I
was left alone as a new mother with a new baby.
Phil had refused Mrs Reseigh's offer to be here.
"It's not your place," he'd told her rudely. He
didn't like her because she had favoured me
from the start of our marriage.'

'Was my father a good husband to you at the
start?' Beth had asked.

Christina hesitated.

'Don't be afraid to tell me the truth.'

'Well, if you're sure. Mrs Reseigh can verify
what I'm about to say. Phil was so proud for the
first few days after we moved into this house,
immediately after our quiet wedding in the
church. Your grandmother stayed with us for a
fortnight. She encouraged Phil to choose the
furniture and décor he liked. He made some

150

hopeless choices but thankfully she steered him in the right direction before anything was delivered. I was so happy to be Phil's wife I didn't care what they decided. She used her contacts to help Phil get a job in an insurance office in St Austell. He quickly developed a good eye for fine taste and he got on well at the job. Well, Phil had a way of charming people.'

'That's why you fell in love with him?'

'Yes, it was so easy to do. He had such a dashing smile. When he wanted to he could change his voice to suit any occasion. Then my mother went home. Phil ventured down to the cove for the first time with his head held high, saying he'd show everyone he'd made something of himself. But he soon came back in a terrible rage. He refused to say why, but I could tell he had been humiliated. He banned me from going down there and refused to speak to me for days.

'I learned the reason why after church one morning. I always went alone. I did everything on my own. I overheard a group of women talking. They were sniggering about my pregnancy and about Phil, saying Phil had been rightfully brought down for thinking he was better than anyone else, that some of the men had put him in his place and told him he was a parasite and a kept man, that he'd have nothing and would never come to anything except for my mother doting on him, and him charming the— well, something rude about me. It must have badly hurt Phil's pride. He started to find fault with me and accuse me of thinking he wasn't good

151

enough for me. I'd tell him how much I loved him and that I didn't care what people thought of me, but he'd shout that I was a liar and I must wish I'd married some toff in my own league.

'Well, he couldn't go down to the pubs for a drink so he started dressing up and went off to the hotels. Occasionally he'd stay out all night. I was so worried the first time he didn't come home.' Christina had sighed heavily. 'He just got angry with me. He misconstrued everything I said and demanded to know if I was accusing him of having an affair. "I was just tired, that's all," he'd shout. "I forgot the time. The manager mentioned they had a spare room and I took it. I needed a break, that's all. Is that too much to ask?" He started drinking a lot more than usual when at home, leaving bottles lying about and falling asleep wherever he was.

'Phil was home when I went into labour. For those next few hours he was like a different man. He was very attentive towards me. I had hopes that once he was a father everything would be normal and we'd settle down as a family. I knew he had hopes for a son, he had already chosen boys' names, but I wasn't concerned if the baby was a girl. I thought he'd be happy to try for a boy next time.

'After you were delivered the doctor went out of the room to tell Phil we had a healthy daughter. I asked the doctor what he'd said.

'"Oh," the doctor replied.

'"Just that?" I asked the doctor. "Was he pleased?" I asked.

'The doctor said, "Of course, Mrs Tresaile. Like a lot of new fathers he was stunned. I'm sure he's delighted. He's slipped downstairs for a little drink. He needs to relax after all the anxiety."

'Then it suddenly became obvious I was about to deliver another baby and the room became frantic. I couldn't be left so Phil wasn't told until after baby Philip was born. Phil ran into the room so excited, but when the terrible news was broken he howled like an animal and tore out of the house.

'Later, after I'd managed to give you your first feed, the midwife put you down in the cradle. The doctor and midwife left, taking my little boy away with them, and I was worried they wouldn't come back to tend you and me. I was completely worn out. My heart was aching for my lost baby. I couldn't rest for worrying about what was on Phil's mind. Finally he came back. I was going to ask him how he was and offer him a look at you but when I saw how furious he was I just froze. He didn't look like my Phil, his face was purple and twisted with rage and he was pointing at me, accusing. "It's your fault my son died," he screamed over and over again. I was so frightened I cowered under the bedcovers.' Christina was crying, her chin wobbling. 'He shouted that he didn't want a daughter, didn't want you or me either. That I should have known I was bearing two babies and should have looked after his son inside me, that it should have been the girl who died.'

153

With huge scalding tears streaming down her face and dropping off her chin, Christina had appealed to Beth. 'It was the first time I let you down, Beth. I was afraid Phil might hurt you but I was too scared to move and protect you. I'm sorry. I'm so sorry.'

'You don't have to say any more.' Beth had been so moved by Christina's agony she could only whisper, desperate salty tears on her own face, and she'd eased her mother's head to rest on her shoulder. 'I understand how it was for you. My father never stopped being cruel to you from that time on, did he?'

'He never stopped taunting me. I tried my best with you but he mocked everything I did. He'd soon crushed me and I couldn't cope. I want you to know all this, Beth, so you have things clear in your mind. I started to take a drink to help me cope. It worked at first and I'd stand up to Phil, and that was when the screaming matches between us started. But soon I couldn't cope again and I'd drink more and more. I'd break things in sheer frustration and temper. I was out of control. I knew what I was doing to you, Beth, to Elizabeth my little girl, but I couldn't stop myself repeating it again and again. I was so ashamed, so frightened for you. But I did love you. I tried to look after you. It was my idea that you take lessons with Muriel Oakley. I knew her to be a kind woman and I was certain I could trust her not to talk about what went on here. Of course, it couldn't be kept a total secret. When you were taken away

154

from me I was heartbroken but I thought it was the best thing for you. I never got on with my mother but she doted on you. I was sure she wouldn't let you down. Like I had so many times. I'm so sorry.'

'I accept that you're really sorry, Mother.' Beth found it so easy to call Christina her mother. 'I really do. You don't have to keep saying it. I understand some of what you went through. You see, I want you to know this, something only Kitty knows.' Now it was Beth's voice that had a tremor.

Her hand on the hot kerbing of Philip's grave, Beth said softly and throatily to her twin, 'I told Mother about my baby, her grandchild, your niece or nephew. She was so good and comforting about it. It was such a relief. Now I come to think about it, our Grandma Frobisher might have been disappointed in me conceiving a baby. She would have considered that it would ruin my life and expectations. She probably would have pressed me to go away and give the baby up for adoption. I couldn't have done that. It might have marred my closeness with Grandma but I would have risked that. She was always awful about Mother. Our brother Joe had something to say like that about her. She wasn't the saint I thought she was.'

Hearing footfalls heading her way, Beth blotted away her tears and got to her feet. It was Mark Reseigh. So far she had only got a glimpse and a respectful nod from him in the gardens of Owles House. He was carrying shears and other tools.

On seeing her, Mark halted. He dipped his head in salute. 'Morning, Miss Tresaile. I'm sorry to have disturbed you. I'll come back later.' He was already turning to go.

'No, you don't have to go, Mr Reseigh. I was about to leave myself. It's peaceful here, isn't it?' Beth had the impression that if she had not asked him a question he would have just walked off. She stayed put, waiting for him to reach her.

'It is peaceful,' he said in his full low voice, stopping close up and resting his weight on one foot. Beth immediately got the impression he was neither stand-offish nor shy, rather he was simply not nosy, intrusive or impatient. She could tell he was a steady sort of fellow. 'Except for the times the vicar is flapping about, but he doesn't do it so often now. He's running out of steam these days, I'd say.'

'He must be getting on a bit. He used to bewilder me when I took my lessons at the vicarage but I was never scared of him. Mrs Reseigh, as a proud grandmother, showed me a photo of your little girl. She looked adorable.'

It was as if the sun itself had lit up Mark. His whole being became animated. He had the typical build of a workman, strong bodied and a little rough and tough round the edges, but he also had a kind consistency to his firm features. His dark brown hair needed a cut and was inclined to curl. 'Rowella's running about all over

156

the place now. Daren't keep a cupboard not tied up or she's pulling everything out of it. She's interested in everything, every sound and movement. She loves animals and the boats and the sea. Course my mother and her other gran Mrs Praed spoil her.' For a man often wordless and of half-expressions he quickly opened up and rambled on happily about his fifteen-month-old daughter. Beth felt the hurt in her heart again at having been rejected from birth by her own father, at having been of no value to him at all. Rowella Reseigh was one blessed little girl.

Beth knew from a dreamy and sorrowful Mrs Reseigh about Mark's romantic history. 'He was sweet on pretty raven-haired Juliet Praed from a young 'un. Courted her from when she was fourteen. Lofty Praed made them keep either side of his garden gate for a couple of years. They got married four years later. They were both young but Lofty and Posy Praed and I weren't against it. Mark and Juliet were right for each other. And when you come down to it, boys younger than Mark was then went off to the Great War and were killed for king and country.

'Mark got them a little place to live up top of the cove. Young Rowella was a long time coming, then we nearly had a tragedy. Juliet fell down the stairs at eight months along and went into labour. There were complications, it was touch and go, we thought we were going to lose both of them. They came through but sadly poor Juliet got an infection and died a week later. It was such a cruel fate for Juliet and Mark. Our one comfort was that she got to see and hold the baby. Mark came back to live with me, him and the baby. Me and Posy Praed take turns helping him with Rowella. That dear little maid means everything to Mark and me. She'll be my only grandchild. Mark says he'll never get married again.' Beth had concluded, in sadness and envy, that her own child, as little Rowella Praed was to Mrs Reseigh, would have been the most precious child on the planet.

'I hope I get the chance to meet Rowella,' Beth said.

'That could be likely,' Mark replied. 'Mrs Vyvyan has us, and my mother, up to the house every now and then. She has us all for a picnic in summer and for a meal at Christmas.' He looked down shyly. 'If you'll permit me to say so, Miss Tresaile, your mother is a wonderful woman. I'm ... um, glad you've seen that for yourself.'

'I shall never doubt it,' Beth said, not offended by his unexpected forthrightness. She was pleased her mother had good and honest people who respected her and sought to protect her. She took her leave.

On the way out of the churchyard she came to Francis Vyvyan's grave. She had stood beside it yesterday with Christina. Fresh flowers had just been arranged there and she guessed Mark had placed them for her mother. She took a moment now to pay solitary homage to the man

158

of whom she felt she knew something from the accounts of him she had heard. It was so tragic that a vital young man of thirty-eight should meet an untimely death.

Beth heard footsteps again, light, slow footsteps. She looked all round. No one was there. Had she imagined them? She heard a sound and rustle coming, she construed, from behind an overgrowth of speckled laurel. She didn't feel it was an animal. Mark was not the type to play stalking games and if it was the Reverend Oakley who was drifting about he'd always done so loudly, oblivious of causing a disturbance.

From behind her came a throaty 'Ahem.'

'Oh!' Beth swung round.

'Oh, my dear Miss Elizabeth, Miss Tresaile, I mean. I beg your forgiveness for alarming you. It's me, Muriel Oakley. I was creeping about to make sure it was actually you before I spoke up. Once I got a glimpse of your face I recognized you at once. It's a joy to see you after all these years. Um, you do remember me?'

'Yes, yes, of course I remember you, Miss Oakley. It's good to meet you again too,' Beth said enthusiastically. She could not help staring at her former tutor, who looked entirely different now. Flesh had fled from the genteel woman's frame leaving her wasted, almost cadaverous, in appearance. Her skin was wafer thin, her cheeks and chest sunken. Her washed-out Edwardian blouse and ankle-length faded black skirt had been gathered in for a better fit

159

under a wide buckled belt of black cloth. Her black, heeled shoes were much patched and mended. Her hair, once pinned up in a cottage-loaf style, had gone a dull grey; cut at chin length from a side parting, it hung as listlessly as the rest of her. She still wore the same wire-rimmed glasses and from the way she strained to focus, Beth could tell they were no longer up to their job. The only other remnant of the younger Miss Oakley was the pleasant smell of rose scent on her. *You poor woman*, Beth thought. Vicarage life had been relentlessly pitiable for her. Beth figured her age to be about forty-two, but she looked so much older – a sorry character. 'I was sorry to learn that Mrs Oakley had passed away,' she said.

'I thank you for your sympathy, Miss Tresaile. My dear mama went on to glory some four and a half years ago. It was a merciful release actually. She went through such suffering.' Miss Oakley floundered apologetically and glanced guiltily towards the church. 'But I shouldn't dwell on that. She's sleeping in peace now until the Last Day. If I may be so bold, you were looking down at Mr Vyvyan's grave. He was very highly respected, you know.'

'So I've gathered. I wish I'd known him.'

'Oh, you would have been, um, well, I mean to say ... M-Mr Vyvyan was a fine example to us all.' Miss Oakley's pallid complexion burned a sickly dusky red and she twisted her hands in front of her in the manner of an embarrassed child.

Beth was filled with compassion for the kind-natured spinster, who had been overlooked indifferently by life and had never gained personal happiness. Muriel Oakley had made it obvious that her admiration for the late handsome Francis Vyvyan had included infatuation. Beth was sure she must be excruciatingly lonely. Muriel Oakley could not have had any life of her own, probably all her hopes had been dashed and she had never had anything to look forward to. 'I'm sure he was. I thought I'd take a look at Mr Jewell's grave. I understand he had reserved his plot beside his parents, quite close to the war memorial. Would you care to walk with me, Miss Oakley?'

'Oooh.' Miss Oakley smiled as if to the highest heavens. 'I'd be honoured to, Miss Tresaile. I get very few invitations anywhere nowadays.'

If any at all, Beth thought, sad for her.

'People are so busy,' Miss Oakley said quickly, as they started off.

Beth remembered Miss Oakley as always being eager not to be seen criticizing others. 'I've never forgotten the lessons I had with you. No one has taught me history like you did. It's given me a lifelong interest in the ancient Greeks, the Roman Empire, and their respective mythologies.'

'Really? That is very gratifying to hear. I've never forgotten you. I taught a few other children after you went away but none of them showed the same aptitude as your good self for learning. None singled out a favourite subject.'

161

'Do you have a pupil at the moment, Miss Oakley?'

'There's been no one for ages. The vicarage is quite run down, I'm afraid to say. It's a rather uninviting place really. My father and I have no servants now. I'm resigned to keeping the house for him. I'm not a very good cook, I'm afraid, but no matter, neither of us has much of an appetite.'

They had reached the war memorial, a tall Calvary cross. A granite beauty befitting the glorious dead from the parish of St Irwyn who had sacrificed their young lives on the seas and Flanders fields, their ranks and names lettered in black on the plinths. Apart from the graves of Beth's twin brother, Francis Vyvyan and a few others, the memorial was the only thing in the churchyard kept in lovingly reverent order. Beth ran her eyes down the names. There were a lot of Vyvyans and Praeds. Perhaps, if he had not abandoned his young family, the name of Cpl P.A. Tresaile might also have been there. Beth felt a yearning sadness, wishing, despite her father's apathy towards her, that she had known him properly, rather than having only unhelpful, poor impressions of him.

'They were all heroes,' Miss Oakley said in hushed tones.

'It's strange to think of my own father dying a war hero. My grandmother told me about his bravery. How he saved a comrade at the expense of his own life. My father had cut himself off from my mother and so I don't know how my grandmother came to learn about it.' It was a matter Beth had not dwelt on, but now she wanted to know all about the mystery.

Beth sensed Miss Oakley stiffen and step back. She had been pale before but now her dry skin was totally bloodless. 'Miss Oakley, are you well? I'm afraid you don't look it. Shall I walk you home?'

'No, no, I – I've just remembered something I must attend to. Excuse me, Miss Tresaile, I must go.' Trembling and twitchy, Miss Oakley took herself quickly off.

When she was out of sight moments later, Beth could hear her running.

Fourteen

Kitty was striding down to the cove. She felt on top of the world. The air was warm and summer-fresh in her lungs. Her long shapely limbs were relaxed yet full of vigour. She was bursting with health and contentment. Behind her was Owles House, where she loved staying with its little reunited family, and she had an adorable faithful puppy to rear. Beth had gone alone to the churchyard, where she needed to be as she made careful progress sifting through all her emotions and setting her old troubles to rest. Beth had no plans to return home for some time. Catching up on her past, Kitty had become aware, Beth had unconsciously fallen into a state of drift. She slowly pondered one revelation after another in her mind, while, partly due to Christina's infirmity, her physical movements had become slower too. Christina was currently resting; a picture of undisturbed poise now so many things with Beth had been resolved. She and Beth were to share a quiet lunch. Joe, joined by his noisy, cheeky pal, Richard Opie, had taken food and drink, and some sort of secret supplies, off to Joe's tree house in the grounds. Everyone, including Mrs Reseigh, was taking turns to watch Grace until Kitty's return.

Swinging a large cloth bag of Christina's, Kitty made a mental shopping list of the items she wanted to get for Grace. The puppy would not need a collar and leash for a while yet, but Kitty was going to buy her heaps of toys, even though a bossy Joe had insisted the little tug rope Kitty had made from plaited rags was enough. Mrs Reseigh had given Kitty an address in one of the little side streets where an old man carved teething toys and made other items for babies and animals, selling them to holidaymakers from his doorstep. Kitty couldn't wait to take Grace for her first proper walk.

Kitty and Beth had discussed with Christina how highly they both thought of Joe for letting Beth become part of Christina's life, and allowing them both to stay in his home. 'He's everything I could wish for in a son,' Christina had said proudly. 'And Beth is everything I could wish for in a daughter. I'm a lucky, lucky woman and I'll be eternally grateful for it.'

Joe still watched Beth avidly for signs that she might yet turn against Christina, but he was astute enough to allow them lots of time together, and he was getting on with the pleasures of revelling in the long summer holiday. One of his main activities was to challenge Richard to race him sprints, pounding up and down the lawn or taking marathon laps around the grounds and through the woods. With Chaplin tearing along beside them they made a happy, noisy troupe. The boys also made high jumps and long jumps, though Christina had drawn the line when they wanted to fashion a pole vault. Kitty was often roped in as timekeeper and she had been willingly cajoled to take part in some of the races. Beth and Christina had sat and watched, cheering and clapping the winner, who was invariably Joe. So far, however, Beth and Joe had advanced little towards bonding as sister and brother.

Kitty reached Wildflower Cottage. Beth was planning to come here next to meet the Praed family, keen to thank them for giving her a safe refuge all those years ago. Kitty glanced over the natural hedging of hawthorn, ash, hazel and elder that divided the cottage grounds from the narrow lane. The hedging was covered with a tangle of honeysuckle and dog roses; so pretty and delightfully old-fashioned. Over the rustic wooden gate Kitty could see bursts of fox-gloves, ox-eye daises, clover, and more. The front of the whitewashed cottage faced the road at a slight angle. The gently winding path up to the scuffed stable door was stony, and would likely be muddy during the winter and on rainy days. Swathes of perennial honey-suckle swarmed over the trellis-sided porch. Kitty took it for granted that the members of the Praed family – eight of them so Mrs Reseigh had said – who squeezed into the modest dwelling, went round the side like many working folk and entered their home at the back.

Approaching a few feet nearer, Kitty got as

close to the hedge as she could and took a swift angled look, which soon hurt her neck, at the back garden. A sturdy lean-to was built on to the full width of the cottage's back wall and plants pressed against the glass. Strings of washing formed a rectangle at the edges of a rough long lawn and laundry belonging to family members of both sexes and all ages wafted in the breeze. There were a few tiny girls' clothes and Kitty mused that they probably belonged to the Praed-Reseigh granddaughter, of whom Mrs Reseigh talked incessantly. Attached to the cottage was a large expanse of ground and there were outhouses, a large shed, a good-sized lavatory and a scrap heap of rusty metal parts, bits of wood and redundant household items. Fishing boat accessories were neatly gathered against the sides of the shed. It appeared that a bicycle was being made from scrap items. Kitty would have liked to get a close-up view of it all. She loved studying other people's treasures. Her brother Stuart laughingly called it her Aladdin's Cave syndrome. 'You might not always discover good things,' he had teasingly warned her.

The long garden patch boasted rows of onions, turnips, banked-up potatoes, and peas, broad beans and runner beans on sticks. On the other side of a narrow path grew salad vegetables, rows of raspberries and strawberries and bushes of currants and gooseberries. There were three beehives, while a large chicken coop and a rabbit hutch and run both held a number of animals. An arrogant cockerel strutted about like a prince. The fishing family appeared both self-contained and enterprising. Kitty had gleaned numerous facts about some of Portcowl's inhabitants, and she knew the Praeds had family living on the quayside where they had their work lofts.

Well, she couldn't stay and stare rudely, invading the Praeds' privacy. She retreated but at once cried out, realizing she was held fast by brambles that clung to her loose-fitting blouse. 'Oh damn,' she muttered, colouring hotly even though, as far as she was aware, her nosiness had not been observed.

'Fine language for a lady, I must say.'

Kitty caught her breath. She had been discovered in the act of spying. That alone was shaming enough, but she knew who owned the husky, mocking voice behind her. It was Rob, the good-looking fisherman. She did not know why, but he was the last local she wanted to make a fool of herself in front of. Then she became cross and defensive, for this man was laughing at her and would probably gain further amusement at her expense by telling his mates all about this humiliating incident. She swung her head round and her sun hat hit him in the face. It would serve him right for being so close to her – and he was very close to her. She smirked at seeing him rub his face, which was unmarked by her action, and loftily met his gaze, his eyes annoyingly still full of amusement. 'I'd be grateful if you helped me to be rid

168

of these brambles.'

Grinning, Rob reached for the front of her body. 'Hold still, don't want to spoil your nice clothes. I'll have you free in a mo.'

Kitty was amazed as he deftly pulled the brambles away from her with firm fingers. He held the whippy branches inside his hands so they couldn't spring back at her. She pulled back out of the way. 'Are you hurt?' she asked, awed. She couldn't imagine anyone else performing such a foolhardy rescue.

Rob displayed his empty, remarkably unscratched hands. They were leathery and bore numerous old scars. 'Not a bit. These hands have spent too many years being drenched by cold salt water and spurred by ropes and hooks and fish scales.' He gazed directly into Kitty's shocked eyes. 'And I'd have done it anyway, for you. I'm Rob Praed and you're Miss Kitty Copeland. Everyone knows who you are, and your friend Miss Elizabeth Tresaile. Very pleased to meet you again, Kitty.'

Kitty knew she was staring at him in doe-like fashion, rather stupidly. Rob Praed was an outrageous flirt, the sort of man who left a string of broken hearts pining for him, but she couldn't help herself revealing the effect he was having on her. She had never seen such a gorgeous, sensuous man before. A tingle as intense as an electric shock went all the way through her when she felt his warm rough hand enclose hers in a firm handshake. He kept her hand inside his and held it close to his body. She should find his provocative manner contemptible but she did not, even while instinctively knowing that Rob was the kind of man who, without particularly trying, made women lose their better judgement.

'You're a Praed.' She tried not to squeak. 'You live here?'

'My Uncle Lofty does. He skippers the family lugger. We're off on the morning tide. I was just going in. Join me and meet everyone, my Auntie Posy, my cousins and my two sisters. And there'll be other fishermen of the fleet and their families. They'll soon be spilling outside with their plates of food and drink anyway. We always have a get-together when we start a new fishing season, pilchards this time.'

Kitty wished his eyes would stop twinkling at her so beguilingly. Calling together her wits she tugged her hand free from his. 'Oh, I couldn't possibly intrude. I was on my way to...'

'Don't be daft, the family and neighbours will be glad to have you. There'll be plenty of grub to go round.' He had Kitty by the elbow and was taking her towards the garden gate.

'But I...' *Oh shut up*, she told herself. *You want to go inside and you want to go inside with him.*

Joe and his pal Richard Opie, the son of a Portcowl hotelier, had left Joe's tree house, climbed over the side hedge and made their way through the woods. Emerging from the trees they had crossed the lane and then, via

170

farmland, they had reached the mean place that was Claze Wyn.

The boys were flat on their bellies, hidden among a mass of wild willow bushes, spying on the rear of the huddle of decrepit buildings. Any garden that might once have been there was long trounced by hordes of stinging nettles and other wild growth. Claze Wyn was the home of the local hard nut, Gabby Magor, an unkempt, hard-drinking woman who dressed like a man and had the physique of a lumbering ox. She was loud mouthed and a determined trouble-maker. Gabby Magor had a criminal record including two prison sentences, one served for receiving stolen goods and the other for causing grievous bodily harm to fisherman Davey Vage, the adoptive father of Beth's as yet unmet half-sister Evie Vage. A row of elder trees in full creamy-white flower backed away from the crumbling cob and thatch, two-up-two-down cottage. Later in the year Gabby Magor would harvest the prolific sprays of tiny black elder-berries for wine making. She produced various wines, which she sold to local outlets. Before-hand she would barter suspect but desirable goods for the fruit, vegetables, yeast and sugar she would need. She would consume none her-self; she was a beer drinker and had a swollen, hard belly as a result.

People said of Gabby Magor, 'She's as mean and cruel as the day is long. Be sure to keep out of her way.' Magor was in effect banned from the cove, for most of the traders refused to serve her. Periodically she ventured down to Port-cowl to show, as she said, that 'I spit on those bastards who dare to look down on me.' She would try to provoke a disturbance, often by baiting and offending holidaymakers.

Gabby Magor was well known for animal neglect and cruelty. An ageing donkey, as well as various cats and dogs – all of which she'd got on a whim then quickly become bored with – and fowl had all suffered at the end of her vicious temper and hobnail boots. Joe was in no doubt it was Gabby Magor who had thrown away little puppy Grace to meet a wretched death in the woods. For that, the Magor hag was going to pay.

Chaplin was dutifully down at Joe's side, panting softly in expectation and as eager to leap into action as the boys were. Joe was peering through binoculars.

'Can you see the old mare?' Richard whispered. His face, like Joe's, was daubed for camouflage with mud scooped from a frog pool en route. Because he had bright ginger hair, Joe had ordered Richard to wear a black kerchief, pirate style, to prevent him being easily spotted. Joe wore a deerstalker hat. He'd say himself that he looked silly in it but he swore it helped him to deduce things, like one of his fictional heroes, Sherlock Holmes. Joe had a tool belt round his waist, the few selected tools for the moment resting on his back.

'No sign of her,' Joe whispered back. 'Or her rickety old bike.'

172

The boys had been to Claze Wyn before and knew its layout. The only things Joe could see moving through the binoculars were Gabby Magor's scraggy hens, roosters and bantams in an inadequate coop and wire run. 'They're easy fox bait. That dragon doesn't care about a thing,' Joe whispered in disgust.

Suddenly Chaplin shot up on his paws and turned swiftly round and growled a low warning in his throat. Joe swivelled his upper body round, afraid that he and Richard had been discovered. He had his fists around a stout pole like a Sherwood Forest outlaw; it would be needed to ward off the thrashing Gabby Magor would mete out over the double trespass. Then he snarled, reached up and yanked down to the ground the girl who had sneaked up on them. 'What the heck are you doing here, Lily Praed? Have you been following us?'

'Only part of the way,' replied the pigtailed, perky wisp of a girl, unfazed by her rough treatment. 'What're you two up to then? What game are you playing?'

'Mind your own ruddy business, maid,' Richard scowled. The glowing redness of his freckled face showed how furious he was with Lily.

Lily merely looked from boy to boy, grinning in self-glory. The boys bragged about their scouting skills but she had outwitted them.

'Keep down,' Joe hissed at her.

'Why aren't you with that stupid gang of giggling girls you're usually with?' Richard demanded, while Joe resumed his surveillance.

'Come to that, shouldn't you be at home? Your lot's about to go off pilchard driving and they'll be having a big get-together. Clear off, Lily Praed, or I'll make you.'

'Huh, just try it, carrot top! Anyway, I'm not always with the girls. Sometimes I play by myself.' Lily got ready to pinch him.

'Shush you two! You'll give us away,' Joe hissed again, and cursed under his breath.

'If you're wondering if Gabby Magor is there, well I can tell you she isn't,' Lily crowed. 'I saw her on her bike arriving at her cousin Barbara Faull's place. That was about an hour ago. She probably went there to scrounge a meal till she goes off to some pub somewhere. So what're you two up to then?'

'Brilliant,' Joe said, referring to the information. He stood up, but still cautiously eyed Claze Wyn. A war widow, Mrs Faull lived in a solitary roadside house only a couple of miles away. Adults said darkly that the women weren't really cousins but Joe had not yet worked out their exact relationship. 'And what we're doing here, girl, is of no interest to you.' He jerked his head. 'On your way.'

'Not till you tell me why you're here.' Lily scurried to her feet and saucily waggled her skimpy hips from side to side.

Joe allowed himself a moment to be amused by the fact that her head came no higher than his chest. She was daintily built, but it was well known that her slight stature and bright-eyed, delicately shaped face belied her playfulness

174

and gritty will. She was the youngest child in the Praed family, and all of them, along with just about everyone else in Portcowl, doted on her. Joe did not share Richard's disgust at girls but he didn't see them as trustworthy. In his view most of them were destined to become gossips. And he hated being halted by anyone's silly behaviour.

'Never. I'd cut my throat with a rusty razor first.' He fashioned a dramatic slash in front of his neck.

'Go on then.' Putting her little grubby hands on the hip line of her untidy dress, Lily made mocking faces at him. 'Do it. I dare you. I'll stay right here and watch. Just don't splash any blood on my dress. I'd have a hard job explaining that to my mum.'

'Oh, for Pete's sake!' Richard seethed between his teeth. 'Get rid of her, Joe. We need to get on.'

Joe gazed down sternly at young skinny Lily. She had dirty smudges on her face but her dimples, either side of her baby-pink lips, marked her as quite a character. She was a pipsqueak of a thing, harmless and funny, but nevertheless a pest. He lowered his eye line to hers and assumed his most deadly serious expression. 'Run home! Run as fast as you can. It's for your own good, Lily Praed. Claze Wyn is haunted, everyone knows that. I bet your mother and father have warned you never to come here, eh?' Lily nodded, her tiny teeth clamped to her bottom lip. 'How the spirits here

175

specially like to get their clammy claw hands on little girls. Run home, Lily, run for your life, before one of those monstrous beings gets angry and rises up and stops you getting away safely.'

'Huh!' Lily replied loud and bravely, although she edged back from Joe and glanced nervously in all directions. 'Ghosts are a load of rubbish. My big brother Linford says so, and my cousin Rob. Rob says you only see spirits when you've had too much to drink. You're just trying to scare me.'

'The ghosts here are as real as we are,' Joe went on in a deep rasping voice, grabbing Lily's tiny shoulder and holding her fast. 'No one but wicked people have ever lived on this site. They were like the people you see in your worst nightmares, people more evil than anyone can imagine. The ghosts here aren't the stuff of the usual silly rumours, like headless horsemen or a lady floating in a white dress. This place was once the hideout of a den of smugglers. After a big double-cross they slit the throats of a riding officer and an excise man. And then there was a mad father who murdered all his daughters in their beds. You must get away from here at once, Lily. Honestly, I'm only trying to save you.'

Joe won the argument.

Lily's bright grey eyes were now shining with fear and her pointy little chin was quivering. Joe Vyvyan seemed so big and awesome, and believable. 'B-but no other girls have been hurt

by an evil ghost round these parts. I would've
heard of it. My mum's only told me to stay
away from here in case Gabby Magor lashes
out at me in temper.'

'That's because—'

'Oh, for Pete's sake, Joe, stop going on and
on. Just get rid of the ruddy little nuisance.'

Richard's cry of impatience let Joe down as
surely as if he had been climbing a cliff face
using a burning rope. Lily saw right through
Joe's ruse. The expression on her pixie face
switched from apprehension to smirking dis-
dain. 'Come to think of it I have heard there's
s'posed to be ghosts here, but not like you're
saying. They're made of cow pee, dung and
piskie dust. You're a rotten liar, Joe Vyvyan!
Now tell me why you're spying on Claze Wyn
or I'll tell my father and brothers you were
trying to scare me to death and delib'rately give
me nightmares. I'll tell my cousin, Rob. I'll tell
him both you boys threatened to hurt me. He'll
get you for that. Rob will "'aave" you in the
sea. Both of you. Drown you dead and good
riddance. Rat bags!'

'Now see what you've done,' Joe growled at
Richard. After nearly succeeding in frightening
Lily away he now had the unnecessary task of
trying to placate her. Any of the Praeds would
deal out harsh punishment to whoever dared
terrify their darling little princess, but Rob
Praed had a mean streak. He didn't easily forgive and forget. Joe couldn't risk his mother
getting upset either if he got a black eye and

177

more retribution for tormenting a supposedly sweet little girl. 'Look here, Lily. Boys do what they do and girls do what they do and they don't really mix, agreed? I'm sorry for trying to scare you. How about I treat you to an ice cream? A large one? I've got a thrupenny piece on me.'

'Yeah, take it and go,' Richard muttered, moodily kicking at a patch of long grass.

Lily puckered her mouth as she considered the offer. Joe, she thought, was genuinely trying to make amends, but Richard's snarkiness was getting on her gidge, as her Granny Praed was apt to say over an annoyance. 'My family buy me as much ice cream as I want. So it's no deal. Tell me why you're here like I wanted to know in the first place. I won't blab to no one else, I swear on my heart.'

'If you don't bugger off this minute, I'll drag you back a way and tie you to a bleddy tree until Joe and I have done what we're intending to, and you can tell the devil for all I care!' Richard bawled. His hands were clawed as if he wanted to put them around Lily's narrow neck.

'Aarh!' Lily shrieked in temper. 'You swore, Richard Opie. You swore two bad words. I'll tell your father and you'll get a thrashing. Your father's a lay preacher in chapel and he'll be ashamed of your bad language, and you bullying a girl four years younger.'

'Stop it, both of you.' Joe threw up his hands in exasperation. 'Keep your trap shut, Rich. You're making it worse. You have to be a leader about these things. We're here on a serious

178

matter and now we're just going to have to compromise. Lily, are you prepared to become an honorary boy for the afternoon?'

'What?' Lily was puzzled at first, but then getting his meaning she squealed excitedly. 'Yes! I'll be anything you like if I can join in your adventure.'

'Joe, are you mad?' Richard protested in disgust.

'A bit, perhaps, but we've got no choice. We need to get on. It's dicey hanging around here. If Gabby Magor was to suddenly come back...' Joe clutched Lily by the wrist. 'You have to swear allegiance to us and you have to swear to never, ever reveal what we're about to do. Got it? Or your guts will spill out over the ground and you'll die a gruesome death.'

'Got it,' Lily replied in awed tones. 'Cross my heart and hope to die.'

'You'd better not let us down or I'll cut off your pigtails and stuff them down your throat. Never forget, Lily Praed, this is an honourable undertaking,' Richard barked, grabbing Lily's other wrist.

'Heads together,' Joe issued in the manner of a commanding officer, which was how he saw himself.

The boys lowered their heads to the little girl, one dark, one red and one wheat-coloured head in a solemn huddle.

'Repeat after me, Lily Praed,' Joe ordered. 'I swear by my flesh and blood that I will never tell a soul about what we're about to do.'

179

Lily gravely made the vow.

'If you break your oath something terrible will happen to one of your family,' Joe intoned with all the threat of an imminent thunderstorm. 'We're here to mete out retribution on Gabby Magor for abandoning a poor helpless puppy and leaving it to die, and we'll also make sure there's no other ill-treated animals here. Before we leave we'll throw the chickens the kitchen scraps we've brought. Right, let's get to it.'

The gang of four, led by Joe and Chaplin, with Lily in the middle and Richard at the rear, crept out of the willows, but not before Lily's willing face and hands were daubed with dirt and her long plaits pushed out of the way down the back of her dress. Hunched over and ready to flee if necessary, they reached Gabby Magor's hard, dusty, nettle-infested ground, and crept over endless rolled-up fag ends and spent matches. They skirted round miscellaneous rubbish, hunks of rusting metal, bits of animal bones and a dead squashed rat. Keeping as diligent as the boys, Lily didn't utter a breath of disgust, but when a short bendy wire washing line came into view at the side of the cottage, she halted to gape amazed at a pair of flannel bloomers, the size of which would make an ensemble of clothes for her.

Richard bumped into her. 'Move!' He pushed her along roughly.

Lily nearly staggered into Joe, but she wasn't cross about the push. She shouldn't have taken

180

her mind off the quest.

Joe made straight for a sort of shed made of rough wooden slats. A quick look through the cracks and he was sure there were no unfortunate animals left to languish inside. There was no point in checking through the filthy cottage windows. Gabby Magor was too rotten to let a creature have the dubious comfort of being inside her manky home. He next went to a privy-sized, stone-walled, slate-roofed outhouse, sheltered under the shade of a hawthorn tree. There was no window and the fortress-strong padlock meant it could only be Gabby's wine store. 'Keep lookout,' he ordered the pair. Tight-lipped and eagle-eyed, Richard and Lily stationed themselves at the corners of the buildings and peered all about the dismal surroundings. Chaplin paced about near Joe, on guard.

Lily was gleeful. If she performed her part well the boys might let her join them on other adventures. She glanced furtively at Joe, who had propped his staff against the wall. What was he going to do? He pulled a screwdriver out of the tool belt. He was going to break into the building, and not by trying to saw through the heavy padlock.

Joe launched himself into the battle of undoing the four rusted screws in the door plate and the fierce effort required soon made sweat break out on his brow and neck. His shoulders ached and he clenched his jaw and panted from the difficulty of getting a firm grip on the screw heads. The screwdriver kept slipping and his knuckles got skinned but he doggedly persevered, grunting, silently swearing to encourage himself. A tiny bit at a time he released each of the four screws slightly then began the easier task of getting each screw out. He didn't ease up for a second, trusting Richard and Chaplin to give an urgent signal if they all suddenly needed to flee.

It seemed a beastly amount of time before he had the door plate and the padlock in his hands. He placed them carefully on the ground. The screws he put in a pocket. Warily but quickly he pulled the door open and peered in through the internal darkness. His nose was hit by an overpoweringly sweet fruity smell. His eyes confirmed what he was expecting to see and he put his thumb up to Richard – Gabby certainly did keep her wine stash in here. Shelves lined the walls and bottles of different-coloured wine stood two deep like proud sentinels. Reaching in and up towards one of the top shelves with his staff, Joe gave the nearest bottle a hefty push then swiftly withdrew the staff and slammed the door shut. Lily wasn't looking his way and her whole little body jumped in shock. 'Oh!'

'Shush!' Richard hissed, but he shuddered himself. Joe had successfully broken into Gabby Magor's wine keep, and now they must get away sharp without leaving any evidence of their trespass here or the hag would dish out some diabolical payback on them. She had never let a grudge rest. And personally, he would get a thrashing off his father, who did not spare the rod.

Hearing the satisfying smashing of glass in one explosion after another, Joe kept his weight pressed against the door so no alcohol could splash out on him. Working fast he retrieved the metal pieces, and following a tricky start he got the locking device back in position. To disguise the places where he had scratched off rust he rubbed dirt in them. Inevitably the strong fruity smell of liquor reached his nose and he saw trickles of the stuff seeping out from under the door. He jumped back to avoid his feet being incriminated.

'Right, she'll discover it sooner rather than later,' he called to the others. 'But she's a short-sighted old mare so it's not likely she'll spot the padlock has been taken off. She'll think it was her own fault. Now let's get out of here.'

He and Richard shot off, with Chaplin in the lead, retracing their journey. Lily scrambled after them, her heart thumping from the sheer excitement of it all. She had taken part in a bold and daring boys' escapade of just retribution. She'd been let in on a secret, and although she would love to tell her grown-up brothers and daring cousin Rob all about it, desperate for them to be proud of her, nothing under the skies would persuade her to give away a single word.

Joe suddenly remembered Lily was with them and he looked back for her. She was lagging well behind on her little short legs. Slowing down, he held out his hand to her. 'Come on, I'll help you along.'

Stretching her hand out to his, Lily put on a tremendous spurt. She leaned forward too far, and then she was falling and the ground was rushing and slammed into her. The breath was completely thumped out of her lungs and her scream was a silent one. Then she didn't move.

'Lily!' Joe cried and tore back to her. Crude horror engulfed him and grew to the heights of terror. Dark red blood was oozing from one side of Lily's face. He fell to his knees beside her and touched her gingerly on the shoulder. 'Lily? Lily?'

Richard was coming back towards them but slowly, his eyes frantic and scared as they looked down on the sprawled little girl. Chaplin reached Lily and went down on his haunches, whining. 'J-Joe ... wh-what...?'

Joe lifted his head and white horror escaped his every pore. 'Rich, I – I think she's dead.'

Fifteen

Clouds were gathering out at sea and the breeze was turning into a persistent wind, chilly in its touch but a welcome relief from the blistering heat of high summer. The air was smoother, kinder. The sky was darkening to a meek bluish-grey. Beth welcomed the mild gloom after the last four stuffy airless nights and searing dry days, when a doleful sluggishness had fallen on all those at Owles House. Beth was in the twin-bedded, Regency rosewood-themed guest room she shared with Kitty. They had insisted on one room to save on housework and each day, to ensure Christina and Mrs Reseigh had no extra workload, they shared the domestic duties. They also brought food delicacies back from the cove and the local farms.

Energized by the fresher atmosphere, Beth had made the beds and dusted the furniture with its scrolling effects, shaped rails and raised mirrors. She got down on her knees while dry-mopping under the half-tester beds to ensure not a wisp of fluff was missed. It was pleasing to restore the room, which faced west and over-looked quiet garden borders, the woods beyond and a glimpse of sea, to gleaming neatness. It

185

was especially pleasing to Beth to see her things and Kitty's dotted about in here, giving the room a personal and homely air.

Beth marvelled how she felt so much at home in Owles House. That she could go to her childhood room and recall the few good memories of bygone years rather than the nightmarish ones. It was important to her to have that little place to retreat to, somewhere she could gather her thoughts and mull over how blessedly different things had turned out than she had expected. She knew if she had left this house, left Christina, the woman she was now comforted and even proud to have as her mother, in a tempest of self-righteous hostility, her life would have been even harder to bear than she could imagine. She had stopped looking for slip-ups in Christina's reformed character. Her mother had vindicated herself. Learning she had been loved and wanted by one of her failed parents was the deepest solace to Beth's bruised heart and soul, to her sadness at facing a future without Stuart and her baby.

Once, however, when she was in the nursery bedroom, Beth's loss had grown almost unbearable. Lying on the little bed, her legs curled up so her feet didn't hang over the footboard, she had cradled the doll in her arms and tried to think back to when she might have played with it. Then she had made the fatal slip of wondering what it would have been like to hold her baby in that way. She'd clutched the thing of bisque and cloth against her chest and sobbed for a lifetime.

Beth would not allow her father to occupy her thoughts. He didn't matter to her. It seemed he had never loved her and he had been a brute to her mother. He had been a chancer. He was dead and could not reject her again. She was glad he had not died a squalid death, and she felt only a fleeting guilt that she was spared the consideration of whether, if he had survived the war, she should attempt to track him down or not.

What did bother her was the bitter history between Christina and her grandmother. Why had her grandmother seen Phil Tresaile in such positive, even affectionate terms? She had obviously loathed her daughter long before the disgrace incurred by Christina's pregnancy out of wedlock. Beth regretted not making the emotional and literal journey to her mother before. In the light of what she now knew, she would have had a lot of questions to put to Marion Frobisher. Beth would continue to probe for answers, but not from Christina, who appeared only to believe her mother had resented her because she had preferred her dead son. Mrs Reseigh would willingly answer any questions but it wouldn't be right to ask her; revelations gained from the forthcoming daily help might upset the close relationship she shared with Christina. Beth's primary plan on arrival here might have been to cause unease, but she didn't want to leave the like behind her when she decided – and she was in no hurry –

to end her open-ended stay.

The first lazy raindrops pitter-pattered on the windowpanes and the velvet curtains stirred from the half-hearted draught. It wasn't necessary to lower the bottom pane pushed up on its sashes. Beth stretched her hand outside and relished the cool wetness spotting her palm. The shower wasn't fated to last long. It wouldn't please the ever-silent Mark. He was hoping for a prolonged downpour to refresh the gardens under his care. He was the opposite of old Mr Jewell. Mark was masculine in stature, uninterested in sharing his botanical knowledge, and most of the time frustratingly monosyllabic.

'I really must go down to the cove and call on Ken Tresaile,' Beth chided herself aloud. He was her uncle; there was no reason not to meet. Both Christina and Mrs Reseigh said he was a good man, and she didn't want him to think she was shunning him. But it had been wise for her to spend lots of time with Christina.

It was more difficult to forge a closer relationship with Joe, mainly because he was still wary of her. For a lone child only twelve years of age it must be hard to suddenly relate to a grown-up sister. Except for the blood tie, Beth found they had little in common and Joe must feel that way too. She wasn't jealous of the camaraderie Joe and Kitty enjoyed. Beth preferred reading and music to chess or grooming the dogs. Kitty was used to having a brother, and it came easily to her to indulge in verbal tussles and exchange daft jokes with Joe. Beth liked looking over the house with Christina, discussing antiques and fabrics and fashion, rather than racing about outside and climbing trees. Dear Kitty, she still had such a lot of endearing youth in her, and she would probably always be like that, bless her. Beth tended to be quiet and thoughtful, while Kitty was a great chatterer, although in the last few days (she couldn't hide it from her friend who knew her so well) she had taken to day-dreaming about a particular rugged young fisherman...

The day after Lily Praed's accident, a contingent of anxious visitors from Owles House had arrived at Wildflower Cottage. Beth had driven so Christina could join a jittery Joe, and Kitty. Richard Opie, who often slept over with Joe during the holidays and weekends, was also with them. Beth had not envisaged that her second arrival at the fishing family's home would find her at the rear of a line of people bearing get-well wishes, flowers, sweets and a chocolate cake.

'I'll never forget the sight of Joe carrying the little injured girl into the cottage's front room.' Kitty had told the sorry tale of Lily's accident after she and Richard had walked home a very shaken Joe. 'She had taken a terrible fall while out playing by herself, and goodness knows how long she would have stayed on the ground if Joe and Richard hadn't come across her. The boys were stricken with fear for her. She was bleeding all over her ruined dress and Joe's shirt. Her bottom teeth were pushed through the skin under her bottom lip, her nose was twice its usual size and she had a lump on her forehead the size of her fist. She had bruises all down the length of her front. She was conscious, but Joe said she was in shock and hadn't spoken a word after he had picked her up.

'Her poor mother Posy went to pieces. Rob Praed, her nephew, rushed down to the Sailor's Rest to ask to ring for the doctor. It was an hour before he arrived. Well, the doctor patched poor Lily up and left instructions on how she was to be nursed. Joe and Richard refused to leave until the doctor assured them Lily wasn't going to die. Lily is so precious to the Praeds after they lost their other daughter, Juliet, Mark's wife. It must be awful for Mrs Praed knowing the men have got to leave to fish away for five whole days. Apparently, at the weekend, they leave their boats berthed at Newlyn and catch the train from Penzance to St Austell, and then take two buses to arrive home,' Kitty had ended wistfully.

For the rest of the day Christina had fussed worriedly over Joe, who was stunned and subdued. Kitty had kept him close company. Beth too had made every effort to reassure Joe but he had not responded to her at all. He had spoken little. Mostly he was switched off in his own horror. With his precocious maturity it was easy to forget he was still a child.

'Hello there, it's good of you all to come.

Come in, come in.' Posy Praed had emerged from her front door and beckoned them into her home. She was a lumpy figure in a faded print apron over a much-worn plain blue frock. Thick-heeled, dull black shoes pummelled by years of wear and repairs accommodated the shape of her wide bumpy feet. Darned fawn lisle stockings filled the scant space between her shoes and long hemline. Her short plain greying hair was tucked in under a hairnet. Her pale eyebrows had been allowed to grow awry. Trickles of red thread veins edged the corners of her nostrils. It seemed unlikely that a trace of titivating had ever been done to her candid motherly face. Beth had thought that Posy wasn't much bothered with her looks anyway.

Taken momentarily back to the time when this woman had scooped her up in her arms and done her best to soothe her fears, Beth recalled a cosy picture of a close, happy family, content with their lot, headed by frumpy but kind-hearted parents who, rather than call each other by their first names or pet names, addressed each other as 'Mother' and 'Father', or even in the Cornish way as 'Maid' and 'Boy'.

'It's very good of you to receive us, Mrs Praed,' Christina had said, all smiles and concern. 'How is dear Lily this morning? We've brought a few things for her, if that's all right.'

'Aw, she's sleeping at the moment. That's very kind and thoughtful of you all, Mrs Vyvyan. Do come in. I'll show you into the front room, and I'll soon have the kettle on.'

191

Posy kept up her welcoming waving in, but Beth could tell she thought it something of an honour to have Christina call at her house. 'Aw, Miss Copeland, 'tis nice to see you again. You were such a help yesterday calming things down and taking care of the boys. Aw, and you must be Miss Elizabeth,' Posy said over her shoulder to Beth, snatching looks at her while she led the way down the broad passage. 'I can see you've grown up to be a fine lady. Oh, mind none of you catches your legs on my son Barry's bits of metal there. He's trying to invent something or other for the boat.'

When they were all in the good-sized front room, which faced the charming wilderness garden, Joe pleaded, 'Can we see Lily, Mrs Praed? Richard and I? We've brought fudge for her. It's soft so it shouldn't hurt her sore mouth.'

'Aw, bless you, Master Joseph. 'Fraid Lily won't be able to see anyone today except me, the doctor and her gran, who's sitting with her. Like I said, she's sleeping. Has been most of the time, praise God. When she wakes she frets and is in pain. 'Tis a hard job to get her to sip a little water. Her head aches something awful, her nose is like a fat tomato and Doctor had to put a stitch in where her teeth came through. Lily will need to rest for some days yet.' Posy dabbed at her eyes, clearly overcome. 'We can't thank you boys enough for bringing her home. She don't usually play in the woods on her own. Well, take a seat everyone. I'll make a pot of tea.'

Beth had noticed both Joe and Richard were uncomfortable with the praise but assumed they were embarrassed by it. Normally, she felt, they would have been pleased to be seen as heroes but they had been thrown by the little girl's distress. She had overheard them mumbling long into the night.

'Please don't put yourself to any trouble, Mrs Praed.' Christina had touched Posy's arm in the sympathetic manner of one mother to another. 'I don't think we should intrude on you. I'm sure you'll be receiving other visitors. We'll leave the things we've brought. If we may, someone will call every day to ask how Lily's progressing. If there's anything we can do, please, please do send word.'

'Yes, please do that, Mrs Praed,' Beth added, eager to return the woman's long-standing kindness to her. 'We'll be happy to take Lily and anyone in the family anywhere that's needed in the motor car. Are you able to keep in touch with Mr Praed?'

'Oh, that's not a problem. Mark, my son-in-law, will pop into the Sailor's Rest every evening where my husband will telephone him from Newlyn. Thank you all very much for coming.'

The Owles House people had quietly trooped outside and returned to the car. Beth had noticed, inside the cottage, how Kitty's eyes kept straying to the mantelpiece where Praed family photographs comfortably sat, her eyes in particular lingering on a rugged, smiling young

193

man in overalls and jersey on the deck of *Our Lily*.

After Beth and Kitty had retired to their room that night, Kitty had mentioned Rob Praed in an offhand manner, but she had done so several times. 'I found when Rob invited me inside his uncle's cottage it was crammed with people getting together for a bit of a do. It's a tradition of the Praed family and their neighbours before the men start each new fishing season. There were more people looking over Mr Praed's well-tended vegetable garden. I was made so welcome and was enjoying myself. I'd barely had time to meet Rob's two sisters when Richard tore inside without knocking and shouted that Lily was badly hurt. It was as if time had stopped for a moment. On seeing the dreadful state of Lily in Joe's arms most people flew into a fluster. It was Rob who took charge of everything. He seems very capable.'

Beth had kept to herself the remark, 'He seems a whole lot more than that to you, Kitty.' Kitty had obviously been deeply impressed by Rob Praed, despite Christina and Mrs Reseigh's description of him in general conversation as the local Lothario. Beth had shrugged it off. Kitty was too sensible to be swept away by such a man.

On the way downstairs, Beth decided to visit three very different addresses. First the vicarage, then the Sailor's Rest. And then to No. 1 Quayside where Evie Vage lived. Only at the vicarage was she sure she would receive a welcome. Beth found the wan figure of Muriel Oakley forever filtering into her mind. The recollection of her encounter with the pale Miss Oakley, and of her sudden scurrying departure, rarely left her. Miss Oakley's goodness to Beth as a child and her careful yet jolly teaching methods meant Beth had not been daunted at receiving lessons, even in a musty, dark, crumbling old place where her outlandish parents stalked the corridors. Miss Oakley didn't deserve to be lonely and listless. Beth had learned that the Reverend Oakley's increasingly bizarre ways, his growing inability to effectively pastor his congregation, had seen their number dwindle to single figures. Having lost virtually all respect for his position, the locals were hoping his retirement was not far off. Perhaps Miss Oakley was longing for that too, envisaging life in some smaller, warmer ecclesiastical home. Miss Oakley would be useful in helping Beth fill in some of the blanks of her formative years, but Beth also felt she owed Miss Oakley something, some of her time and a little companionship.

Beth wasn't particularly worried about meeting her uncle. Mrs Reseigh had said that according to the local grapevine he would be very interested to see her. Beth would be interested to see the home where her father had grown up. It would be nice if Ken Tresaile could offer her a few good memories of his brother. Mrs Reseigh couldn't say whether Evie

Vage would welcome Beth on her doorstep. No one, apparently, had put the question to Evie. It would be a waste of time, she would not answer. Like Davey Vage, Evie was known for keeping her opinions to herself. Davey Vage was unlikely to welcome Beth into his home, so the best time to go there was when he was working out at sea. Beth thought she might not get in touch with Evie at all if her mother was still alive, felt it wouldn't have been acceptable to all the Vage family. How would Evie receive her, Beth wondered, nervous about it. With lack of interest, unfriendliness, even resentment? Evie might be offended at suddenly having memories that might be sad or even horrid thrust upon her. On the other hand, Evie might be wondering whether Beth wished to see her. The last thing Beth wanted was for Evie to think she was too stuck-up to want to know her. Beth's last destination would reveal what a visit to Evie would be like.

Beth went straight to Christina, knowing that at this time of the morning she would be in the study at her desk.

Christina was ending a telephone call and smiled warmly at Beth, an expression which Beth returned. It was a fantastic heart-warming pleasure to both of them. Each was awed and amazed at their new relationship, but each felt a measure of guilt about the past. For Christina, and it would be so for evermore, over the dreadful ways she had failed her daughter. For Beth, over her long-held beliefs that her mother had never really loved her.

'Ah Beth, I've ordered plaice for dinner this evening. I'll make a creamy herb sauce. Joe and Kitty are picking the vegetables from the garden. I'll do my speciality lemon sorbet for dessert. How does that sound?'

'Really delicious. I'm going to have to put my thinking cap on to cook something so tasty for us tomorrow. Ready for me to fetch us coffee?'

'Oh, yes please,' Christina smiled in supreme joy.

Mother and daughter always enjoyed this part of the day, a brief period they were able to spend exclusively in each other's company.

At that moment Kitty popped her head round the door. 'Sorry to interrupt. Could I borrow the motor please, Beth? I've just had a brilliant idea. Lily is a lot better now. I thought I'd offer to run her and Mrs Praed down to Newlyn to see Mr Praed and Lily's brothers before they set out on their next fishing trip.'

'Oh, I don't think you should do that, Kitty.' Christina's frown cleared the brightness from Kitty's eyes. 'It isn't really done, the wives and family going to the fishermen, unless one of the men is seriously injured. Mr Praed will have been assured by Mark that Lily is recovering well and he'll be happy about that.'

Kitty's disappointment was glaringly apparent from her deep scarlet blush. 'Oh ... I'll, um, take Grace out to play in the garden then.' She hurried away.

'Poor Kitty,' Beth said to Christina. 'That was

really about her hoping to see Rob Praed.'

'It could be poor Kitty indeed if she's fallen for that individual,' Christina sighed, with feeling. 'He's not a settled type and I should think he'd look to a local woman if he wants a wife.'

Kitty had discovered the peace of one of Beth's favourite old spots for herself. She was under the willow tree, lying on a rug with little Grace snoozing on her chest. Her eyes closed, she was reliving a secret, a wonderful memory, of Rob Praed kissing her. On taking her into the busy kitchen of Wildflower Cottage, crammed with women preparing heaps of food for the traditional gathering – cakes, splits, pasties, sweet and savoury flans and tarts and assorted sandwiches – Rob had introduced Kitty to his ever-smiling Aunt Posy, his dainty, wise-looking Grandma Praed, and his two sisters, Judy and Alison. The two younger women were wearing aprons over what appeared to be their best dresses and shoes. They had shingled their hair. Short and slender, not needing make-up to enhance their clear features, they were attractive, and to Kitty they were welcoming and curious.

Also in the room, which was soaked in mouth-watering baking smells, the heat from the black iron cooking range eased by the open door and windows, had been a medley of neighbouring housewives of various ages, and infants watched over by young girls. Rob introduced them all to Kitty, even telling her the babies' names, proving to Kitty how much family meant to these people. One beautiful black-haired toddler proved to be Rowella, Mark Reseigh's daughter and Posy Praed's granddaughter. Kitty had never felt so immediately at home in a new place. It was cosy and comfortable here with a pervading sense of closeness and fun. Kitty declined a cup of tea offered by Posy from the huge, ever-ready brown and beige teapot but accepted a glass of blackcurrant cordial. Rob had said, 'I'll get a drop of ale later.'

'It's a pleasure to meet you, Miss Copeland,' Posy Praed had said. 'How're you finding it staying up in Owles House? I've met Miss Elizabeth, many years ago that was.'

'Miss Tresaile has talked often about your kindness to her,' Kitty had replied, a little uncomfortably aware of so many avid eyes suddenly on her. 'She does intend to call on you and thank you personally.'

'Aw, she needn't do that. We're always glad to help anyone out. We don't turn no one away,' Posy smiled. 'Have you known Miss Elizabeth long?'

'We've been friends since she moved up to Wiltshire with her grandmother.'

'Is it right that her grandmother is now dead?' Grandma Praed asked, her dark eyes beady and piercing.

'Miss Kitty didn't come in here to answer a barrage of questions,' Rob laughed. 'I'll take her outside to meet Uncle Lofty and the other men.'

Kitty wouldn't have minded chatting with the

women and girls and cooing to the babies, but she was pleased to be swept out of the cottage. It allowed her to avoid any personal questions about Beth and Christina, which she would have had to sidestep.

She was amused to find the gathering of men lounging behind the sheds. They had been out of sight to her while she stood in the lane. They bantered and smoked while drinking mugs of tea or passing round a flagon of ale. Kitty found Lofty Praed, his sons Linford junior, Douglas, and the twins Barry and Andy, an amiable lot, as were their fishermen neighbours.

'Your garden is amazing, Mr Praed,' Kitty said to Lofty. 'I've never seen so many rows of ripe produce. Your raspberries look luscious.'

'Aw, thank you, Miss Copeland. Taken years of hard work and a bit of knowhow to get 'un this good. We're lucky here to have our own bit of ground and not to have to go up the cliff to the allotments. You're welcome to take a dish of raspberries away with 'ee. Give me a minute and I'll go pick some for 'ee.'

'I'd love to have some, but don't put yourself to any trouble,' Kitty said, totally unfazed by all the male faces gazing her way. Among the older men there seemed to be some real characters. One had an opulent full set of pointed whiskers, another was a cheeky gurner and a third a chuckling talker of entertaining gobbledegook. The young men were more ordinary, one or two of them bashful. Some were nice looking but none outrageously handsome like Rob.

'I'll pick some for Miss Kitty,' Rob pitched in. 'I'm sure she'd be pleased to help me.'

While Rob went back inside to fetch a dish, Kitty looked over the green plants with Lofty, enthusing over the large healthy specimens. 'Bet my son-in-law Mark don't produce beauties like these savoy cabbages up in yonder big garden, eh, Miss Copeland?'

'I should say not, Mr Praed, but I wouldn't say so to Mr Reseigh,' Kitty grinned impishly. 'I saw his little girl, your granddaughter, in the kitchen. She's gorgeous.'

'She is that, and bright as an admiral's button,' Lofty nodded, full of pride. 'Mark will be along as soon as he's finished his work up at the Dunn Head Hotel. Our late Juliet can look down and rest assured he's done well by Rowella, our little angel.'

Kitty had wondered if Evie and Davey Vage would make an appearance here among their neighbours, but in view of Beth's connection to them she would not ask.

'Ready?' Rob interrupted his uncle, with his eyes rooted on Kitty in a manner that made her feel strangely squirmy inside her tummy. This man was becoming a powerful draw on her.

'Of course,' Kitty said jauntily. 'Excuse me, Mr Praed.'

As she walked with Rob over the well-stamped path down to the bottom of the garden Kitty knew the men had formed a huddle and were guffawing about Rob's blatant move to get her alone with him. She did not care. Being alone with Rob was all she had wanted at that moment, and was all she wanted now.

They had reached the end row of raspberries. The moment they started off down between the prickly-leaved, pale-red fruit and a high hedge of privet, Rob had smiled directly into her eyes. 'You hold the bowl, Kitty. I'll pick the berries. I don't want you to get your fingers red and sticky. Watch out for the bees.'

His fingers working quickly, Rob soon had the large enamel bowl half filled.

'Mrs Vyvyan and Miss Tresaile will be thrilled with these. I must ask your mother about a recipe. I'm sure she'll have a delicious local one,' Kitty had said, concentrating on his gorgeous face rather than on what he was doing.

Rob faced her and held a fat raspberry up in front of her. 'I prefer them as they are,' he murmured, his voice slow and husky. 'With lashings of cream on them.' Before Kitty's mesmerized eyes he fed the raspberry into his mouth and leisurely ate and swallowed it. 'Now you try one.'

Kitty had felt herself tremble as he picked a plump raspberry and made an unhurried journey with it towards her mouth.

'Open up for me.' His tone throbbed in her ears.

Kitty had no will except to obey him. She parted her lips. Her heart raced as his thumb and finger reached her mouth and then he put his thumb and finger right in and rubbed the raspberry on her tongue.

202

'Taste it,' he murmured. 'Tell me if it's a wonderful experience.'

Again she had obeyed him, and because he did not take his thumb and finger away she closed her quivering lips round their warm roughness as well as the raspberry. The fruit melted in the heat of her mouth. Finally he drew his hand away, leaving her to chew the fruit and feeling she would choke with the invasiveness of the whole act. She managed to swallow but red juice trickled out from the corner of her lips. Mortified, she raised her hand to wipe it away but Rob caught her wrist.

'No, let me.' He had placed the bowl on the privet hedge. Then, without seeking permission, he had pulled her into his arms and close against his body. Bending his head to her face, he put out the tip of his tongue and licked away the juice reddening her tender skin. He kissed her on that damp spot. Then he looked into Kitty's eyes. 'You really are a most beautiful woman, so very beautiful.'

Kitty felt light-headed and she stopped breathing for those few intense moments. She was in raptures to be imprisoned in his tight grip. Her arms were hanging limp but she brought them up and circled them round his strong neck. She opened her lips for his kiss, the kiss that was surely coming. His mouth came down claiming all of hers, a deep and intense experience nothing like the few kisses she had received before, which had been chaste and innocent in comparison. There was nothing

203

innocent in the steady pressure, movement and demand of Rob's mouth.

He ended the kiss. He had been the creator and master of it and the timing was his. He laughed and retrieved the enamel bowl. 'We'd better get on before I ruin your reputation.'

There had been no other chance to be alone with Rob after that, but Kitty had found herself part of the whole crowd and had enjoyed every moment. She had hoped desperately that Rob would ask her to meet him somewhere quiet again but no such invitation had materialized, for Joe and Richard had crashed in with the badly hurt Lily Praed. Now Rob was away at sea and Kitty was left hoping that he would seek her out when he returned over the short weekend. At least for now she had her wonderful secret.

Sixteen

Evie Vage stepped out of the back door of her home, locked it then slipped the key into one of the two deep pockets stitched on to a cloth bag, one of the two she was carrying. It was almost unheard of to lock one's door before bedtime, but Davey Vage insisted that the privacy of his small whitewashed cottage should be meticulously preserved. The embroidered bag, with its pair of strong curving cane handles, contained Evie's purse and shopping list and was the only bright thing about her. The rain had petered out leaving the clouds washed pristine white and fewer in number. It was pleasantly warm, so she did not need a cardigan. As usual she wore an uninspiring low-waisted, loose frock, a watered-down version of a fashionable style and sewn herself from a Butterick pattern. She was in muted pink, the bodice loose and extending to her ankles.

Others might think her clothes joyless and austere but everything about Evie had an appealing innocence, and like that of her mother, her dark prettiness could not be dampened down. Some people, even those who had once reviled her, thought of her as a decent, honest, obedient little body and believed she would make some fortunate man a good wife. An undecorated straw cloche was pulled down and half obscured her face. Her one deliberate concession to attractive wear was a pair of shiny grey ankle-strap button shoes. Her father always said, 'Never be afraid to fork out for good shoes, Evie. It shows you're a well brought up young lady and that we're not poor!' Evie would never wear clothes that drew attention to her, but she was proud of her shoes and they gave her confidence.

She carried the cloth bag carefully. She treasured it. As a young child, Evie had watched her beloved mother, Iris, cut out its shape from pale blue linen and embroider on it raised sea scenes, with sky and clouds and waves and boats and seashells, mermaids, sea horses and much more. Intricate beading had also been added. The Vage home was plain and basic but similarly crafted cushions, table runners and pictures made by Iris, who had spent most of her married life shut away indoors, lifted the ordinariness of every room. All made from the generous allowance for materials and sewing silks Davey Vage had gladly given his wife. Evie and her father were proud of Iris's accomplishments and cherished them, as they did her memory.

'I couldn't have had a better wife than your mother,' Davey had oftimes said since Iris's untimely death from pneumonia. 'She gave me you, Evie, and a man couldn't wish for a better and more loyal daughter.'

As the years passed Evie had realized that, unlike every other mother and father, her parents did not share a bedroom. Her mother had a twin bed in Evie's room, the larger of the two bedrooms, the one that faced the sea. Her parents had never called each other by pet names but had always been Davey and Iris. Sometimes her mother had even referred to Davey as Mr Vage. Evie understood more before school age when the taunts from other children started.

'Old man Vage isn't your real father, my mother said so. Your real father's no good. Ran out on his wife and little maid, he did. You've got rotten blood in your veins, Evie Vage.'

'No, you can't play with us, not your sort, born wrong side of the blanket.'

When she grew older she had even been jeered loudly to her face, accused of being 'Phil Tresaile's bastard'. Evie was grateful it was not thanks to the bullying that she found out who had sired her. Iris had told her the truth as soon as she was old enough to understand. 'But always remember, Evie,' Iris added earnestly, 'Mr Vage *is* your proper father. He was good to me when I was in trouble and my parents threw me out. I was their only child and they had high expectations of me and I let them down. They moved out of the cove before you were born and I've never heard from them since. Mr Vage has given us a nice home to live in and we shall never be in want. I shall always be grateful to him and so should you, Evie. I'll never let him down and neither must you, swear that to me, Evie.'

Evie, happy in her life apart from the bullying, had so sworn.

'Evie, darling, you'll always be safe and secure as long as you remember that. You have a home here for life. This cottage will be yours one day. Mr Vage has it written in his will. I can't exactly hold my head up in Portcowl but you can, never forget that. Just don't make the same mistakes I did.'

Evie had not forgotten a single word of her mother's urgings, but from that time onwards she had, by her own choice, kept herself to herself. From then till now she had totally ignored those who reviled her and her mother. Contrary to common belief she wasn't aloof or lonely or as timid as a mouse, and she certainly wasn't ashamed of her origins. There was an element of self-preservation in her stance, but mainly she just could not be bothered to pander to the small-minded, the backbiters, or to listen to people who suggested she was 'lucky in the circumstances' to be allowed to mix with them. Evie was content. She had a caring father, and everything she needed for her material comfort, and she had a settled future. Her faith in God meant she was certain that one day she would be reunited with her beloved mother. She had all she could ever want, now and in the Hereafter.

Evie had a few good friends, all women. She

lived at No. 1 Quayside and next door to her were Judy and Alison Praed. She enjoyed sitting outside the front of the cottages, knitting with Judy and the Praeds' next-door neighbour, the elderly widow Mrs Coad. Rob Praed had built a bench against the wall adjoining the Praeds' and Mrs Coad's homes, and Evie would join them for an hour or two nearly every morning. It was while there knitting a few days ago that she had seen, across the quay, Rob Praed and the rest of the crew of *Our Lily* chatting to a striking-looking woman who, it turned out, was the companion of someone who had not been expected ever to return to Portcowl. A person Evie had heard about almost as a legend, whose childhood suffering had led to her rescue and a well-deserved happy-ever-after ending. Elizabeth Tresaile, Evie's younger and more privileged half-sister.

Her father had brought home the facts to Evie. They had been at the tea table the next evening. 'I've got news, my handsome.' Davey's sombre tone told Evie it was serious news. The leathery colour of his balding head drained away leaving his rounded cheeks grey and blotchy, and his monobrow crinkled into the likeness of a scrunched-up insect.

'What's wrong, Dad? Not problems with the boat, is it?' Davey was the engineer of *Morenwyn* and he felt his responsibility in that regard very keenly.

Davey had put down his knife and fork, leaving his steak and kidney pie virtually uneaten.

209

'It's nothing like that, Evie. There's someone come to the cove. It's the Tresaile girl, Elizabeth. You know all about her. You're related, of course. Half-sisters. She's moved in with her mother. Don't know the full story about that and nor do I want to. If she learns about you, I'm concerned she might be curious about you and try to see you. How would you feel about that? Would you want to see her?'

The suddenness of the question and the issues it raised also wiped out Evie's small appetite. 'I don't know ... she might not be interested in me at all, we can't have nothing in common.'

'Exactly,' Davey had stressed as if brushing aside the fact that the women had the same biological father. 'She was brought up by her stuck-up grandmother. She'll be posh. We're ordinary people.' Stretching across the little kitchen table Davey had placed his heavy rough-knuckled paw over Evie's stiffened hand. 'We've been all right, eh, Evie, just the two of us, with our own routine, our quiet life, since your mother died? I've always tried to do the best for you, Evie. If there's anything you want I'll get it for you, and if there's anything you'd like to do, I'll not stop you. Life must be a bit boring for you sometimes. I mean if you want to go to the cinema or have a meal out we can go together, or you could go with the girls next door. We've never had a holiday. We could go away for a few days somewhere between the fishing seasons, if you like. I'm not being self-ish keeping you just about all to myself, am I?

It's just that no one can hurt us if we stick together, just the two of us.'

At the end of her father's pleas and kind promises, Evie smiled at him. 'Don't worry about me, Dad. I'm perfectly happy with my life just as it is.'

It was true, but during the next few days Evie had thought often about Elizabeth Tresaile. Posh or not, Elizabeth was, except for Ken Tresaile, her only blood relative, and Evie could not help being curious about her half-sister. If she was to find herself face to face with Elizabeth and Elizabeth did speak to her then Evie would certainly respond, albeit cautiously, and take it from there. If it happened she would tell Davey. She had no need to be scared over his reaction. He was too kind to be disappointed in her. Evie had never seen Christina Vyvyan and had caught only the odd glimpse of her strapping, confident son. The people of Owles House, past or present, including the man who had fathered her, were nothing to Evie. As for Elizabeth Tresaile, time would tell about that.

In Evie's second bag, a large straw one, were various finished items of her other craft, lace making. The local shops eagerly bought her traycloths and tablecloths, doilies, furniture runners and handkerchiefs and sold them on in the summer season. Today Evie was delivering to Richard Opie's mother a private commission, lace curtains for her sitting room. All the money Evie made from her lace she saved to buy presents for Davey's birthday and Christmas, and the rest she put away for 'a rainy day'. Davey insisted she also keep the profit she made on the fishermen's jerseys she knitted. Evie walked across the tiny backyard that only took two short strings of washing line and three tubs of begonias. Dozing on the low stone wall, either side of the little cast-iron gate, were two of her four cats, Smoky and Fluffy. She stopped to smooth their fur and kiss their soft lazy heads. 'Biddy's inside, Where's Sly, eh? Out looking for fish tails? Now you two must help Biddy look after the house. I shall only be out for a short while.'

The ground rose immediately into the short, cobbled Dunn Alley, a hair's breadth wide and flanked on either side by the end walls of the homes of Old Street. Once through the alley she reached Half Street, where Mrs Reseigh and her son and granddaughter lived. Evie had knitted a matinee coat for Rowella and she loved seeing the little girl. Theirs was Thrift Cottage, half hung with slates, half painted pale pink, the middle dwelling of just seven homes, hence the street name. Its tiny front garden was bursting with summer colours in pots and hanging baskets. There were pinks, hollyhocks, lavender, poppies, lupins, begonias, lobelia and geraniums. The cottage was much photographed and admired by holidaymakers who climbed up this way, and to Mark Reseigh's pride it was featured on souvenir postcards.

Next was Crescent Street where the cottages,

in groups of four to six, formed the shape of its name. The gradient cut out of the cliff was quite steep but softened where the dwellings stood. All the streets and alleys were flagged or cobbled or were just rough ground. Evie's lively strides made quick work of the journey.

Leaving Crescent Street behind, Evie was near the top of the cove. Here were the finer dwellings, owned mostly by tradespeople. A motor car was parked grandly outside one house. Cliff Way Road, newly built this decade, afforded a panoramic view of the sea and nearby Dunn Head, and of Coggan Point way across the cove. The chimney tops of Owles House could be seen. The road was paved and flat, affording the better-off easier passage, but it lacked the olde-worlde feel and wonderful quaintness of the rest of the cove.

Mrs Opie, whose husband owned the Grand Sea View Hotel, had waved hair flat against her scalp, long rows of pearls and no apron. She had seen Evie coming and stood smiling delightedly on her doorstep. In her rather affected voice she said, 'You've finished my curtains, Miss Vage. How splendid. Please step inside so I can take a look at them. Then I'll fetch my purse.'

Evie was faintly offended that the pretentious Mrs Opie should doubt the quality of her work, which had taken her hours to make. The evidence of her gifted handiwork in the shops proved her unsurpassed excellence. Minutes later, however, she left Cliff Way Road carrying not only her payment of three pounds ten shillings, but an unexpected two and six bonus thanks to Mrs Opie's utter delight with the curtains. Evie was delighted too and went straight off to buy a box of coloured beads to add to a shawl she was making for herself.

Evie was humming a ragtime favourite she had heard on the wireless but went quiet at hearing the cries of a new baby coming from three houses along. She was happy with her life as a single woman but she did find her maternal strings occasionally being tugged.

Judy Praed had begun to teasingly advise her about looking around for a future husband. 'You don't want to end up a sad old spinster like Miss Oakley, do you?' chirpy Judy asked. 'You'd regret missing out on having children, wouldn't you?'

'I suppose so, but I'm satisfied with my life. Me, Dad and the cats.' So Evie would ward off the suggestions.

'But Mr Vage and the cats won't be here for ever, Evie,' Judy persisted. 'And the day will come when you'll be too old for children. I don't want you to end up horribly lonely. Why not give love and a family a chance? I've found my true love, Bernie and I are getting engaged. And Alison is casting her eye round. There's some nice young men about. There's my cousin Linford and the rest of the boys. One of them would be suitable for you, Evie. They're all steady and not bad looking.' Judy gave a little wicked laugh. 'What about Rob? He's a bit full of himself but he's totally family orientated.'

'Everyone knows your brother's got a roving eye,' Evie had returned. She disapproved of Rob Praed. She sensed he had a mean side to him and she did not like him at all.

'He'll stop all that when he settles down,' Judy had said confidently, only the day before. 'It's about time you started looking for a husband, Evie. What do you think, Mrs Coad?'

Mrs Coad had long ago lost her fisherman husband to the cruelty of the sea. She had a son and a daughter and grandchildren living in Portcowl, who looked in on her almost every day. 'Time will tell, I suppose,' the elderly woman had issued her usual saying. 'But after I lost my Gordon it was a blessing to have my children with me. I've never regretted the hardships I went through bringing them up alone. Going back to the matter of spinsters, there is one who's not exactly old yet but she's certainly very sad. I got a letter from Miss Oakley yesterday. She's calling on me tomorrow afternoon. If you ask me, visiting the old and sick is the only thing that keeps her going. S'time her father was put out to pasture, better fit her not to be living any longer in that musty old vicarage.'

'You'll make good company for her, Mrs Coad,' Evie had said. 'Miss Oakley must be really lonely rattling round in that gloomy old house where it's said not even the water taps function properly. When she comes down to the quay she often heads for my cats. It's like they take pity on her and let her make a fuss of them.

215

When Fluff was having her last litter I asked her if she'd like a kitten. She looked so grateful then got into a fluster. "No, oh no, thank you for your kind thought but it would never do," she said. She was like a little girl, sorrowful at having to refuse a treat. It's awful really. Can't be many people in Portcowl sadder than Miss Oakley.'

Evie left the baby's cries behind her but the possibility of having babies of her own stayed in her mind. She knew Davey would hate to lose her but he probably wouldn't mind too much if she brought a nice fisherman husband to the door. She mused about possible husbands from among the young men she knew and felt shy and a little scared at doing so. Of all the possibilities, Linford Praed kept coming to her mind. He was a few years older than her, and sensible and steady. He had always spoken respectfully to her. He had walked out with about half a dozen girls. Judy had said none of them had been the right one for him. Could she, Evie, be right for him, or he for her? Evie felt a nervous fluttering in her tummy and found she was blushing. If she ever were to marry Linford, or one of his brothers, it would be nice being Judy and Alison's cousin-in-law. But their sister-in-law, never. Deciding it was time to end these nervy thoughts, Evie began humming again.

A strange vision appeared just ahead of her. A woman in creased, rather shabby clothes, her felt-brimmed hat askew, was stumbling along

Cliff Way Road seemingly hot and flustered, as if she was lost. Evie's mouth dropped open in shock to recognize the vicar's daughter. Miss Muriel Oakley had blood on her leg and her stockings were ripped. Evie hurried to her, hoping no one living behind these nobler windows would spy Miss Oakley and be appalled by her dishevelment. 'Miss Oakley, have you had an accident? Can I help you?'

Muriel Oakley came out of her dithering stupor and threw up her hands in horror. 'Oh, Miss Vage! I'm so sorry. I – I seem to be going to the wrong address. I'm meant to be calling on ... on, um, Mrs Coad ... I – I think.'

Evie saw there was a deep graze on the lady's cheek, and the side of her loose cardigan was covered in grit and dust. 'Miss Oakley, you're hurt. You are meant to be calling on Mrs Coad today, but not until this afternoon. Please let me take you home and tend to you. I think you need the doctor to call. You're hurt, Miss Oakley,' Evie repeated, for the lady was slipping back into confusion.

'Really? I am? H-how kind of you, um, Miss ... Miss ... ow! My knees are stinging.' She looked down and seemed to crash inside and shrink in size. 'Oh, no, look at the state of me, I'm so ashamed. Yes, I really must go home. What will people think of me?'

Evie put her arm round the lady's sagging bony shoulders; a gesture unthinkable in any other circumstances. 'It's going to be all right, Miss Oakley. You mustn't worry. You've taken

217

a fall somewhere and it's left you dazed. Let me knock on a door and explain what's happened. Then we could ring for a taxicab to take you home. I'll go with you if you like.'

'No!' Miss Oakley flew into a tremendous panic. 'Don't do that, *please*, Miss Vage. I'm terrified of motor cars, of anything that has noisy machinery. Could you walk me home? I'd be so grateful to you.'

'Of course, don't worry, I won't leave you.' In one quick movement Evie straightened the lady's hat, then she turned her round about and slowly led her off.

'Oh, yes-s,' Muriel Oakley suddenly whimpered, clinging to Evie's arm so hard she pinched her. 'I remember now. It's coming back to me. I – I was walking through the churchyard. I go there every day to talk to my mama, you understand. Then suddenly *he* was there. He was right in front of me. I screamed, I think. I turned and tried to run away but he was there again. He laughed. He pushed me over. He always laughed when he did ... when he did it to me! He's a terrible man. He's evil. I can't get away from him. I don't want to go home, he might be there!'

The horrible rigidity that had gripped Muriel Oakley just as abruptly left her. She went limp and retreated again into a stupor, her mind shutting out the horror of the terrible incident.

It was a relief for Evie to have her hurting flesh released, but it was getting harder to move Miss Oakley along and soon they would have to

218

start climbing the hill. 'Dear God,' Evie thought with revulsion. 'Her father's hurting her, and in the worst possible way by the sound of it. I shouldn't really take her home but I can't really take her anywhere else. I've got to think of a way to help her.'

Seventeen

It was a shock to Beth to be suddenly faced with her half-sister. She had arrived at the Gothic-style iron gates of the vicarage, which were partly hanging off their hinges and thrown against the perimeter wall, and there, trailing just feet ahead of her, was the evidently accident-befallen Muriel Oakley, being supported round the waist by a slender young woman. Instinct made Beth certain she knew who the stranger was.

Beth rushed over the weedy gravelled ground to reach them. Miss Oakley was sagging at the knees, groggy and mumbling to herself. Beth hailed the stranger. 'Good afternoon, can I help you with Miss Oakley? Oh, and are you Evie Vage?' Beth's second question was out of her mouth before she had time to consider the wisdom of it, and she was embarrassed to feel her face burning.

'Hello, I'd be glad if you could take Miss Oakley's other side. She's had a fall and badly needs to lie down. I've walked her up from the cove. I tried to get her to allow me to call for a taxi but she utterly refused. Said motor cars frighten her. How do you know my name?' As soon as Evie took her first good look at the well-dressed, posh-speaking Good Samaritan she knew the answer to her own question. Her colour too rose highly. 'Are you Elizabeth Tresaile?'

'Yes, yes I am. I'm pleased to meet you, um ... I've been planning to call on you. I hope you wouldn't have minded. Well, now we've met. I – I suppose we'd better get Miss Oakley safely inside.' Beth knew she was making a weak impression but she didn't know how to be with her half-sister. She was reassured that Evie Vage was polite and had not refused her offer to help. Tucking her clutch bag under one arm, Beth folded Miss Oakley's flopping arm through hers and lifted her flagging weight. She smelt not of rose water but of sour perspiration. 'What happened to her?'

Pace by careful pace, Evie and Beth led the vicar's daughter past a jungle of tangled shrubbery and neglected rhododendrons, towering weeds and wild herbage, to her front door. 'Miss Oakley told me that she'd fallen in the churchyard this morning,' Evie explained, putting on hold her personal feelings at suddenly being faced with her half-sister. 'It seems after that she got confused. She was meant to be visiting a neighbour of mine but she had gone down to the cove far too early. As you can see she's hurt, but she's flatly refused to allow me to call the doctor. She said she doesn't trust doctors. She became really upset. It's taken me well over an hour to get her here.'

Evie would never betray the full story that Miss Oakley had told her, least of all to the woman she had just met. On the arduous journey here, during many necessary rests, Miss Oakley, in her confusion, had rambled out a terrible story. She believed Phil Tresaile had appeared to her in the churchyard and taunted her and deliberately pushed her over. Evie was fearful Miss Oakley was more than just confused and was actually beginning to lose her mind. That would be no wonder to her, given the monotonous, seemingly abnormal life she had been leading for so many years with her potty father.

'It's fortunate for Miss Oakley that you were on hand to bring her home.'

They had arrived at the wide granite doorstep of the vicarage. Beside the iron foot scraper was a pair of large rubber boots with mud drying on them. Apparently the Reverend Oakley had been gardening (and about time, Beth thought, having noticed the wild state of the flower beds and shrubbery) and he was within. Inside the dark, drab porch was a dusty coconut mat lagged with dead leaves, and on it were several pairs of scuffed and dirty male shoes, all neatly lined up, an odd combination of carelessness and care.

'Miss Oakley, we're at the vicarage door, you're home,' Evie said loudly and soothingly, when they were inside the musty porch. 'Miss Tresaile is also here to help. We'll just knock on the door for Mr Oakley.'

'He won't be there,' Muriel said faintly, emerging out of her daze, but her legs were sagging more and more after the long uphill struggle. 'Papa doesn't come inside until I call him in nowadays. The door won't be locked. We can go straight in.'

'I'll open the door,' Beth said, suppressing a shudder. On her last entry here, as a child, the brasswork had been gleaming and the tiled porch floor scrubbed. Now the porch seemed like a gloomy neglected cavern and the thought of stepping over the threshold into the old house was wholly uninviting. Glancing at Evie, Beth saw she too was apprehensive.

The heavy door, hanging untrue, creaked and whined on its hinges as Beth pushed on it, and she was forced to let go of Miss Oakley so as to be able to push harder. As the door opened a history of fustiness and human staleness hit Beth full in the face. Her eyes stung and her nose felt contaminated with something rotten, like an insult. She failed to hold back the instinct to clear her throat and try to eject the damaging air. She heard Evie gasp in horror and then gasp again as if struggling for breath.

'Are you all right?' Instinctively feeling concern for her flesh and blood, Beth looked round Miss Oakley at Evie.

Evie nodded, grateful for the genuine consideration. Her eyes were full of unease. Her pity for Miss Oakley grew. Surely no one would remain completely sane for long if they had to live in such overpowering gloom. It would suck away all a person's hopes and desires and crush them until eventually they'd never rise again.

The nervous company shuffled into the hall. Beth and Evie shared the feeling that it was like entering the middle of the night. For some reason the mirrors and paintings had been covered with swathes of dark cloth. Half-tables and chairs, cabinets and the umbrella stand were huge vague shapes in the dimness, suggesting echoes of misery hidden behind them and threatening to pounce out on the humans at any moment and drag them into some nightmare existence. The drapes at the windows were drawn across; moth-eaten and ragged, they looked like witches' cloaks. Looming to the left of the huddle of women was the great wooden staircase. Its gargoyle-like newels seemed to stare at them.

'She shouldn't have to live here,' Evie whispered, with exasperation and sympathy.

'No, she shouldn't,' Beth agreed, with pity for her former teacher. She put her face near Miss Oakley's ear. 'Where would you like us to take you, Miss Oakley? The drawing room? Your bedroom?'

'I – I need to wash and change my clothes,' Muriel murmured, her feebleness taking on an edge of shame. 'My dear papa would be most alarmed to see me like this.'

'We'll take you up to the bathroom,' Beth said. 'I've got a rough idea of the layout of the upstairs rooms.'

'No, oh no, you mustn't!' Muriel was suddenly energized and insistent. Embarrassed horror at the suggestion screamed out of her every pore. It had brought her to a trembling lucidity, and she pulled away from her carers and put distance between herself and them. 'I m-mean I couldn't put you good ladies to any more trouble. You've been so kind, so charitable, and I am so grateful to you, but I can manage now, honestly I can. I just need to compose myself and lie down in my room. I need to pray. The Lord raise me up over this.'

'Well, if you're sure, Miss Oakley,' Evie said, using the soothing tones she had employed since discovering the lady's plight. She had the same sort of faith in the Lord, but she was worried that Miss Oakley would soon plunge again into bewilderment and terrifying delusions. 'Can we do anything for you? Make some tea? Do some tidying up? We could prepare a meal for you.'

'Oh, bless you, Miss Vage, but really I'll be fine, and you and, um ... oh, it's you, Miss Tresaile ... have your own affairs to attend to. Everything here is fine, really it is. Please don't let me detain you both. Please go about your own business, and thank you for inconveniencing yourselves on my behalf. If you don't mind I'd like to be alone now.'

Beth and Evie knew their presence was now upsetting Miss Oakley, who was mortified with humiliation on every level. They offered her a quick polite goodbye and went back outside into the fresh air that was so welcome in their

225

lungs. Behind them the front door of the vicarage was shut with a firm thud. Beth and Evie had no need to tell each other it was a huge relief to be out of the morbid old building.

Silently, with their eyes on the derelict ground, they hurried out beyond the forsaken gates.

'I feel so sorry for her,' Beth said, taking another long reviving breath of clean air and adjusting her embroidered cloche.

'Me too,' Evie said, straightening her clothes which had become ravelled up in the recent journey.

'Well, you did what you could for her, Ev—' Beth was shy now. 'Um, may I call you Evie?'

'Of course,' Evie found herself saying. 'I tend to keep myself mainly to myself but I'm always happy to help anyone who needs it ... Beth.'

The half-sisters gazed at each other deeply, aware they did not share the slightest physical likeness, aware too of the subtle differences in their dress mode and hairstyles – Beth chic and Evie a little homely. But it did not matter. None of their differences mattered, at least not for now.

'You did a lot for poor Miss Oakley. I'm sure she'll bless you for your willing kindness.' It was strange to Beth to have met Evie in such odd circumstances and to be feeling quite comfortable with her. She had the need to express praise to Evie. She had only just met her but she liked her greatly.

Evie felt a little reticent now; there was the

matter of her father not wanting her to ever meet Elizabeth Tresaile. But it was not at all daunting to meet Beth and it did not feel wrong to linger with her. Beth was not stuck up in the least, and Evie liked her and wanted her to know it. 'You must want to show kindness to Miss Oakley too. You came here today to see her specially, didn't you, not Mr Oakley?'

'I was fortunate to have her as my first teacher. She was very kind to me.' Beth was smiling broadly and she felt the same lightness in her heart she'd had when she'd bonded with Christina. 'Evie, this is so strange to be here with you, but I feel comfortable about it, don't you? I thought our first meeting would be strained, perhaps even a disaster. I was a little scared about it, in fact.'

'I didn't think I'd want to meet you and I was worried that you might turn up on my doorstep, and to be honest I wouldn't have cared if you'd returned home without contacting me. It's nice that you intended to meet me, and yes, I do feel comfortable with you, Beth. It's strange for me to be feeling this way, I mean, I haven't any family except for my dad, and my uncle, our uncle Ken Tresaile.'

'I'm so glad you think that. So glad this is so easy for us both.' Beth held back the desire to embrace Evie. It was too early for that, and it was not the sort of social intimacy that came naturally to the humbler class. She reached out her hand to Evie. Evie offered her hand. They kept their hands together for a long while, smiling and both still a little inhibited.

They strolled off side by side along the sunny lane.

'Perhaps we should get the one matter out of the way that links us together, Evie?' Beth ventured, hoping it would not put a wedge between her and her sister. She liked it, revelled in it now, having a growing family. 'Phil Tresaile, the man who should not have rejected either of us but did so through his rotten selfishness.'

'He means nothing to me, never has,' Evie said firmly, telling the truth, but finding it disturbing that he was somehow terrorizing Muriel Oakley's mind from the grave. He had had a bad effect on many people. 'Davey Vage is my father. I love him as my father. I'm sorry if your father hurt you a lot, Beth.'

'He did, but it's not important to me now. But I've learned that he was instrumental in my mother's fall from grace, and I hate the fact. She didn't deserve any of the cruel treatment he handed out to her, Evie.'

Evie waited for Beth to say more. When Beth kept silent Evie understood. The relationship and reconciliation between Beth and her mother was private to them both. 'No one deserved to fall foul of Phil Tresaile. Let's mention him no more. I'm glad your mother knew happiness with Francis Vyvyan. He was a very fine man.'

'I'd like to have met him. Since I've arrived here it's been a shock to discover I have a brother and a sister, and had a twin. It's only been a short while but now it feels natural. It

228

feels like I've never really been away from Portcowl. Strange, I know, but it's true.'

'I'm glad for you. It's up to each of us to make the best of our lives.' It was something Evie's mother had often said, and Iris had made the best of life for Evie and herself as Davey's wife and homemaker.

'Well, what shall we do now?' Beth said, happy that the awkward matters had been addressed and that thereby she and Evie seemed to have gained some closeness. 'I also intend to call on Ken Tresaile today. It's time I approached him. May I walk down to the cove with you, Evie?'

Evie hesitated. If she were seen with Beth, her father would soon get to hear of it. 'Well, the thing is, I'll be honest, my dad was hoping we wouldn't ever meet. Not that I'd mind,' she added quickly as Beth's face shaded with disappointment. 'I'd welcome it, but it's difficult. I hope you understand, Beth.'

Beth was heartened at seeing her disappointment reflected in Evie's expression. 'I understand. Mr Vage is worried I'd intrude on his home and upset you in some way, Evie. I've only been back in my mother's life for two weeks. I didn't know you existed, Evie, until a few days ago. We're strangers, although it doesn't feel that way any more. Mr Vage doesn't know me at all. Hardly anyone in Portcowl does. I hope to change that, Evie. I'll make a point of meeting the local people. Perhaps if I bump into your father some time and he gets to know and trust me...'

'Perhaps,' Evie echoed Beth, but without a lot of hope. 'But my father is a very private man.'

'We can wait and see and hope. We've plenty of time. I've no plans to return to Wiltshire for a very long time yet. Evie, what's Ken Tresaile like? I understand he's nothing like his brother, our father.'

'He's always been nice to me. I'm sure he'd be very interested to meet you, Beth.'

'That's good to hear.' Beth halted reluctantly. 'Well, you'd better go on ahead, Evie. Hopefully we'll find a way of keeping in touch, perhaps through Miss Oakley. I shall try again to help her. I'll wait here a while then dawdle on my way.'

'All right then,' Evie said, and Beth saw she had an engaging smile.

Beth held the gaze of Evie's pretty eyes. 'It's been wonderful to meet you, Evie. Take care of yourself. I'll say goodbye – but just for now.'

Evie returned Beth's lingering look. She nodded to convey that she shared the same sentiments. 'Bye then.'

After a few long moments Evie left. She went a dozen steps then looked back. Beth had not moved. The sisters' smiles to each other lasted a very long time.

Eighteen

The prow of *Our Lily* sliced cleanly through the dark waters as the six-man crew of Praeds set off for the run-in to the fishing port of Newlyn. The sea was calmer now but most of the night the surf had been heavy, making the boat lurch and roll drunkenly and the mizzen light wink dementedly. It had taken nearly five hours to haul the nets in over the roller with both motors in play. Their eyes smarting and reddened by wind and salt spray, for the men it had taken more hours of muscle-breaking work to shake and unravel the nets to send the quivering pilchards showering down into the fish berth. It was an age before the fishermen finished stowing all the gear away and headed for the warmth of the cabin, where they cast off their long yellow oilskins and leather sea boots.

Lofty had announced philosophically, 'We had a bad night of it, nets come up so light they didn't reach nowhere near the bottom, catch won't fill twelve maunds when we go alongside the market. But we're all safe and sound, and that's it.'

The stuffy cabin had an almost tangible combined stink of sweat, tobacco smoke, pungent

231

wet leather and oilskins and the crabbiest socks that had ever steamed on the planet. Lofty, Linford Junior and the youngest son Douglas, and Rob, were long accustomed to the rank smells. Nor did they notice the motion of the lugger, even during the periods when it pitched and tilted in high-running seas. 'Wonder how our dear little maid is,' Lofty voiced his daily concern.

'You know she's getting better, Dad,' Linford answered patiently from the bunk where he was sitting, rolling a smoke. He was lulled now by the vibration given off by the propeller, as were the others. His two middle brothers, twins Barry and Andy, were in the wheelhouse. 'Mark's said so every time over the phone, 'cept for the first day and night.'

'Lily's as tough as the Wolf.' Rob, already smoking, grinned at the memory of his tomboy niece running gleefully into the house one summer with a colony of snails crawling up her skinny bare arm. She'd put them there and exclaimed she liked the tickling. Horrified but unsurprised and giggling, Aunt Posy had disappointed her daughter by pulling off the snails, throwing them out the door, then lathering Lily's arm with enough warm water and soap to clean every child in the cove for a week. Doting on her as much as her immediate family did, Rob had joined them in plying Lily with treats and promises of treats to replace the fun she'd had with the snails. Lily was precious because she was a surprise late baby, and she had become even more so after the family tragedy of losing Juliet. And Lily was treasured because despite all the attention lavished on her – and she knew exactly how to work on each member of her family – she was not at all a spoiled brat.

Douglas guffawed. 'She'll be up and about shrieking as loud as a flock of gulls. No gale nor spring tide would get the better of our Lily.'

'You worry too much, Dad,' Linford said. 'Mother'll be taking good care of her.'

'And she'll have Judy and Alison fussing over her too,' Rob declared.

'Maybe, and that's all very well,' Lofty murmured, preparing to eat a hunk of yeast cake. 'But I've told Mark to tell Mother not to let Lily out of her sight till we get home.' Finally some of the tension left Lofty and the deeply etched lines on his hardy brow were a little less obvious. With white cake crumbs tumbling down his shirt, he spoke loud and hearty. 'When we get home we'll have a big family roast and later an even bigger tea party. Invite them boys, Joe and Richard, to join us. If not for them ... well, I don't want to think about that. As long as Lily and Mother are all right then I'm a happy man.'

'What about that Miss Kitty?' Linford made a sussing noise of male appreciation between his teeth. His eyes, edged like all fishermen's with crow's feet from staring endlessly against the elements, gleamed horny and in awe. 'She's a smashing piece of stuff.'

'You can say that again,' Douglas remarked,

with his usual guffaw. He passed a coarse glint on to his brother and cousin, but furtively, for his father came down hard on lewd behaviour. Lofty saw all unattached women as pure princesses who ought not to be tainted by pre-marital attentions. 'You going to invite her, Dad? She was a brick to us that day.'

'Why not?' Lofty replied happily, washing down the cake with a mug of strong black sweet tea.

Later, when Lofty slipped out to take over at the wheel so Barry and Andy could get a bite to eat and drink, Linford leaned towards Rob. 'Are you planning to see the delicious Miss Kitty Copeland again?'

'Don't know,' Rob shrugged his powerful shoulders. 'I thought she'd be good for a shag but she's obviously a virgin. That means emotions might be involved on her part and she'd want more than a good time from me. Can't stand being chased after. Comes with accusations and the try-on of guilt and intimidation.' The tight expression of extreme annoyance vanished from Rob's face. Now he was quietly serious. 'Got a wedding to plan soon now Judy's engaged to Bernie Crewes—'

'And it's a good job for he that you approve of him,' Linford cut in, with a knowing nod.

'And Alison's on the lookout. Will find myself in an empty house before too long,' Rob said, as if he had not been interrupted. 'So I think it's time for me to cast out my net for a wife. I want a big family.'

'Well, you'll have plenty to choose from. Just about any woman would have you, though I don't know why, you ugly swine,' Linford jested, in envy.

'Got anyone in mind?'

'It would have to be someone who'd make a good fisherman's wife. Not some flighty piece I couldn't trust while working away. Someone like Judy and Alison and Auntie Posy.' Rob ran possibilities through his mind. There was no lack of suitable candidates in Portcowl or the other local fishing villages. Suddenly it was obvious to him.

Rob gazed levelly at his more easy-going cousins. 'Evie Vage would make a good choice.'

'Evie?' Linford and Douglas exclaimed in unison.

'What about Evie?' the twins asked, squeezing into the cabin and leaving barely space for anyone to move. Andy spoke alone. 'Father said, no need for anyone else to go out. He's quite happy on his own. So what's going on then?'

The others shuffled up to give the twins a few inches of a bottom bunk. Linford thrust a crib box at them. Barry lifted the tin lid and cut off a large slice of yeast cake for his twin and himself.

'Rob's thinking of marrying Evie,' Linford scoffed, staring at his confident cousin as if he thought Rob, for once, would be out of his depth.

'What?' Both of the twins had wolfed down a chunk of cake and both nearly choked on it. 'That would be the biggest challenge of any man's life.'

'Yeah, exactly.' Douglas confirmed his own amazement. 'He's got sea madness. Davey Vage would rip his head off before he allowed that to happen.'

'And Evie wouldn't give the idea the time of day.' Linford shook his head. 'She's devoted to Davey. He brought her up as his own and she loves him for it. She'll be happy to care for him till the day he dies, and that could be a long way off. He's in his sixties but he's hale enough. And apart from that, from what I've seen, Evie doesn't care all that much for you, Rob. She's the only woman I've ever known to look at you with, well, something like distaste, I'd say.'

Rob lit another cigarette on the end of the one he was finishing, then he leaned back, his hands behind his head. 'You're all talking wet and you know it. Evie's shy, a bit overawed by me, that's all. She'd be ideal for me. Doesn't gossip, doesn't want a high life.' He rubbed his taut stomach. 'Her cooking smells are mouth watering. That's a big plus, and I'm sure she'd make a good mother.'

'There he goes,' Douglas wailed in reverential admiration. 'He's at it again. When someone says he can't have something or isn't likely to get it, Rob's all the more determined he damned well will.'

'And he usually succeeds,' the twins said, in

236

hero worship. After a stern look from Rob they added, *'Always* succeeds.'

'Oh well,' Linford said knowingly. 'Trouble full steam ahead then.'

Nineteen

'Joe, I'd like to make a suggestion to Mother,' Beth said, watching him carefully. 'But before I do I'd like your opinion about it.'

'Go on,' Joe replied bluffly, throwing a red rubber ball for Chaplin, or rather hurling it, far away towards the shoreline.

Beth had expected his wariness over the mention of their mother. Joe had accepted Beth's invitation to go down to the little Owles Beach, but neither of them was entirely comfortable with the other. He did not have to say he would prefer it if Kitty was with them. He would have mentioned fetching bathing suits, and he would have splashed about in the waves with her, leaving Beth holding the towels. Beth, as usual, would have felt sorely left out. This morning though, Kitty had put on her prettiest casual summer dress and sun hat, and just enough make-up to add lively sophistication to her natural beauty, and then she had hastened off down to the cove. To browse in the shops, she had said, but Beth knew Kitty was really hoping to come across Rob Praed. She had tried to bring out her friend's feelings about the fisherman but for once Kitty was being reticent. Beth was concerned about the whole matter. Kitty and Rob Praed were worlds apart, and he had a fly-by-night reputation in regard to women.

'Well, you overheard me telling...' Beth paused, then said, 'Christina' – Joe had made it plain he was opposed to her calling Christina her mother; humouring him was more likely to provoke in him a more relaxed attitude – 'about Miss Oakley's confusion yesterday.'

Chaplin came charging back with the red ball in his jaws and dropped it eagerly at Joe's bare feet. To be polite to Beth, Joe made Chaplin wait for the next throw. 'I did, and Mum felt sorry for her, and suggested you both go to matins tomorrow to try to gauge if the old vicar is disturbing her. If you ask me, they're both batty. It's time the Church retired them into some quiet little house somewhere. If my father were here he would have stopped the Reverend Oakley from dragging the village down. My father was a parish councillor and he arranged lots of activities jointly between the cove, the chapel and the church. My father said it made people feel connected and gave them something to look forward to. Now the church might as well not exist.'

'That's very sad, and it's a shame some of your father's excellent work in Portcowl has been undone.' Beth wanted to point out that the Oakleys could not really help their respective conditions and that someone should have supported them ages ago, but Joe's stance with regard to them would not allow that. It saddened Beth how easily she could irk Joe, but it also annoyed and hurt her that he did not seek to establish the same closeness with her that he shared with Kitty. Rather, Joe generally made it evident he was still suspicious of her; otherwise he just about ignored her.

Joe threw the ball and spent several moments watching Chaplin dive after it. Then he looked squarely at Beth, unblinking. 'What's this suggestion you have?'

Beth could tell he was ready to argue with her. She had suddenly endured enough of his surly unfriendliness. Damn it all, his mother was her mother too, they were completely reconciled over past sorrows, and it was time Joe accepted and acknowledged it. 'Please do not take that tone with me, Joe. I've done nothing to deserve it. I'm trying my best to get on a good basis with you. You don't have to accept me as a sister but I would like us to be friends. If you're worried that I'd try to take our mother away from you then let me assure you I wouldn't dream of it. I'm delighted she met your father and knew real love and that she has you in her life. I'm not jealous of your devotion to each other, if that's what you think.

'What I was about to suggest to *our* mother, and bear in mind I'm asking you about it first, is, do you think it would be a good thing if she started to have a bit of a social life? Like having lunch down in the cove or at one of the hotels. To become a little involved in local life. People know all about the family past. There are no

240

more revelations, no nasty surprises at all. Our mother has the right to go where she pleases with her head held high. It would help her to grow in confidence. And before you bring up the question of Evie Vage, I've talked at length to our mother about Evie and she has no problem about me meeting my half-sister. Joe, please, I'd like you and I to be friends. What do you say?'

'You obviously want the truth so here it comes. If Mum wants to go out a little, as long as she is never left alone and is well supported, then yes, it wouldn't hurt if it were suggested to her. But she must *not* be persuaded in the slightest against her will. I won't have her upset or frightened. She goes to church occasionally, and watches school events, but if that's all she's happy to do then it will not change. I don't care about Evie Vage. She's none of my business. If you're glad to have met her then I'm glad for you. I'm not worried that you'll try to come between Mum and me. I don't believe that's on your agenda. What I don't like about you is why you've made no attempt to find out why your grandmother – my grandmother too, I know, but I've never thought of her as that and never will – ostracized Mum and made her life hell. Why did Marion Frobisher always take your rotten father's side over her own daughter? It's fine that you've established a good mother-daughter relationship with my mother, but my mother was denied that for herself and she's suffered all her life because of it. Marion

241

Frobisher and Phil Tresaile wantonly tried to destroy her, and you don't seem to care!'

Beth's head was down and her shoulders drooping. At the beginning of Joe's reply, because of his frostiness, she had braced herself and had been prepared to argue the points, but his hostility at the end was too much for her. Feeling guilty and damned over his accusation, sure he loathed her and they would never be on good terms, she stumbled a few feet away to the rocks at the base of the cliff. Clutching for the sun-heated granite, not a scrap of energy left in her, she slumped down on a low hard rock, and putting her face in her hands she burst into tears of wretchedness.

'Beth.'

She barely heard Joe say her name. She didn't know he was standing close to her, puzzled and remorseful. She had no idea that he had lingered uncertainly on the sand, biting his bottom lip for some time before sidling up to her.

Seconds passed.

Beth wept miserably.

Joe hung about not knowing what to do.

Beth felt something weigh down on her knee. She registered that Chaplin had put his head there and she took some small comfort from that. But she went on sobbing. Perhaps she should never have come here. It was selfish of her. It had done some good, made Christina happier, but her presence was hurting Joe. It might hurt Evie if it caused problems with her adoptive father. And Kitty was hankering after an unsuitable man who was likely to break her heart. And now she was faced – and she was ashamed to have kept brushing it aside – with the fact that her beloved grandmother had been a horrid and cruel woman. If her grandmother had harboured selfishness in her heart then Beth had inherited that baseness. Beth's selfishness had led her to gladly rush into an affair with a married man without a care for his innocent wife and children, with no concern that she was betraying her best friend. Her wantonness had led her to conceive a child who, if it had lived, would have been forced to live a life under the cloak of shame and secrecy, denied its father.

'Beth, please stop crying. I don't know what to do.'

Hearing Joe's plea, she knew she must put his feelings first. Gulping and sniffing and breathing deeply she brought herself under control. 'I – I'm sorry, Joe.' Her voice was wobbly and tear-laden.

'Got a hankie?' Joe asked, with obvious relief that she was all cried out.

She nodded and pulled out the scrap of linen from her dress pocket. Wiping her eyes, she took a lengthy steadying breath. 'I'm sorry for the exhibition, Joe.'

'I'm sorry I upset you so much.' Joe dropped down on the sand at her feet and sat cross-legged. 'I'd never really thought about what coming here meant to you. I'm sorry for saying such harsh things about your grandmother and father. It must be upsetting for you to be faced

243

with it. Mum doesn't seem to care about what they did to her. Meeting Dad enabled her to put it to the back of her mind, I suppose. But it niggles me and makes me so angry. Yet if things had been different she would never have married Dad and had me. Life's really strange, isn't it?'

'Yes, it is.' There was so much she wanted to say but her mind was in a muddle. 'I don't really know what to say now. Except that I will try to discover why my grandmother was so cruel to Mother and so positive about my father.'

Joe let out a sigh of the sort a grown-up might give when resigned to something. 'You don't have to. Perhaps it's better not to dredge things up. Things might be learned that would be better left unknown. It shouldn't matter anyway. You don't seem horrible.'

'I'm glad you think that. I hope one day you will trust and like me.'

Joe shrugged his broad shoulders. The conversation was getting too intense for him. 'You're OK. Want to go for a paddle? I warn you that Chaplin loves to splash about and you'll get a thorough soaking.'

'That would be nice.' Beth had never been so grateful for an invitation. Joe was warming to her and the soaking she would get would explain her reddened eyes.

'Stuart sends you his love.'

'What do you mean?' Beth stared open-mouthed at Kitty. Her heart felt as if it was being squeezed by a cold grasping hand, her stomach flipped sickeningly and dizziness swept over her. After her distress with Joe earlier in the day, the blood drained out of her. A little while ago Kitty had returned from the cove downhearted. Whether she had seen Rob Praed she was not saying. She had changed her clothes and washed off her make-up and mentioned she was going to telephone Stuart. Talking to Stuart rarely failed to make Kitty laugh and she would stay cheerful for ages, but it had not worked so well this time. Now Kitty had, to Beth's fragile mind, set accusing eyes on her. Had Kitty's remark held an edge of sarcasm? Did she know about Beth and Stuart's affair? Was Kitty about to go wild with anger and accusation?

'Good gracious, Beth, are you all right?' Kitty tore across the sitting room to her friend. She sat on the sofa beside Beth and felt her forehead for unnatural heat. 'Are you going down with something, do you think? You've gone as white as a ghost.'

Relief flooded Beth and the icy anxiety fell away. It was her guilt that had made her fear so. 'I think I've had too much sun and got a little dehydrated, that's all.' Beth managed a wan smile in the hope of avoiding a further fuss. But how dare Stuart send his love to her, it was unfeeling and cruel.

'Kitty's right, you don't look well at all, Beth.' Christina leaned forward from her arm-

245

chair, where she had been sewing missing buttons on one of Joe's shirts. 'I'll fetch you some aspirin. Then I think you should lie down and have a rest. If you don't feel well enough to attend matins tomorrow, you must stay at home. Perhaps Kitty would like to drive me to church and accompany me.'

'I'd be pleased to. I want to hear one of Reverend Oakley's famous, or should I say infamous, rambling sermons, and I want to keep an eye on poor Miss Oakley, whom I've yet to meet. I've been invited to high tea at Wildflower Cottage. May I pick some flowers from the gardens for Mrs Praed, please?'

'Pick as many as you like, anytime you like,' Christina said. 'And thank you, Kitty.'

Beth swallowed down two aspirin. She had liked Christina saying 'you must stay at home'. Owles House wasn't her home, it was Christina and Joe's. But Beth felt at home here. She allowed Kitty to see her up to the bedroom and dig out her silk pyjamas. I should be happy, Beth told herself. She was on a closer footing with Joe, and Christina had tentatively agreed to take a quiet lunch in the Dunn Head Hotel. But Stuart sending her a loving sentiment had broken and bruised her heart all over again.

Kitty put Beth's sponge bag on the bed for her. 'I spoke to Connie too over the phone. She was so excited. The children are going to spend two weeks with her parents because Stuart is about to take her to Greece for a second honeymoon. She says Stuart's promised not to work such long hours any more and he's being very attentive towards her. She said it's like the early days of their marriage. They're even hoping to start another baby. Stuart used to say two children were enough for any family, but Connie always longed for at least one more. That's really good news, isn't it? Wish we could meet someone as wonderful as my brother, eh, Beth?'

Beth was shredded in the pits of her being. Kitty's innocent remark had stamped all over her soul and she couldn't stand any more. 'Do stop going on!'

'Oh, I'm sorry, Beth. How thoughtless of me, me and my big mouth. You thought you had met someone like Stuart but it all went wrong for you, and then you lost your baby.'

'Kitty, please! For goodness sake just go and leave me alone.'

'Oh Beth.' Kitty dithered, wringing her hands. 'I'm so sorry, I'm going, I'm going. I'll pull the curtains over first. You try to have a good sleep. I'll check on you later. If you want anything just bang on the floor.'

Beth gritted her teeth while Kitty darkened the room and finally left, with a soft click of the door. Then she threw herself on the bed, curled up tightly on her side, clutched a pillow to her face and screamed silently into it. 'Damn you, Stuart. How could you be so cruel? How dare you send me your love while all the time you're giving it to your wife? Didn't you realize how much that would hurt me? You were the other half of our affair so why aren't you missing me? Why aren't you feeling guilty? Why must I take on all of it? Now you're gaily dashing off on a second honeymoon and planning a new baby, of all things. While I'm left without my baby and left like this, a wreck! Damn you. You've betrayed me. I hate you. I never want to set eyes on you again.'

She cried a second wave of tears that day but this time it did not turn into a flood. She was surprised at how soon the tears petered out and stopped. She felt humiliated and cast aside but it did not feel like it was the end of the world. She would always mourn her lost baby but she had other, more important people than Stuart in her life now. She had her mother and Joe and Evie, her flesh and blood. She still had Kitty's faithful friendship and she had Muriel Oakley to befriend properly and to champion. There was no need and no point being up here as limp as a dead fish while her mother was downstairs probably worrying about her. She could freshen up and simply enjoy being with Christina, and with Joe. Richard had gone shore fishing with his older brothers today and Joe was at a loose end. She could challenge him to do something for fun. Kitty was feeling a bit down. She needed Beth, her best friend, to confide in, and Beth would take the time to gently get Kitty to open up about the (no doubt, today) elusive fisherman.

She had a headache, but a cup of tea, something to eat and some fresh air would soon make it go. She got up off the bed, flung back the curtains and washed her face and combed her hair. It was time to get on with the present and leave the past behind. First, though, there was one bit of it she must still confront. The subject Joe had brought up on the beach – her grandmother's lifelong cruel attitude towards Christina – was haunting her now as much as it did Joe.

Twenty

Loud snores were rattling round inside the
shambolic living room at the back of Claze
Wyn. It was late on Sunday morning, and the
lumpy heap of humanity that was Gabby Magor
lay solidly prone on her back on her wreck of an
antiquated settee. The volume of her regular
snorting rivalled the decibels of a steam engine
and the puttering that followed each snort
puffed out her foul beer-reeking breath to further contaminate the rancid atmosphere. A
scientist's dream of bacteria bred at lightning
speed in the dim dank room, and on and in
Gabby, but it didn't harm Gabby, she seemed to
thrive on it. Every so often her snoring halted
and she would smack her bulging lips together,
whereupon her entire hulk would shudder like a
dying engine. Then she would cough on the
putrid tobacco tar choking her lungs, her
spreading bulbous nose would twitch, her top
lip would ride up and her exposed grey front
teeth would give her the semblance of a dangerous rabbit.

Gabby had woken in the early hours, due to a
pressing need deep in her loins. Cursing and
grumbling, she had struggled to heave herself

250

off the stinking, lumpy, crumb-infested settee and stagger, while rubbing at her blurry red-rimmed eyes, to pee in the enamel chamber pot set in a makeshift commode. She was still dressed from the day before – she changed her clothes about once a fortnight and never bothered with nightwear to sleep. Eventually she would bundle up her dirty, stained clothes and take them to her cousin's home for laundering; always an inadequate job as her cousin was equally slovenly.

After pulling up her massive drawers – inherited from her mother – round her flopping stomach and hauling up her workman's trousers, once her late father's, she had hefted round and stared down into the tarnished chamber pot. 'Mmm, time I bleddy emptied that. I'll do it tomorrow. Now where's me fags?'

After a quick drag on a pre-made rollup, Gabby had flopped back down to sleep again. She never put out a cigarette butt, and as so many times before, she cheated death while the lit ash burnt into her fingertips and went out. Gabby was beyond feeling the blisters now on her blackened, destroyed flesh. She slept on, snoring, puttering, spluttering, coughing, and occasionally scratching where a flea had bitten.

Something suddenly landed on Gabby's enormous sagging bosom and she flailed her arms in her sleep to swipe it off, muttering angrily. The nuisance went. But it came straight back and now it was tugging on her shirt front. Gabby's befuddled mind was hauled out of her rest and she was furious. 'What the bleddy hell...?'

She half-opened an eye. The weight shifted to her neck and chin. Four hard things were pressing in and choking her, and wetness was being spread over her nose and cheeks and brow. 'Eh? What's happening?'

She felt a sharp pull on her greasy hair and a sharp nip on her ear lobe. Rising like a monster from the deep she sat up and knocked the nuisance clean off her. Blinking and screwing up her globular features, she made out a cowering and whimpering little white patchy thing where it had thumped down and skidded against the badly scratched chest of drawers nearby.

'You!' She pointed accusingly at the shivering tiny young mongrel. 'I forgot all about you.'

Gabby wallowed and fought until she was perched on the edge of the settee. 'I forgot I brought you home yes'day.' Her mood lightened, as it always did when she had a new interest. She softly clapped her hands and made friendly clucking noises to beckon the dog to her. 'Did I frighten you? Sorry about that, boy. I forgot I got you, naughty me, eh? Come on now, come to Gabby. You must be hungry, eh? Let naughty Gabby see what she got you to eat, eh? Could do with a bite meself.'

The young mongrel slowly, slowly got up and sneaked forward cautiously. It backed away and whimpered in fear when Gabby suddenly thudded upright on to her feet, towering over it. 'Come on, little one,' she cooed, her delighted smile more like a grimace. 'Gabby's hungry too. Into the kitchen for us then. Think Barbara gave me a bit of ham the other day, we'll share that, eh?'

The mongrel trailed after Gabby, crossing the square of bare flagged floor that led to the kitchen. Opposite the dirty, mildewed front door were the steep, impossibly narrow stairs that led to two bedrooms. Gabby had slept in the back room for years, after her father's sudden death, a few weeks following her mother's merciful demise from years of being bedridden thanks to a stroke. Gabby used the bedrooms to store junk and hide stolen goods. A mouldering stench seeped down from above but would only be noticed by unfortunate visitors or intruders.

Glancing over the filthy flagged kitchen floor, Gabby noted where the dog had relieved itself. Avoiding the puddles and soiling, she patted a chair and then the bare pine table, and the dog first climbed up on one then the other. With the dog in comfortable reach, she petted and hugged it. Reassured and wanting to please and be accepted, the unattractive but appealing little dog jumped up to her and returned the affection by licking her, then indicated its loyalty and submission by lying on its back and showing its tummy. Gabby tickled its tummy then picked the dog up into her arms. 'What did I call you yes'day? Can't think. Don't matter, I'll call you Tickle. You like a tickle, don't you, eh? We're going to be the best of friends, me and you, Tickle. I've never had a friend, ever. I was an ugly brat and people used to tease me, said I smelled and called me fleabag. Never thought I had any feelings. Got me cousin Barbara, she just about puts up with me, lazy cow. But then she got to, or I'll punch her one. Got to get to these people first, Tickle, or they'll walk all over 'ee and crush you down. But we'll get on like a house on fire. Now you sit there like a good boy and let Gabby get us summat to eat.' She put Tickle back down on the table and laughed merrily when he sat still, his little head up and waiting expectantly.

Lumping her way to the built-in food cupboard she pulled out some stuff. 'Well, Tickle,' she told her new friend, who was now excitedly on his feet with tongue out in hope. 'We got a bit of bread, bit stale but never mind. Ham's gone off, sod it.' She tossed the ripe-smelling meat into the stone sink. 'But there's some potted meat and some golden syrup. There's some lemonade for me. I'll pour you a drop of water from the butt later.'

Plonking her mass down on a chair Gabby put the food directly on the table. Tickle sniffed the half loaf of hard bread and licked it. Gabby laughed. 'Can't wait, eh?' Picking up an unwashed knife she hacked the bread into four hunks, two of them larger for herself, which she lathered with golden syrup.

The potted meat went on the two smaller pieces of bread. 'Here, get that down your guts, Tickle.' It was a very generous gesture for Gabby to make. His curly white tail wagging joyously, hungry Tickle started by rapidly licking off the potted meat.

Gabby bit off a large chunk of her bread, the syrup at once making her chops sticky, and she talked while chewing open-mouthed. 'This'll do us for now, boy. We'll go out later and get something else. Farmer Read will always sell to me, even on a Sunday, and that lot are bleddy chapel goers! Some people round here are stuck up and think themselves respectable, but I could tell 'ee more than a tale or two. And I'll kill a hen. I'm getting rid of that lot out there anyway, they're terrible layers and don't earn their keep. So we'll be scoffing chicken for days. I've got an order for half a dozen bottles of wine off some campers, so we'll take it to 'em and we'll be quids in. Lovely. Got to be more careful how I store the wine in the keep though. Didn't set some up prop'ly and lost 'lem bottles.' Gabby's jowls dropped and her tight eyes became moist. 'Life jumps up and kicks you in the bleddy face at times.' While Tickle gobbled down his bread she fell into a stupor.

She came round when Tickle went up on his hind legs and licked at the syrup dribbling from the sides of her mouth. Looking down she went cross-eyed to see what was happening. 'Oh ... Tickly, Tickle, whatever I bleddy called you. You love me, don't you? You won't turn against me, will you?' Tickle continued licking at her face and she took that as his 'yes'.

She eased him away then found a piece of

255

sweetened bread that had fallen inside her shirt and fed it to him. 'We'll go to cousin Barbara's drekkly and scrounge a bit of supper. She likes a drop of wine too, you know. I'll get some beer for meself, don't like wine, funny isn't it? I'll get you a 'normous great bone. And we'll get sozzled and have a bleddy good time. We'll sleep there tonight. Life can be good, Tickle, just got to make the effort. You'll enjoy yourself with me, oh yes you will.'

Pulling Tickle into her arms she held him close against her chest and rested her face against his little warm body. Tickle snuggled in. Gabby shut her eyes and leered, although the leer was actually a smile of contentment.

Twenty-One

Davey Vage was in his allotment, situated alongside nineteen others up behind the houses on the Coggan Point side of Portcowl. He had got there just after dawn and put in four hours of hard but satisfying work, pausing occasionally to exchange with other gardeners a few sentences on horticultural matters. He was now relaxing in a deck chair outside the little tool shed he had built, drinking a tin mug of strong sweet tea from the flask Evie had made for him. As much as Davey preferred to be alone he missed his late neighbouring allotment holder, Bill Jewell, the former gardener at Owles House. He and the tiny-boned, pipe-smoking Bill had surveyed others' rows, the vegetables in cold frames, and compared them unfavourably to the larger produce of their own greener fingers.

Davey had occasionally invited Bill, a childless widower, to join him and Evie for a Sunday roast meal, but Bill had always refused, not minding to spend most of his time alone. The years had shrunk Bill's short skinny frame and he no longer reached above four feet eight inches; he had shortened his wide trouser braces with clumsy black thread stitches. Beth's childhood impression of him looking like a goblin had been remarkably accurate. Bill had been a prolific chatterer and the name Elizabeth Tresaile had more than once trickled off his tongue. Davey had listened, not much interested, but glad the girl had been out of the way. 'That Miss Elizabeth was a dear little soul, you know. No child should have seen and heard the things she did. But her mother was pushed into the drink, cowed down she was by Phil Tresaile and her wretched mother. And that Marion Frobisher, there was a right bitch, if I should say the word. Two-faced didn't come into it, I can tell you, Davey. Marion Frobisher was a right bint despite all her high and mighty ways, I can tell 'ee,' Bill had muttered with feeling.

'Oh?' That had drawn Davey's full attention.

Bill had leaned his capped old head towards Davey's ear. 'I could tell poor Mrs Vyvyan one reason why her mother was so nasty to her. She was jealous of her daughter getting Phil Tresaile as a husband. Liked young men, Marion Frobisher did, and she fell under Phil's spell before Miss Christina did. I know that for a fact. I'm telling you this, Davey, 'cus I know you'll keep it a secret, and 'cus it might help you feel more amiable towards dear Miss Elizabeth if she should ever return here. Mrs Frobisher used to meet Phil for hanky-panky in various places out in the gardens. I used to see 'em slipping off separately and meeting up. I nearly fell over 'em once while they were in the throes of passion, the dirty buggers! They used language that would disgrace a barrack room. I heard her once demanding why he'd availed himself of her daughter after they had already become lovers. "Why aren't I enough for you, Phil?" she said. "Why do you have to have that little cow? Christina is good for nothing." What a way for a mother to behave. Marion Frobisher has a lot more to answer for than poor Mrs Vyvyan ever did.'

Bill had puffed angrily on his pipe. 'Bet that old woman was only good to Miss Elizabeth to spite her own daughter. I only hope she doesn't succeed in poisoning Miss Elizabeth's mind against her dear mother. I got a lot of time for Mrs Vyvyan, she's held herself together for the sake of young Master Joe. She deserves credit for that. There's some wicked people in the world, it's sad to say, and Marion Frobisher is one of them.'

Well, Elizabeth Tresaile had not held out bad feelings towards her mother. Davey cursed the day she had returned to Owles House and the fact that she was staying for God knew how long. And damn it all, Evie had met the wretched Tresaile girl. Evie had mentioned in a slightly embarrassed and offhand way how, while she was on an errand of mercy taking home the pathetic daughter of the useless vicar, the Tresaile bane had turned up. He wanted Evie all to himself. Iris, her teenage mother, had been seduced by the braggart Phil Tresaile, but Iris had gone on to be the perfect wife for Davey and the most devoted mother a girl could have. Iris was responsible for the sweet-natured, honest, obedient girl Evie had turned out to be. Davey had protected Evie against the worst of the prejudice over her illegitimacy. If the Tresaile woman came fully into Evie's life she might make Evie feel inferior, even if she did not do so deliberately. She might invade his and Evie's home. And Davey hated the thought of all the gossip that would inevitably circulate, spread mostly with relish. Evie would have to ward off all the curiosity and the underhand remarks. Evie should not have to cope with all that. Davey was not going to allow Evie to be tainted by the sordidness involved in Elizabeth Tresaile's life.

Davey finished his tea and went back to his hoe, which he had left leaning against his shed door. He caught a whiff of strong sweet tobacco smoke and looked over his shoulder.

Rob Praed was there.

'Never seen you here before, Rob,' Davey said, holding back his annoyance at being halted from getting on. He liked to do things to an exact timetable. 'Can't see your Uncle Lofty running out of veg to pass on to you. Something up?'

Rob worked his finger and thumb to put out his cigarette and kept it inside his hand. He held himself up straight. 'No, not at all, Davey.' Rob smiled his friendliest smile, then looked a bit bashful. 'Just hoping to have a word with you, that's all.'

Davey was on the alert. Rob was mostly thought of as a decent young man and admired for the way he had cared for his two younger sisters after they'd been orphaned when Rob was seventeen. People generally saw his sowing of wild oats as natural for a good-looking young man. True, Rob was amiable and fun, and helpful and generous to families when other fishermen had a poor season, but Davey neither liked nor trusted him. To Davey's mind, the times when Rob was suddenly hard testified that something nasty lurked beneath all his good humour and camaraderie.

'I'd be glad if you said your piece. I've got tatties to hoe.'

Rob cleared his throat.

For the first time Davey saw Rob blush and shift as if uncertain. Davey's pale eyes became slits. What was his neighbour up to?

'It's like this, Davey.' Rob again cleared his throat. 'I want to ask you something man to man. You see, I'm hoping to form something serious with Evie. Evie's a wonderful woman, she'd make an ideal fisherman's wife.'

'What?' Davey's eyes bulged as horror crammed into him. 'Over my dead body. You know what my daughter means to me, what she meant to her dear mother. How can you think for a minute I'd *ever* consider letting a fly-by-night like you court my Evie? Just you keep away from her or I'll rip your ears off and stuff them down your bleddy gullet.'

Rob shifted his weight on his feet but he was

261

not particularly ruffled. 'Please hear me out, Davey. I know you have reservations about me but I can put your mind to rest about them.'

'Huh, never.' Davey was feeling sick and panicky at the thought of losing Evie to this cunning sort, and no man was good enough for her anyway. 'Now clear off!'

'I'm asking you to listen carefully to me and to think again.' Rob's tone grew firmer and his demeanour became resolved. 'Yes, I got a few rough edges but no one can deny that I've been good to my sisters, that points to me making a good husband and provider. I've played the field but now I'm ready to settle down. I can be edgy but I'm not an out-and-out troublemaker.' Rob fixed his eyes on Davey's, and his voice was barely above a whisper. 'If I was, Davey, then I'd have spread something round all about – your secret.'

'Secret?' Every last muscle in Davey's body tightened. 'I haven't got any secrets.'

'There is one, Davey. I saw it for myself some years ago. You were with someone, inside your shed. I was a kid back then and didn't know what was going on, but I knew it was something I'd best keep my mouth shut about, and I have done ever since. I'm no longer naive about what you were doing, of course. People wouldn't tolerate that sort of thing. You'd have been run out of the cove. Iris and Evie would have suffered even more over that than through the scandal involving Phil Tresaile. Evie wouldn't know how to cope with it if she ever found out.

So you see, Davey, I'm not such a bad man. Am I?'

Having gone paler than a bleached fish bone, Davey stumbled to his deck chair and slumped down into it. He held his chest in shock, his breathing ragged. 'I didn't ... think anyone ever knew. And now you're saying if I don't let you have access to Evie you'll blab my business all over Portcowl and beyond.'

'No, never, Davey, I swear on my life. I don't want to destroy you and I certainly don't want Evie to ever be hurt by anything. I think no less of you, Davey. Life is hard. We find love where we may. I'm sorry he lost his life in the war. I understand why you want to cling to Evie. Without her you think your life would be unbearable. All I'm asking you for is the chance to approach Evie with the view to us finally getting married. I'd take things slowly, show her the utmost respect every step of the way. If Evie isn't interested I'll leave her be. You don't really want to deny her a husband and children, do you? Evie would make a wonderful mother. Think of it, Davey, having grandchildren on your knee. And you'd not really lose Evie. She'd only be living next door. She can bring your meals round or you can join us round the table any time you like. You can still spend lots of time together.'

Davey ran his shaking hands several times down over his face, dragging down his jowls and loose lower eyelids. He was like a man defeated. 'And you say you promise if she doesn't welcome your attention you'll leave her be?'

'Of course, I wouldn't dream of forcing her into marriage. It would be miserable for all of us. What would be the point in that?'

Davey was silent for some time. He was crying noiselessly, and Rob thought he was probably crying over his lost love, a young fisherman who had worked on *Morenwyn* with him, and whose ship had been torpedoed in the war. When he looked up with puffy red-streaked eyes, wiping at his nose, he spoke in raw rasps. 'I love Evie so much, like she's my own flesh and blood.'

'And I'll love her too, Davey.' Rob went down on his hunkers in front of his intended father-in-law. 'And honour her, and see she never goes without, if she'll have me. All I'm asking to start with, is when Judy and Alison come round to your place later today and invite Evie to have tea at my Uncle Lofty's that you encourage her to go. Evie will probably want to stay at home, but you could encourage her by saying it would do her good to go out.'

Rob Praed had given a fine speech laced with admirable sentiments, he had made promises, but Davey would never trust him. When he was after something, if one way didn't work out he'd try another, then another, like a dog never giving up on a bone. Davey had been put in an impossible situation. Praed had given him no choice. But out of this wretched mess was something Davey could use to his advantage.

'You can send your sisters round today, but just be warned that I won't ever force Evie to do something against her will. And I'll kill you and hang for it if you ever hurt Evie. But there's something you can do for me in return, something easy enough for a wily man like you.'

'Fair enough. What is it?'

'Evie's told me that she's accidentally met that Elizabeth Tresaile. Evie seems to have liked her. I don't want my girl ever having anything to do with her or her bleddy lot. There can be nothing but trouble or heartbreak for her. I want you to swear, Rob Praed, that if Evie returns your interest you'll always keep her away from them.'

Grinning straight into Davey's stricken face, Rob spat on his hand then offered it to be shaken. 'Put it there, mate. It's as good as done.'

As Rob strutted off, relighting his smoke, Davey stumbled into his shed and wept for his past loss, his present horror and humiliation, and his revulsion and dread at Evie's possible future. She was soon to be faced with guile beyond her understanding.

After a while he looked up out of his watery eyes. Those eyes glowered and dried in the heat of his fury and then they glared into an evil fantasy that might become a reality of his making. He was seeing Rob Praed with his mocking face no longer handsome but bloody and smashed beyond recognition. 'You might not have mocked me over Cyrus like that

265

upstart bastard Francis Vyvyan did the day he discovered my secret here, but you're threatening my precious Evie's peace and well-being. I've not tied her down to me. She knows her own mind and she's enjoying a life of freedom in the way that she wants. She won't want you, you piece of shite, and if you don't quickly get that message you'll end up in the sea, all rotted away and apparently smashed up by the rocks. Just like Francis Vyvyan did, out on his boat.'

The succulent aroma of roasting lamb filled the Vage kitchen and wafted out of the open windows and the open top of the back stable-door. Evie had not long basted the sizzling meat and potatoes and put the roasting tin back in the oven. Saucepans of lightly salted vegetables were prepared and ready to put on the hob to bring to the boil and simmer. Her father would be back in about an hour with the Sunday newspaper, which, after he had changed and washed up, he would read in his comfortable little armchair; the armchair in which three former generations of Vages had sat. Davey and Evie were the last to bear the name of Vage locally.

Evie spread over the table a pure white, lace-edged square tablecloth, one made by her mother, following in her mother's Sunday tradition of laying the table with the best cloths and cutlery. She fetched the rosewood canteen that held the silver, a wedding present to her mother from her father, and one which Iris had been

266

very proud of.

Three of the cats were indoors, washing themselves or snoozing. It was a cosy, safe scene that Evie loved. For five days and nights she had missed Davey, praying for his safety at sea and good catches of pilchards on *Morenwyn* – prayers that had been answered. From the corner of her eye Evie noticed the most fastidious cat, Fluffy, pause in her preening on the hearthrug, seeming to listen. Nothing unusual in that, but some instinct made Evie keep still and look towards the door.

A large tall shape appeared at the open top half of the door and then Evie was rushing to the door in alarm. 'Smoky!' Her youngest cat was streaked with blood and shivering, wrapped up in a shirt in the muscular bare arms of Rob Praed from next door. 'Oh, my goodness, what happened?' She opened the lower half of the door and beckoned Rob inside.

'Somehow he got stuck in some old drainpipe. He was scared and howling like a banshee. He was just as scared about being pulled out,' Rob said, grimacing to indicate the long deep scratches on his arms and chest, revealed by his ripped vest. ''Fraid he got a bit scraped and mangled. I'm sorry but he got hurt more during the rescue than I think he did getting stuck.'

'Thank you so much, Rob,' Evie said gratefully, her eyes on Smoky's de-furred wounds. 'Come to the sink. Are you all right holding him a bit longer?'

'Of course.'

'If I can manage to bathe him with some salt water and put on some healing salve, Smoky can go down in his basket.' Then she said, in a lower voice and with her head down, 'After that I suppose I'd better see to your scratches. They look very sore.'

'They are stinging a bit.' This was no lie, but the soreness was nothing to Rob in comparison with his flesh being ripped by a fish hook or getting a net or rope burn. Picking up a trusting Smoky had been easy, but pushing him into the narrow, foot-long piece of drainpipe in a quiet unobserved spot, while Smoky spat, howled and fought, had taken a full bloody three minutes of pandemonium. Then, gripping Smoky's rear end, Rob had hauled the cat out, while it was thankfully stunned, and wrapped it in his shirt. Smoky had stayed in shock. Rob had been pleased to be seen as the animal's rescuer by some local kids. 'Keep back, can't stop, I'm rushing him home to Miss Vage.' The gleeful interested kids had followed on Rob's heels until he had told them to 'Run along now.' The morsel of news would soon pass round the cove. Rob would be called a hero, and the thoughtless person who had supposedly tossed away the drainpipe would be the stupid villain.

Evie fetched a bag of cotton wool and a bowl of hot water from the kettle. She put in three good pinches of salt then without glancing at Rob – she was aware of him watching her with a smile – she carefully eased away parts of the ruined shirt and bathed Smoky's wounds. He wailed in pain and protest but Rob's vice-like grip stilled his struggles.

'Please, Rob.' Evie gave him apologetic eyes for a moment. 'You're hurting him.'

'Sorry,' Rob gasped as if mortified. 'I didn't want him to scratch you.'

Finally Smoky was clean and his wounds were covered with a herb salve. 'I'll take him from you now,' Evie said, again not looking at Rob. She was uncomfortable having him this close to her. It felt like an invasion. 'Still inside your shirt, if that's all right.'

'Of course.' Rob would have given her his deepest smile but he knew his nearness to her was disturbing her. He would have to proceed very slowly to get Evie to see him any differently than a male neighbour she would rather keep distant from. He would have to prove to her that she could trust him and that he was genuinely interested in her.

He had never been this close to Evie before, and he had not particularly wanted to be until considering who would make him the best wife. He had always thought her pretty despite her plain attire and modest ways and he preferred her longer hair to the short styles. Nearness to Evie, and now feeling her careful arms touching his body as she took the damned cat from him, was a sweetly sensuous experience. She smelled clean, of the essence of sweetness. He would take a bet that she was a better cook than his sisters, who were good in the kitchen. Her housekeeping was homely and immaculate, a necessary part of Rob's specifics in a bride. As was her reserve, aversion to gossip, and respectability. Evie would bring up strong dutiful children. He wanted at least four. Her only downside was her love for these useless annoying furry creatures. They could stay living here with Davey. If she wanted a pet once married to him, she could have a dog.

Cooing, and stroking Smoky on the one small place on his head he was not creamed, Evie gently placed him near the range on a knitted green and blue patchwork blanket in the large round basket that her family of cats shared, although rarely all at the same time. 'Poor Smoky, you poor thing, rest now. You can have some poached pilchard when you're over the shock.'

She rose, still anxiously gazing down on Smoky while addressing Rob in her soft voice. 'If you don't mind waiting, I'd like to give Smoky a drop of water. Shock dehydrates, you know.'

'You see to Smoky first, Evie. If you don't mind though, I'd like to sit down for a minute.'

'Oh, of course. Take my chair.' She pointed to the tiny stuffed chair next to the cat basket. 'I'll bring some fresh salt water to you.'

'That's good of you. I hope I'm not interrupting your dinner preparations. Don't suppose you've got a cup of tea in the pot? Don't make a fresh pot. I like my tea as it comes.

'Lovely tea,' Rob said appreciatively, a short

while later. The tea was lukewarm and over-steeped but he still enjoyed the taste. He did not watch Evie closely while she poured steaming water into a clean bowl and put salt in it. If he embarrassed or unsettled her he wouldn't get far with his campaign for her, so he simply took the odd glance and enjoyed her light economical movements. Evie was wholly feminine and she was the sweetest thing. He could actually say he really was interested in her. It was a sublime feeling to be considering a woman who was not a pushover. He would not be able to take his time wooing her, despite Davey's word at not getting in his way, even with the condition to keep the Tresaile woman at bay from Evie. Davey would not tolerate his attentions to Evie for long if she did not soon reciprocate his hope of forming an attachment. So after a time Rob would have to steamroller her towards marriage.

Evie tore off a wad of cotton wool from the package and approached Rob uncertainly. She was trying to ignore his half-naked torso, the well-toned muscles of his fine physique, but she could not help herself admiring it. She was not entirely averse to the attractions of the finest masculinity. How she wished the evidence of her eyes, which she kept mostly down, would stop making her tummy fold over and squirm so. Where should she start on bathing this man's deep scratches? 'Um, the water needs to cool a bit.'

'I'll tend to myself, Evie,' Rob said, knowing

she would find this a tremendous relief. He had to repress an improper shiver at the thought of her fingers touching his bare skin. Evie was growing more appealing by the moment. 'Won't take a minute. Then I'll go out and get rid of that drainpipe so it can't do any more harm.'

'Thank you,' Evie said humbly, feeling a little less awkward. 'I'm very grateful to you for saving Smoky. He must have been so frightened. That's the thing about cats, they're so curious and love to squeeze into small cosy places, not that a drainpipe should seem cosy.' She went to Smoky and leaned down to him. 'You are a silly boy, aren't you?'

This sort of thing would usually bore Rob, but he thought it a charming scene as Evie was involved in it. It was time he took himself off. Quickly, he wiped the salted water across his chest, hands and arms, not feeling the heat of the water. Years of immersion in bitterly cold seawater and handling fishing gear and fish had killed off the nerve endings on his fingertips, but the cat's scratches were damned sore. Needing a smoke, he got up and made for the door. 'Thanks for the tea, Evie. I'll leave you in peace.'

He couldn't resist smiling into her eyes. Such pretty eyes she had. Not unexpectedly she couldn't hold his gaze and looked down at the cat. 'Thanks again.'

'Bye then.' He left, shutting the lower half of the stable door after him.

272

Evie stared at the stable door for some time. Smoky's self-pitying mews finally drew her attention. Evie swallowed to wet her dry throat. Just for a moment her everyday life seemed somehow strange. She snuggled Smoky up in the blanket and caressed him until he fell asleep. 'Well, Smoky,' she found her voice at last. 'That was quite an experience for both of us. Please don't get into any more scrapes like that.'

Twenty-Two

'Papa, may I speak to you please?'

Muriel Oakley had run after her father and stationed herself in the porch of the neglected church before he could enter to intone his duty of morning prayers. It had always come down to her having to make an appointment to gain her father's time, but that usually proved a failure for he always forgot. So today she had chased after him.

Fluttering his scrawny arms, which made his black robe and cloak flap and gave him the look of an ancient rook – a habit some found alarming and some mockingly mimicked – the elderly clergyman blinked down over his half-glasses. 'What is it, daughter? You mustn't stop me from going about the Lord's work.'

He was half kindly and half reproving, and it was frustratingly evident to Muriel that his mind had already left her. 'I just want to remind you that I've been invited to luncheon at Owles House today,' Muriel elucidated loudly. 'I'll leave you some cold meat and salad on a tea tray in the kitchen. Don't forget, Papa.'

'Yes, um, my dear,' the Reverend Oakley murmured vaguely.

Muriel stood aside and let her father flutter past her. She jumped in her skin as he clanked the church door shut heavily after him. Hugging her drooping cardigan to her body, head dipped low, she trudged back to the vicarage. She was feeling guilty about going out. Her father would forget to eat and drink unless she stayed in his presence and reminded him to chew and sip every mouthful. But she so wanted to go to Owles House. Muriel still felt honoured and a little elated to have been invited to dine by Mrs Vyvyan herself, after matins nearly two weeks ago. Her house guest, the very beautiful Miss Copeland, had seemed genuinely interested in Muriel too and had generously encouraged her to attend. It was such a change for Muriel not to be overlooked. Falteringly, she had accepted and had shyly suggested the date ahead to give her time to sort out something appropriate to wear, to brush up on her manners and simply to get used to the idea.

During the intervening time she had dug out all her clothes and pairs of shoes. They were all woefully out of date and smelled either musty or of mothballs. Mrs Vyvyan and Miss Copeland had appeared in church utterly chic and exuding ladylike confidence. Muriel saw herself as an ugly faded marsh moth to their tropical butterflies. Miss Elizabeth would also look stylish and polished at the luncheon today. She had written to say how much she was looking forward to Muriel attending the meal.

Muriel had sat down on her bed and cried large round tears of shame and desperation. She would look like a freak in the company of those three women. Part of her shame was over her father's behaviour after the church service that day. All had gone well during the service; somehow he always managed to perform admirably well. He tended to rattle through most of it, but the faithful flock of Mrs Reseigh, a few elderly ladies, and a serious-faced young man, a permanent guest at the Grand Sea View Hotel who would never offer his name, did not seem to mind. Her father's prayers were dignified and his sermon, given with drama and emotion, albeit rambling on too long, always seemed to go down well.

'I thank you for the Word, Reverend Oakley. I have a greater understanding of the Lord's words to the Samaritan woman at the well now,' Mrs Vyvyan had said with a gracious smile.

Muriel, nursing sore fingers after grinding out the hymn tunes on the creaky old organ, had been glad for her father to receive some sincere praise. Usually all the small but faithful congregation said was, 'Thank you, vicar,' and off they went. Her father had brought out a flurry of extra points to Mrs Vyvyan about his sermon, but then he had muttered, 'Thank you again, dear lady,' before shooting off abruptly through the graveyard, whooping and flailing his robes as if a boy pretending he was an aeroplane. Her father was losing his mind, and was only his normal self during an increasingly small part of each day. Sometimes he went off for hours after dark, leaving her anxious about whether he would ever come home.

Mrs Vyvyan and Miss Copeland had generously behaved as if they had not noticed her father's childish antics. 'It's been a pleasure to meet you, Miss Oakley,' Miss Copeland had said.

'Oh, it's very nice of you to say so.' Muriel had twisted her hands bashfully in front of her body. 'I'm so sorry Miss Tresaile was unable to come today.'

'She wanted to spend some time alone with Joseph,' Mrs Vyvyan had put in.

And then the luncheon invitation had come on behalf of all three ladies. Muriel was embarrassed to remember how twittery she had become. She had even curtseyed at one point. She had immediately accepted the invitation, of course; at the very least it would have been terribly rude not to.

A short time later she had asked why such refined ladies would want to bother with the shabby likes of her. She was as plain and as dull as stagnant pond water. Except for having looked after both her parents, and now just her father, her life was pointless. If Mrs Vyvyan and Miss Elizabeth and Miss Copeland knew everything about her they would shun her with disgust. She was disgusted with herself, was so every day, and had been so for many, many long years.

Having made her way up to her bedroom she dropped down on the edge of the bed and gazed gloomily at the garments laid out beside her, which she had chosen to wear today. She had laundered the outfit and rinsed it in strong rose water, but it was awfully dreary – a white and fawn striped blouse with smocked panels above the bosom and a small shawl collar, and a long, gored, high-waist skirt – and well below par for socializing in. Even her cameo brooch and her mother's pearls did barely a thing to prettify the effect.

She sat there and sat still. Willing herself to attend the luncheon. No one would mind her clothes, it was she they wanted with them, she was their exclusive guest, they had said so, and they would not care what she looked like. But she couldn't go looking like a governess – that's what it amounted to. She should have made polite immediate decline. She must cancel and do it now. Leave it any longer and it would be unspeakably discourteous. She sat and brooded, rubbing the sleeve of the blouse between her thumb and forefinger.

She realized she had allowed an hour and a half to drift by. She should be at Owles House now, the sherry should have been sipped and the meal should have begun. She could hear the telephone ringing down in her father's study. It would be one of the three ladies, but she continued to ignore it. She was now unforgivably disrespectful. But she had no respect for herself and nor should anyone else respect her. And she

278

was unforgivable. Years ago she had done an unforgivable thing and she was doomed for it.

Suddenly she jumped up and saw with despair her reflection in the mirror. She was a drab. She was an ugly, useless, good-for-nothing sinner and decent people should have nothing to do with her. She hated herself. She couldn't stand it. 'Why did you have to invite me to your fine big house?' Muriel screamed at the image in her mind of the three hostesses while beating the sides of her head. 'You should leave me alone. I wish I could be left alone. If only I was all alone!'

A huge involuntary sob escaped from her throat, like a regurgitation of darkness and despair from her soul. And then against her will her eyes were drawn to the wardrobe. She had left the doors open and on the wardrobe floor she could see it, the evidence of her crime, which she had kept as a penance.

She let out a soul-deep cry of utter desolation. 'I shouldn't go anywhere.' Muriel fell down on the bed and coiled up in a foetal curl. 'I mustn't. I'm not worthy. I won't go anywhere ever again.'

Beth and Kitty were on their way to the vicarage to find out why Miss Oakley had not turned up for lunch or telephoned to cancel or postpone. The calls Christina had made to the vicarage had not been answered. The three women were worried about Miss Oakley. It was not her nature to be discourteous and simply not show up. Beth and Kitty were taking the motor car as a precaution in case Miss Oakley, or the Reverend Oakley, was ill and needed help or a doctor.

'If we find all is not well, Mum is going to inform the church authorities. It's their responsibility to ensure everything is well in each parish and to take care of the incumbents,' Beth said grimly, adjusting her sunglasses as strong sunlight flashed through the high hedgerows and trees. Kitty, also wearing sunglasses, was driving fast but safely, her chin set grimly.

'It's a crying shame, the waste of Muriel Oakley's life,' Kitty muttered crossly. 'One glance was enough to show she'd dried up and wilted away to almost nothing years ago. I hope we won't be too late. I've a bad feeling about this.'

'Me too,' Beth admitted. She glanced at Kitty. 'I agree with your pessimism over this but I'm only used to you being cheerful, Kitty. You've been down ever since your disappointment over that Rob Praed fellow. Are you sure there isn't more to it?'

'He snubbed me in front of his whole family. It hurt, that's all. I felt such a fool.' Kitty shrugged off Beth's concern but her hurt was running with unaccustomed depth inside her.

A sense of shame mingled with Kitty's hurt, and not a little anger. How dare that man treat her like someone he could pick up and drop at will, drop as if she was a damned nuisance to him? She was ashamed at how, a fortnight ago, she had eagerly dressed up and presented herself, with Joe and Richard, at Wildflower Cottage for afternoon tea. The boys had been shown into the front room where a perky, excited, slightly battered Lily was still being made to rest, and the children began a noisy game of Snap. As Kitty was a guest, Mrs Praed and Mrs Reseigh, who was also there, kindly refused her offer to help with the food and she was shown into the front room with a glass of parsnip wine (delicious), where she had to suffer the squeals and shrieks born out of the card game. Through the window she had seen Rob outside on the front lawn with the rest of the men, smoking and drinking from bottles of beer. The windows were wide open and the ultra-sweet heady scents of the riot of flowers were drifting inside, and she could hear their talk about the previous week's fishing and other male-orientated stuff. Mark was with them, sitting on a bench, holding his gorgeous little black-haired girl possessively and proudly. While sipping the wine, Kitty had unsuccessfully tried to catch Rob's eye. She was confident she was looking her best. She'd overheard Mrs Praed mention to Mrs Reseigh, 'Miss Copeland's some beautiful, isn't she?' Surely Rob would notice her in that way when his eyes finally alighted on her. He kept peering towards the garden gate and over the hedge.

'Won't be long till the food's served, Miss Copeland.' Judy Praed had popped her head round the door. 'We're just hoping one particular guest will turn up.'

Hoping one guest would turn up, Kitty thought. It was not certain this guest would arrive for tea.

'Judy, she's here!' Alison Praed had called to her sister. 'She's actually turned up.'

Kitty got up and looked out of the window to see who this somewhat illustrious guest was. A beloved elderly relative brought by some form of transport, she had assumed it would be. She was surprised to see a slim, modestly dressed, slightly hesitant young woman being met at the gate by Rob, who had hurried to open it for her. The stranger looked vaguely familiar to Kitty. 'Joe, can you come here please?' Kitty appealed to him.

Joe had just triumphed in a game and he reached her at once. 'Yes, Kitty?'

'Who is this who has just arrived?'

'That's Evie Vage,' Joe said quietly. 'Beth's half-sister.'

'Oh, yes, of course, I remember seeing her knitting with your cousin Judy outside on the quay. It's a pity Beth isn't here to get another opportunity to meet her. She's getting quite a welcome.' Rob had been joined by his sisters, his Aunt Posy, Uncle Lofty, and Mrs Reseigh in the welcome party.

'It's unusual for her to go out much,' Joe said in that same small voice.

'It must be strange for you to have a sister who is sister to someone who has lived all her life in the cove.' Kitty had put an understanding hand on Joe. 'You've had a lot to get used to.'

'You can say that again, and strange doesn't even come into it. I'm even playing a childish game with a *girl*. But my father taught me to just get on with things. When Mum is happy, it's all that matters to me.'

Kitty ruffled Joe's hair. 'You're such a good person, so strong. I'm proud to have you as my friend.'

'And me you.' Joe had palmed down his hair. 'Well, I'd better get back and thrash this lot at another game.'

Kitty had gone outside keen to meet Evie Vage, the sister Beth was so eager to see again. It was Mrs Reseigh, beaming and rosy-faced, who had introduced Evie to Kitty. 'It's a great pleasure to meet you, Miss Vage.'

'And for me to meet Beth's best friend,' Evie had said shyly.

'Beth has talked about you a lot.'

'I think about her a lot.'

Rob had been up close behind Evie, and Kitty had flashed him a sultry, hope-to-meet-you-alone-later smile.

In return Rob had given her a glowering short stare then tossed his head away, as if flicking away a troublesome insect. Kitty's heart had plunged as if her whole self had been pushed off the cliff. Rob was not interested in her at all. His previous flirting and their kiss had meant nothing to him. But then, why should it? If things had gone further with him and there had been the chance, he would doubtless have tried to have full sex with her. To him it would have been only a fling with some well-off holiday-maker. She felt ashamed, because although she had hardly known him, and had been warned by his own kin that he was a womanizer, she had been so drawn to him, she knew that at some point she would have willingly given away her virginity to him. She had held off the men of her own circle from intimacy beyond kissing and cuddling, yet she would have thrown away her self-respect on a man who was simply not worth it. She had not learned from the glaring evidence of how this sort of shallow encounter had ruined Christina's young life and come close to destroying her. How Beth's probable affair with an unavailable man had caused her nothing but heartache. Rob Praed was a user of women and he was as rotten as Phil Tresaile had been.

She had been saved from revealing her agonizing embarrassment and resentment thanks to Posy Praed, who had announced the food was ready and invited the children and the women to go to the table laid out in the kitchen to help themselves. 'I've made a cake to celebrate Lily's recovery. There's a candle on it for her to blow out, and we can all sing "For She's a Jolly Good Fellow".'

'You'll enjoy Aunt Posy's baking, Evie,' Rob had said to her in a kind voice before retreating back to his place among the men. 'Judy and Alison will take you in.'

Mrs Reseigh had escorted Kitty back inside. From then on Kitty had not glanced in Rob's direction. There had been no more chance for her to speak to Evie, who was swept away by one Praed after another to look at the flowers and the vegetables, 'As good as anything your father grows in his allotment,' Kitty had overheard Lofty Praed laugh. Evie had brought a little gift for Lily of a knitted black and white cat, and the recuperating girl and the gift were much gushed over.

The boys had got bored, and it was with absolute relief to Kitty that after the cake had been cut and served she could suggest they should now all quietly give their thanks and say goodbye and head back up the hill.

Kitty said, as she expertly swept the car round a sharp bend, 'Beth, how long are you thinking of continuing your stay with Christina? You see, I'm thinking of returning home very soon. Stuart and Connie have just arrived home, and I'm missing them and the children. I'm missing everything at home. I love it here in Cornwall but now it's time for me to leave. You'll be perfectly fine at Owles House without me now, won't you?'

'Is that what has been on your mind?' Beth looked pained. 'I'm sorry, Kitty. I've been selfish, haven't I, being so wrapped up in my own concerns. Of course you must feel free to go home as soon as you'd like. You're bound to be missing your home.' Beth could not bring herself to add, 'And Stuart too.' She didn't want to think about him ever again. 'Will you be all right on the train if I drive you to the station? I'll be so sorry to see you go. I've been thinking a lot about my future and now I'm reconciled with Mum, and have Joe and Evie, and now I'm on good terms with my Uncle Ken, it's without question that my future lies here in Portcowl.'

Just as her meeting with Evie had taken place unexpectedly, rather than having to knock on the door of Ken Tresaile's living quarters at the Sailor's Rest, Beth had come across her uncle out of doors. After ambling on slowly after Evie in the lane so they wouldn't be seen together, Beth had reached the cove and was rehearsing in her mind how she would greet her uncle. She was hoping it would be Ken who she would see right away rather than one of his staff. She had arrived at a shop selling new and second-hand books, just the sort of place she liked browsing through. She marked it for her next excursion down here. A burly middle-aged man in a blazer and knitted patterned waistcoat and a blue tie emerged from the low doorway with a packaged book tucked in his hand, and he lifted his trilby to her. He was looking at her intently and kindly. 'Elizabeth, do you know who I am? It's your uncle, Ken Tresaile.'

She had known instantly who he was. Ken shared many of her father's masculine features, so clear from the photographs her grandmother had kept for her, but with a milder edge. His hair was greying and his outline was less defined with the passage of time but he was still a rather attractive man. 'Uncle Ken.' It came

286

naturally to her to call him that. 'It's Beth now. How strange, I was just on my way to call on you.'

'You were?' His eyebrows shot up. 'Well, I couldn't be more delighted, Beth. Would you like to take my arm while we carry on to the pub? I'd be proud to show you off, my lovely young lady niece.'

Beth had felt proud to walk so close to her uncle. It felt good and important to be under the protection of an older male relative, something unknown to her before. She got to know many locals that day.

It had been strangely fascinating to see her father's childhood home, the rooms homely with net curtains, chenille tablecloths, and linoleum and floral rugs. Phil's little back bedroom, now a storeroom, had beams and a sloping ceiling. None of his things were left there. Ken had explained how Phil had thrown everything into the harbour waters on starting his new life. Beth had studied sepia photographs of her late grandparents and aged great-aunts and great-uncles. Relaxed with her uncle, feeling she had known him for years, she had asked him, over coffee and ginger fairings, to tell her everything about her father's rebellious childhood. 'And please don't keep anything back. I'm resigned to the fact he wasn't a good man.'

'It was fun at first watching what Phil got up to.' Ken had gazed wistfully at Phil's wartime medals, sent to him as next of kin after his brother's death. 'Like knocking on people's doors then running away, silly things like that. But then he became – and goodness knows why – wilfully disobedient, stealing, breaking people's property, scaring the elderly. He even holed a dinghy once and there was nearly a disaster. He caused my parents no end of worry. They would have loved to watch you grow up, Beth, but sadly the hostility between all of us here and Phil was too great,' Ken had voiced sadly. 'It's all such a shame when families don't get on. Can't tell you how pleased I am that's all well with you and Christina, and to have you here, Beth.'

'You'll be seeing me again, Uncle Ken. I shall come here often,' Beth had promised when she had said goodbye.

She had kept that promise and when she'd gone down to the pub she had usually managed to pass a few words with Evie while her half-sister had been outside knitting. The sisters had agreed to patiently hope Davey would come round to them wanting to be close, which would enable Evie to invite Beth into her home. Beth was resolved to somehow win over Davey Vage so she and Evie could enjoy a fully open relationship.

'I'm thinking of selling up in Wiltshire, Kitty, and buying something here in Portcowl, but I'd still like to stay on with Mum and Joe for some time. In fact I was going to speak to you, Mum and Joe about it after we'd had lunch and Miss Oakley had gone home. I thought I was an only child but now I've discovered my father had other children. Now I know about my twin Philip I feel a more complete person. I hope he somehow knows he's got his sister's love as well as his mother's. You will come down and visit us all often, promise me, Kitty? I'd hate to think of my life without you in it.'

'Of course I will, dumb head, you couldn't keep me away.' Kitty glanced at her with a huge sunny smile. 'I couldn't be more pleased for you, Beth. All my hopes and wishes for you have worked out better than I could have imagined. I was so afraid we would be driving back with you in pieces, that if things had gone badly with Christina you would have been more frustrated and upset than before. I'm going to miss you so much when I get home, but it's time for me to move on too. I love all the local craftwork here and I might open a shop selling country crafts, choosing from all over the country. It will give me scope to travel around Britain and buy the best. It will be fascinating.'

'It certainly sounds it, Kitty. I'm delighted for you, and I'm glad you saw how uncouth that fisherman was. We'll make a pact that sometimes I'll join you on your travels. Who knows what adventures we might have.'

The friends were suddenly laughing, all the tensions amassed in the past weeks lifted away.

'Perhaps Miss Oakley just got cold feet,' Beth said, chewing her bottom lip, as they pulled into the vicarage grounds. 'I mean, she hadn't been invited anywhere for years. She must have been so nervous about it. I should have rung her first thing this morning to encourage her. I should have come here before but I didn't want to crowd her. Evie mentioned she's been here twice since bringing her home that day, and although Miss Oakley thanked her she put Evie off both times. Poor lady, she must be so miserable.'

Kitty stopped the motor car in front of the battered old door and turned off the engine. The women got out and gazed all about, peering at the windows.

'It's so quiet,' Beth said, feeling chilly despite the pleasant heat of the day. 'Too quiet.'

Kitty shivered the whole length of her body, and like Beth she wished she had brought a cardigan. 'I found the church dark and creepy but this place is like something out of a horror movie.'

Beth nodded grimly. 'Well, we'd better knock on the door and see what we find.'

Twenty-Three

Beth and Kitty stood uncertainly in the vicarage hall, edging closer together until they were linking arms. 'Hello!' Beth called out. 'Miss Oakley! Reverend Oakley! Are you here?'

They received the same response as they had to their knocking on the door. Nothing. The silence in this bleak place was heavy, not a brooding sort of heaviness but one of waste and terrible sorrow, and there was the sense of something like decay. Decaying lives, Beth thought gravely.

'We took the decision to step inside, Kitty, so we might as well look in some of the rooms. Miss Oakley or the Reverend could be dozing somewhere. Somehow I doubt we'll find him at home. I've a feeling he goes off and isolates himself for most of the day.'

'Let's try the study, the drawing room and the kitchen. They're the most likely places we'd find someone,' Kitty replied, trying to stare through the gloom. She waved her hand in front of her face in the vain hope of avoiding the cloud of dust motes apparent in the faint daylight. 'Where did you take your lessons? It's possible Miss Oakley might be in there.'

'OK,' Beth said. 'I know where the rooms are, but we might as well glance in all the downstairs rooms.' Beth dearly hoped one or other of the Oakleys would soon be located. She felt a dread of searching for them upstairs. As Kitty had mentioned for herself, she had a bad feeling about this.

A little later, she and Beth had returned from their search and stood at the foot of the stairs. Kitty declared as if choking, 'My God, this place is worse than I thought possible. There's dust and cobwebs everywhere, and the grime in that kitchen ... It's no wonder no one is invited inside. Miss Oakley must feel so ashamed and hopeless.'

'Come on, no more pussyfooting,' Beth said grimly, putting aside her dread. 'We're going to search the upstairs rooms. If we don't find her, there might be some clue in her room to where she's gone.'

The stairs creaked and heaved at their every step, giving the impression someone was creeping up behind them, and both Beth and Kitty kept glancing behind. 'The atmosphere gets more and more depressing as we climb,' Beth whispered to Kitty, wanting to put a handkerchief to her nose and mouth.

'Let's just look in the first bedroom,' Kitty answered grimly.

'Miss Oakley, Miss Oakley, are you up here?' Beth called out on the landing. All that could be heard were two different clocks chiming a quarter past three. Feeling like an insolent trespasser despite being here out of concern, Beth turned the first dusty glass doorknob in the dark, airless upstairs hallway. She pushed the door open wide enough for herself and Kitty to fully view the room. The curtains were closed, but there was just enough light for the women to conclude that this room had been the late Mrs Oakley's. The room was tidy, reverently so – left, they were sure, exactly as it had been when the old lady died. Once it had been congested with Victorian furniture, most of which was pushed back against the walls to make room for Mrs Oakley to be nursed at the end of her life. A large gold cross, likely brought from the church, stood in the middle of a long table at the foot of the bed. Numerous candles had been burned in vigil. 'Miss Oakley?' Beth enquired, in case the daughter was somewhere in the shadows of the room.

'She's not here,' Kitty said. 'We must keep going.'

The next room was a cold, functional bathroom, obviously boarded off from the first bedroom; once, when vicarage life was grander, it had probably been a dressing room.

'It's the next room, I feel it is,' Beth said with a sigh, feeling morbidly stifled. The longer she spent in this house the more the atmosphere dragged her spirits down. 'I hope Miss Oakley's in there and she's just resting and forgotten where she should have gone today.'

'Me too,' Kitty agreed heartily. The next door was at a sharp right angle in the corridor and

Kitty went straight into it, Beth tight beside her. The room, kept fairly neat, appeared empty but on the bedcovers was a small heap of crumpled clothes. The women knew at once that these were the clothes Miss Oakley had intended to wear to lunch today.

'So she was coming and something changed her mind,' Beth murmured. 'Kitty, we've got to find her. I just know something bad has happened to her.'

Kitty nodded, the gloom and sense of despair in this bleak old house telling her that too.

Beth went to the foot of the bed. She saw more discarded clothes on the floor, scrunched up oddly against the wardrobe. Then she knew it wasn't clothes she could see. 'Oh no! She's here, Kitty, on the floor. I fear we might be too late.' Beth rushed to the hunched figure and sank down on her knees. Kitty followed suit but made a detour first and threw back the curtains that dragged on their heavy rings. Daylight hit the room, making Kitty and Beth blink heavily.

'Miss Oakley?' Beth was grateful for the improved visibility and she took Muriel Oakley's drooping head in her hands. 'Thank God, she's a little warm. She's alive, but she's collapsed and she's very ill. Help me get her into bed, Kitty. We need to get her warmer. And we need to call the doctor – I know his number – and find her father. The Reverend Oakley needs to face the fact that this cannot go on. Miss Oakley needs help and I'm going to see that she gets it.'

Muriel suddenly opened her eyes and stared directly at Beth. 'You always were such a dear girl, Miss Beth, but I don't deserve your help. I'm not ill.' Her voice was cracked but strangely accepting. 'I'm wicked, you see. I've done some very wicked things and I deserve to be punished. I want to confess. It's time for me to confess and find my peace and then let justice be done.'

'I advise you to see a priest a little later, Miss Oakley. First let Kitty and me get you comfortably in bed. You need something warm and nourishing inside you and a hot water bottle, and please allow us to call the doctor for you. Do you know where your father is likely to be? He needs to know you're unwell.'

'No, no.' Muriel pushed Beth away and Beth was amazed at the strength in her. Gone was the mumbling, apologetic woman she had known since her return to Portcowl, but it was plain she was in terrible distress. Tears loitered at the corners of her stretched, reddened eyes and her face muscles were twitching. She straightened to prop her sagging weight against the wardrobe and pulled her knees up. It was then that Beth and Kitty saw she was clutching something in her trembling hands against her chest, a small box that perhaps had once held a pair of new gloves. 'Please do what I ask you, Miss Beth and Miss Kitty. Sit on the bed and listen to me.'

Glancing uncertainly at each other the friends did as she bid. 'You don't have to tell us what troubles you, Miss Oakley,' Beth said softly.

'I need to tell you, Miss Beth, because it is connected to you,' Muriel rasped, firm but stricken.

'To me? How?' Beth was baffled and apprehensive.

'I didn't mean it to happen, believe me. I couldn't stop him. He was too strong for me. I...'

'Who are you talking about? Did someone hurt you?' Beth prompted. She was afraid for her former teacher, for Muriel Oakley was remembering something that had clearly thrust dark and terrible shades over her, and Beth knew how dreadfully that could affect a life.

'Beth,' Kitty whispered in her ear. 'I don't think you should interrupt her. Her mind is not with us. She needs to bring out what is mentally torturing her.'

Beth nodded and braced herself, like Kitty, to listen. And to wait, for however long it took for Miss Oakley to reveal her appalling secret and how it involved Beth.

'I ... I didn't like him, I certainly didn't approve of him. He didn't take any notice of me for years.' Muriel let out a terrible moan. 'Then one day when I was alone cleaning in the church he was there. He told me some story about wanting help and would I go with him. I didn't want to but I couldn't refuse a plea for help. He led the way outside. It wasn't far, he said. Then he did it to me, he hurt me so much. I cried and pleaded with him to stop but he just laughed. I was so ashamed. Of course, I couldn't tell anyone. He said it was my fault. I'd smiled to entice him every time we'd met and led him on. I tried to avoid him after that but the shame happened again and again until he suddenly left the area. I thought my prayers had been answered but...'

Beth and Kitty traded looks of pure horror. Both had to resist the urge to go to comfort the distressed woman. 'Poor Miss Oakley was raped, but what has it got to do with me?' Beth whispered.

Kitty gripped Beth's hand and entreated her with her eyes to understand. Then Beth was gasping in utter shock and revulsion as she grasped the truth. The rapist had been her father! Knowing how cruel and heartless he had been, she knew there was no doubt. How many more people had he tried to destroy? Beth was overwhelmed with shame. Had she inherited some of her father's indifference to the suffering of others? She had willingly embarked on an affair without a thought for her lover's innocent family. 'It wasn't your fault, Miss Oakley,' she cried. 'Please don't believe that. There's no need to let your agony go on. Let us help you, oh please let us help you. It's what we want to do. We can take you away from here where all your terrible memories are, to somewhere quiet and private for you to recuperate. I'll stay with you. I promise I won't leave you.'

Beth's desperate imploring broke through Muriel's great sorrow. 'Bless you, Miss Beth, but you don't know the full story.'

'I don't care what it is. It was my father who violated you, wasn't it? He nearly destroyed my mother but she managed to survive. Don't let him ruin your whole life. You have nothing to confess. You did nothing wrong.'

'Oh, but I did.'

'How? How could you possibly have done anything wrong? You've been honourable and caring all your life. You cared for your mother like a dutiful daughter and you've done your best for your father. Forgive me for saying this but your father is old and getting senile. He needs help too. You both need looking after, your father for the rest of his days and you, Miss Oakley, until you are rested and well. Let me and Kitty take you away now to Owles House. My mother will be glad to have you there until proper arrangements can be made.'

'I know what you're saying is right. My poor papa should be in a nursing home. He wanders off every day and one day he'll get lost and might not come back at all. Bless you for wanting to help me too, but you see I've committed an unforgivable sin and I must be punished for it by judge and jury.'

Beth was having a hard task to stop herself from weeping over the woman's misguided belief. 'What was it you did, Miss Oakley?'

'I've never told anyone what happened to me, of course. I tried to put it all behind me, and I thought I would in time by serving the Lord. My womanly function had ceased and I thought

298

it was judgement on me for my shame and that I was being denied having children. It was unlikely anyone would want a plain woman like me anyway, so I wasn't too upset. Then it happened. Pains throughout one night like I never knew possible. And I gave birth, you see, in this room, in my bed. There was this little baby and stuff. The baby was all blue and about four inches long, dead of course, born too soon. I cried so much. I wanted that innocent little child of mine, you see. If it had lasted longer inside me and been born alive I would have placed it on the doorstep and told my parents it was abandoned by a desperate mother. It's not unknown for babies to be left at a vicarage. I would have convinced my parents somehow that we should bring the child up, that it was God's will. Its life had come about by sin, but I believed God would have blessed it because it wasn't its fault it had been conceived, and through that little life I hoped I would have been happy and fulfilled. It was a little girl. I named her Martha Mary. Years before I had dreamed of having a daughter called Martha Mary after the two sisters faithful to the Lord.

'I washed and dressed her in my old doll's clothes. I held her for a while. She was pretty and had a little fine hair. Then I baptized her with water from my wash bowl. St Philip baptized the Ethiopian eunuch in roadside water, there was just the two of them. The Ethiopian's actions were sincere and so were mine, so I hoped God would understand. I couldn't tell my parents of course, the shame would have killed them. Then I wrapped Martha Mary up tight in silk with potpourri and put her in this little box. My wardrobe has a false bottom to hide valuables and I put my baby in there, and there she stayed until my mama died, when I took her from her hiding place and hid her in the folds of my mama's wedding dress which she was buried in. So finally Martha Mary took part in a Christian burial and I went to her secret grave every day.

'I was quite at peace for a while. Then he started appearing to me, to torment me. It was my punishment for concealing Martha Mary's stillbirth. I'll only get away from him when I finally confess to the law and am punished by it.' Muriel's eyelids fluttered and slowly closed, her voice grew fainter. Beth and Kitty were both wiping away tears of sorrow for the poor tragic woman. 'Papa wouldn't really understand it, and if he does he'll soon forget for ever. He won't remember the disgrace. I don't think I'll be sent to the gallows and I shouldn't think they'll want to exhume my mama to search for my baby's remains. It will be prison or the asylum for me and I won't mind at all.'

Muriel's body slumped and Beth and Kitty jumped up off the bed. 'She's out of it, thank goodness. We can get her into bed now,' Beth said. Then she added defiantly, though still weeping freely, 'I'll be damned if I let her go to rot in prison or an asylum. I've just learned my evil father was responsible for fathering yet

300

another child. I would have had another sister. I shall convince Miss Oakley that her secret is safe in God's love and with us. And I'll be damned if my sister Evie is kept from me. Davey Vage might be a good man but he has no right to insist that Evie should have nothing to do with me.'

Twenty-Four

'I can't believe what I'm seeing out in the lane!' Up in Joe's tree house, standing on an old upturned crate, Lily was using Joe's spyglass.

'Don't tell me. Mark Reseigh's on his way to garden here,' Joe said, uninterested. He was sitting pow-wow-like on the timber floor with Richard, where they were proudly discussing Joe's recent athletics club wins and his acceptance into the county team. Richard had recently achieved an impressive third in the hurdles, and a win with Joe in the relay races at that successful meeting. Joe had been photographed for the newspapers thanks to his achievement and he was lauded down in the cove. Joe's headmaster had been in touch and once the autumn term began the school was to put on a ceremony for him.

'It's not him,' Lily piped on. 'It's a she and she's got her stupid legionnaire's hat on and even sunglasses, but I don't know what else she thinks she's wearing, they're either long shorts or short longs. Still, it's better than those old long johns she was once seen wearing.'

'Can't you just shut up for once, maid?' Richard shouted at her, his freckled cheeks growing nearly as red as his hair. 'Joe, why do we have to keep having her around? She's a ruddy nuisance! She filches all our grub. She never stops chattering and then she only spouts nonsense. We look blimming fools letting her tag round with us. I mean, who cares who's out in the ruddy lane?'

'You can't speak to me like that.' Lily twisted her neck round to poke her tongue out at Richard. 'Tell him, Joe, I'm part of this gang.'

'We don't really have a gang, Lily,' Joe said, hardly knowing himself why he was so patient with the fidgety little girl. Lily could be such a pain, but she did make him laugh and she was as tough as old boots. 'Just get to the point, eh?'

Lily looked again through the spyglass. 'It's Gabby Magor.'

'So what?' Richard seethed, gritting his teeth and making strangling motions with his hands.

'The point is,' Lily announced in her maddening gloating way, 'she's got a little dog with her.'

'She's what?' Joe bawled, scrambling to his feet. 'Why didn't you say so in the first place? This is serious. Right, out into the lane!'

'Stupid ruddy girl!' Richard raised a fist at Lily, pushing her aside so he was second down the rope ladder. 'One of these days I'm going to half drown you.'

Under the shade of a large parasol, Christina was relaxing on the terrace. Beth and Kitty were fetching morning coffee, and because it

303

was her last day before she left for home, Kitty had been down early to the shops and brought back cream cakes for a treat for everyone. Christina had told Joe to bring the other children to the terrace table at ten thirty. Their constantly ravenous tummies would ensure they wouldn't be late. It amused Christina how Joe allowed cheeky Lily to trail round after him and Richard. Beth and Kitty thought Richard's irritation with Lily was a hoot.

Christina stretched out her bad leg and rubbed it gently, smiling, for the arthritis didn't shoot half so many aches and pains through her hip joint nowadays. That was because she was relaxed and so happy now. Beth was staying for good in Cornwall. She had her daughter back and Beth was never going away again. Chaplin and Grace were side-by-side dozing in the sunniest spot on the terrace, and Charlie was chasing a butterfly on the lawn. If Francis were here things would be idyllic.

At the weekend, Beth had said she was going to knock on Davey Vage's door and ask nicely if she could see Evie. Beth's determination – although Christina was concerned about it – suggested that she was not going to rest until she had succeeded in nothing less than claiming Evie as her older sister. If all ended well Christina would be glad to have Evie, even though she was Phil's child, in her house. When asked how he felt about Evie Joe had expressed the horror of being always 'surrounded by women', but as long as he was left to do things his way, and he still got time alone with Christina, which Beth was sensitive to allow, he was fine about it.

One day soon, Christina thought, without flinching from the notion, she would get involved in local life. A curate was to take services in the church until a new vicar was appointed. No doubt he would see a swelled, curious congregation. Christina had received praise, as had Beth and Kitty, passed on via Mrs Reseigh, for their kindness to the Oakleys. Miss Oakley had stayed at Owles House, under complete bed rest, for two days. Christina had called in Mark Reseigh to search for the Reverend Oakley, and Mark had tracked down the confused clergyman sitting beside a farm stream, talking aloud to his dead wife as if he could actually see her. Now both of the Oakleys were in the same Christian-run nursing home, and after some soothing words from Beth and Christina, Miss Oakley had gradually been persuaded she had nothing to confess to anyone. 'God knows everything,' she had said in the end. 'Only he can judge me.'

He would certainly have passed severe judgement on her rotten first husband, Christina had thought fiercely, glad to have this latest episode of Phil Tresaile's evil doings brought to a satisfactory end. Evidence – old potpourri and a few fine hairs – that Miss Oakley had not imagined she had given birth to a baby had been discovered in the forlorn little glove box. Sorrowfully Miss Oakley had agreed to allow it to be burned in the fire lit in her sick room and she had tearfully watched that part of her harrowing past disappear. 'Fire cleanses,' she had said. 'One day when I go to the Lord I'll be fully cleansed. Martha Mary didn't deserve what happened to her. The Lord is merciful and she might be with Him waiting for me.' Then she had fallen into a proper restful sleep.

Christina saw Joe and his cohorts tearing across the lawn, making for the drive. 'Joe! Where are you going? It's time for the cakes!' Chaplin was up on his paws stretching his legs and watching the tearaways. Christina called Grace to her.

Beth and Kitty arrived with the trays of coffee, lemonade and treats. Mrs Reseigh was with them; more than ever, she was regarded as part of the family. 'What on earth are the children up to?' Beth said in astonishment.

'Must be something serious for them to forget their tummies,' Mrs Reseigh frowned.

The women forsook the goodies, and with Chaplin – and Grace, scooped up in Kitty's arms – they all started off for the lane. They soon heard shouting and screaming and a dog barking out there. Christina let Chaplin run on ahead in case Joe needed help.

'How dare you take my bleddy dog from me! Get your bleddy hands off him, or I'll kill ya!' Gabby lunged at Joe to try to wrest Tickle out of his arms, but Joe was faster in backing away from her towards the driveway. Tickle was growling at Joe and struggling to get free

306

of him.

'You're not fit to own a dog!' Joe yelled at her. 'I rescued one you'd abandoned in the woods on the cliff just a few weeks ago. You've got fed up with every pet you've ever had and then you dump them. I'm not going to let you do that to this one.'

'Hush, little one,' Lily soothed the little fretful dog. 'It's for your own good.'

Joe fended off Lily's reaching grubby hands. The dog was snarling now and Lily would likely be bitten. Richard grabbed Lily by the shoulders, wrenched her round and gave her hearty push. 'Go back to the ladies, you!'

'Joe! Joe! What's going on?' Christina shouted to him, riddled with worry because she couldn't see anything beyond the hedgerows. She couldn't keep up with Beth and Kitty's pace, and taking Grace, urged the younger fitter women to run and find out what the bedlam was about.

Mrs Reseigh stayed with her. 'That's Gabby Magor's big mouth we can hear. Dear God, that woman's language indeed. And in front of children! Shall I ring the constable? Mark must be on his way, hopefully he'll reach them soon.'

'Oh my God, I hope we won't need the police. Joe! Come back here at once!' The riot out in the lane continued. 'Right, my son, you're in a lot of trouble this time.'

Beth and Kitty came upon the melee to see Mark running the last few feet towards the struggle. Joe dodged past the women pell-mell

307

with a small howling mongrel in his arms and Gabby Magor used her thick sinewy hands to push Richard violently out of her way. Richard was sent skidding along the ground and ended up in the ditch. Lily was now in Gabby's path and she stood transfixed, her eyes large and bright at what the wild woman might do to her. Mark reached Lily and shovelled her up, dropping her safely out of the charge.

He positioned himself in front of Gabby, his stance rock solid and his eyes on fire. 'What are you doing to these children? Get away from here!'

Gabby spat on her fists and raised them at Mark. 'Not on your bleddy life.' She let out the vilest profanities. ''Tisn't me what's in the wrong. Those bleddy kids stole my dog from me. I'll get the law on them and 'tis those little bastards who'll go to clink. I'll kill 'em if they don't give me my dog back. And I'll knock you into hell if you don't get out of my bleddy way!'

Mark put up his hands in conciliatory fashion. Without looking round, he asked, 'Is this true, Richard?'

'Not really.' Richard was up and rubbing himself down. 'Joe took the dog from her because she's cruel to her animals. We're saving it from suffering, that's all.'

'See!' Gabby yelled. 'That brat's admitted it. His rotten bleddy mate stole my Tickle and if he's not brung straight back to me this minute I'll knock all your blocks off. Including they two shitty hoity-toity tarts there.' She gave Beth and Kitty a lewd gesture.

'That's enough!' Mark growled. 'Mind your language, woman. I think we'd better all go and see Mrs Vyvyan about this.'

'You, matey, can think what you bleddy like! But I'm getting my Tickle back or you'll all soon be dead meat.' Gabby glowered at all the company in turn then pointed at Lily. 'Starting with that little shower of shit first.'

'Awp,' Lily gulped and half hid behind Richard. He put a protective arm round her.

Beth had never seen such a fierce and furious woman, or one as ugly as Gabby Magor. She was like a hideous raging bull. Beth might have been afraid of her but this she-bull had threatened the children. 'Miss Magor,' she said frostily. 'Joe should not have taken your dog. I'm sure Mrs Vyvyan will deal with him accordingly. Would you care to step inside the grounds and speak to Mrs Vyvyan about this?'

Some of the raw wrath seemed to die down in Gabby but she was still like some venomous menacing hulk of machinery, the stuff of children's nightmares. She snarled, 'Yeah, let's get this over with. And she had better do the right thing by me.' Gabby lumbered past Beth and Kitty, making the ground shudder. 'And I want that bleddy big kid thrashed for what he done.'

'Thank God you came along when you did, Mark,' Beth said, holding out her hand to Lily. 'That woman seems capable of anything.'

'She is,' Mark replied grimly, motioning for Richard to go on ahead of the grown-ups. 'She once beat Davey Vage up for no reason at all.'

Evie's father had been beaten up? Beth loathed the woman even more.

'I'm going to miss all the dramas when I leave here tomorrow,' Kitty said.

'Now, Miss Magor, let's talk about this reasonably and sensibly, and please refrain from swearing,' Christina said, amazed at how in control she was. Before Beth had forgiven her and returned her love she wouldn't have been able to deal with this. 'First I'll tell my son to give you back your dog.'

'I should bled— think so too,' Gabby rumbled with animosity, shooting out her rough paws for Tickle. 'Come to Mummy, Tickle. How dare this bled— lot accuse me of 'tending to kick you out.'

Now the initial battle was over everyone was aware of Gabby's ripe odours. Lily had her hand up over her screwed-up face.

Tickle was struggling to get to his owner but Joe clamped the dog to him. 'Mum, you have to listen to me. Remember Grace? This woman was responsible for the dire circumstances Kitty and I found her in.'

'What's he talking about? Who's Grace?' Gabby screeched. 'I don't know no bleddy Grace. The boy's mad.'

'This is Grace,' Christina said, 'here in my arms. My son and Miss Copeland found him abandoned in the woods almost starved to

310

death. Because of your previous neglect and lack of interest in animals we had reason to suspect you were responsible.'

'I've never seen that mutt in my life,' Gabby roared. 'You got proof it was me?'

Gabby had the high hand here and everyone glanced wryly at each other.

'There you are then. Hand my Tickle over to me at once or I'll get the law on all of you.'

Christina had no choice and ordered reluctantly, 'Joe, do as Miss Magor says.'

'Mum!' Joe protested.

'It's the right thing to do. Put the dog down.'

'Yeah, put him down,' Gabby crowed. 'I'll prove to you how much I love Tickle and how much he loves me.'

Slowly, scowling, Joe started to lower the dog down and Tickle soon struggled out of his grip. Gabby was clucking to Tickle, and Tickle yapped in delight and tore over the grass to her and jumped straight up into her arms and licked her all over her face, his little body trembling in excitement.

'See, we love each other,' Gabby gloated with a variety of ugly sniggers. 'I've taught Tickle to sit and stay and roll over and everything. Now I want an apology from the bleddy lot of you. You better not be too stuck up to do it 'n' all.'

'I apologize for the trouble that has been caused to you, Miss Magor,' Christina said, none too friendly. 'Now please leave my property.'

One by one Joe, with a hard stare, and then

Richard and Lily muttered that they were sorry.

'You have my apologies,' Kitty said ungraciously. At least the foul woman had denied any knowledge of Grace and she could never put a claim to her by saying Grace had wandered off and got lost.

'I'm sorry too,' Beth said. 'But let me tell you this, Gabby Magor. You may have taken a fancy to this little dog but we'll be keeping an eye on you. If there is the slightest notion of you hurting or neglecting Tickle I'll see to it that you are prosecuted.'

'Oh, will you now,' Gabby rounded on Beth. 'I know who you are, Miss toffee-nosed Elizabeth Tresaile. You needn't think yourself so bleddy wonderful. I 'spect you know your father was nothing but a whoremonger, but do you know about all the women he was screwing, eh?'

Beth's expression of horror made Gabby bellow with laughter. 'No, not me.' Christina hurriedly told Joe to take Lily and Richard away and Joe reluctantly complied. 'He weren't interested in me 'cus I had nothing to benefit him. It was your high 'n' mighty grandmother, the stuck-up bitch, that he was tupping reg'lar. I saw them. She was ravenous for him. I watched and I heard her rowing with him after. "What do you want my wretched daughter for?" she said, all tears. "Aren't I enough for you, Phil? Christina's nothing, she's too weak for you." Well, that got proved right. Sent you off your head, didn't he, missus?' Gabby jeered

312

at Christina. 'Your mother really hated you but I 'spect you already knew that. Well, I'm off. You can all drop dead, the lot of you!' With an angry toss of her fist Gabby lumbered away.

'Excuse me,' Mark said, looking down then walking away. Mrs Reseigh followed on.

Beth and Christina had paled considerably, but they didn't need a discussion about Gabby Magor's spiteful words to know she had been telling the truth. It echoed loudly down the years now, explaining why Marion Frobisher had always taken the side of Beth's father, Christina's first husband.

Kitty was mortified for them to have learned these disturbing and humiliating facts in such a brutal manner. 'I'm so sorry for you both. I'll leave you to talk.'

To Beth it was as if every last scrap of her being was twisted then torn apart and destroyed in a storm. It had been the last thing she could have thought about her beloved grandmother, that she had pursued her father when he was a young single man, first as a holiday fling and then as a besotted older woman. For some reason she had never loved her own daughter – perhaps Christina had been a burden to her – and then she had come to hate Christina for falling, like herself, under Phil Tresaile's spell. Had her grandmother's love and care for her been genuine or merely a way of causing endless heartache to Christina? Beth was numbed through right now. When the full impact of this revelation hit her, would she ever be able to forgive her grandmother? Beth had received shock after shock as she had learned of the tragic innocent babies her father had sired. What if he had impregnated her grandmother? The thought was too horrible. Were there any other Phil Tresaile offspring in the world? She had to end these musings or she'd go mad.

Christina was watching Beth closely and was sure she knew Beth's thoughts. 'Will you be all right, darling? You were so close to your grandmother. Can we walk back? My hip...'

Beth immediately took Christina's arm. 'The question is, will you be all right, Mum? Did you have any idea or has this been a total shock to you too?'

'I had my suspicions. I knew my mother liked younger men, but before Phil it had been rich men. Don't hate her, Beth. Your grandmother really did love you. I think she was glad when my own father died young. She had never had a good word for him, perhaps that's why she couldn't tolerate me. Francis taught me to leave the past behind. Please don't let this latest thing continue to disturb you and steal your peace.'

Beth gave herself a mental shake. 'I won't, because no matter how bad my father was all his children were wanted and loved by their mothers. It's made me more determined to have Evie in my life. Let's reconvene the coffee and cakes, shall we?'

'Yes, lovely, and I must think about how I'm going to deal with Joe. He did something wrong but for the right reasons.' Christina smiled and affectionately tidied Beth's hair. 'And I can't help feeling so proud of him.'

Beth took Mark his 'crib' of a mug of bark-strong tea and a rock cake. Mrs Reseigh repeated Mark's preferences every time he worked in the gardens and Beth knew he didn't like coffee and ate only plain food. He was mowing a side lawn that had at the sides beds of fuchsias, red-hot pokers, rich pink and salmon-pink pools of sedum, and bright yellow and red begonias. High, spreading blue and purple mop-head hydrangea bushes added shelter, and then there was a natural higher hedgerow in front of the woods. It was the perfect place to bring a rug and lie down to sunbathe.

Seeing Beth on the way, Mark left the mower and joined her where she had placed the little tin tray on a small well-weathered stone table. 'Thanks, Miss Beth,' he said in his respectful yet distant way.

'I made your tea today. I hope you find it to your liking. I've put two sugars in it.' The curious side of Beth always had a yen to draw the virtually silent Mark into conversation on some subject other than his young daughter. This time she had something to ask him and she would not allow his reticence to stay his tongue.

'Thanks,' Mark said again, and that was all.

'Mark, I need to talk to you quite bluntly. I'm sorry.' She felt the need to apologize because it was him.

'Go on.' He looked at her without expression,

and she had no hint as to what he was thinking.

'There was something I noticed about you during that unfortunate incident with that dreadful woman when she mentioned my father's and grandmother's affair.'

Tightening his mouth Mark looked away and gave a small sigh.

'There it is again, that certain turn of your head, that regretful sigh,' Beth plunged on. 'I'm sorry but I can't spare your feelings. You knew about the affair, didn't you? I'm sure of it. But how?'

'You've been straight with me, Miss Beth, so I'll be the same. When I was due to take over from old Mr Jewell he showed me round the grounds and he told me what I should think was all your family's secrets. Like Gabby Magor he saw things that should never have gone on. He said he trusted me to keep my mouth shut but thought I should know it all so I'd have nothing to feel I wanted to dig into. That's not my way. There was no need for Mr Jewell to insist I listened to him, I didn't want to know. I swore to keep my peace and I have. I didn't even tell my wife. So there's no need for us to ever speak of this again,' he ended firmly. He picked up his tea mug.

Beth knew he wanted her to go but she had one last question. 'I thank you for your integrity. Do you think any others know?'

'There's no way of knowing that, but if it was common knowledge it would have been all over the cove.' Mark was looking straight across the

316

lawn, cut off from Beth, but then he suddenly settled his eyes on her. 'This must be hard for you and Mrs Vyvyan.'

'We'll not let it get us down.' Beth was pleased at his show of concern, to see this kind side of him. If only all men were as faithful to their wives and as caring towards their children as he had been to his, then she and Christina, Evie's mother and Miss Oakley would never have known their respective horrors. 'What I don't understand is why an infamous trouble-maker like the Magor woman didn't spread round what she knew long ago. It doesn't make sense.'

'Does anything?' Mark muttered, a tarnish of pain shading his rugged features. 'What sense was it that my Juliet died? Or Francis Vyvyan? Gabby Magor insults people about their physical looks but she doesn't often spread malicious gossip about their personal lives. She ill-treats lots of animals then she takes to one and dotes on it. There is no sense in the real world.' He offered Beth a faint smile of irony. 'Is there?'

'No,' Beth replied after a moment's reflection. 'Just shades of light and dark, and we must learn to leave the darkest ones behind us if we are to get on with our lives.'

Twenty-Five

Evie tried to ignore the drawer in the kitchen dresser but her eyes again wandered towards it. Inside the drawer, slipped under a box of bills and receipts, was a letter she had received, a rare thing for her. When it popped through the letterbox three days ago she had been both wary and excited about it. The postmark was Newlyn. She had been a little scared. The writing wasn't her father's – he always sent messages to her by phoning the Sailor's Rest – so had someone written to her to say her father was ill or had had an accident? No, that didn't figure either. Even such a message would have been passed on via the pub. Or her uncle, Ken Tresaile, would have sent someone or turned up himself on the doorstep.

Taking the letter from the drawer, Evie ran up to her room and sat on the deep cut-stone window ledge, on the long sun-faded cushion her mother had made. The blustery wind was driving scatters of noisy raindrops against the pristine clean glass and there was a bit of a draught, but Evie stayed here in one of her favourite places. She glanced up and down the quay, furtively, guiltily, not wanting to be spied at what she was doing. Not that it was anything wrong. It couldn't be wrong for her to read again the letter sent to her by Rob Praed.

Dear Evie,
I hope you don't mind me sending you a few words. This is hard for me because I've never done this sort of thing before. I've always gone straight to the point with a woman I've taken a liking to. But things are different with you, Evie. I more than like you and I'm feeling a bit shy about asking you to walk out with me. I've really enjoyed seeing you those few times since I rescued Smoky. Please will you consider me as a boyfriend? I know I'm rough at the edges but I swear on my heart I will always respect you. You have nothing to fear from me.
When I'm back at the weekend, I shall come round and ask you out for a meal, and ask Davey's permission too, of course. Please, please think about saying yes.
I'm looking forward to seeing you again.
Sincerely, Rob Praed

Just as when she'd first read the letter, Evie shivered with a fusion of horror and delight. The first time she had thrust the letter in the drawer as if it was burning her fingers. It had certainly burned her sensitivities. During the next three days followed by hard-to-sleep nights, she had turned over her every thought and feeling about it. She had resented Rob for putting her in the most awkward position of her life. It was foreign to her to think about wanting a boyfriend and a husband. She was happy just to remain with her father. She didn't need a family. Davey had assured her that, if or when the time came when she was left on her own, he would leave her the cottage and ensure she was well provided for, and she would carry on with her craftwork and quiet life.

Thinking about children, watching the local ones and the holidaymakers' and day trippers' families, and mothers with new babies, was now making her think what holding a baby of her own would be like. 'Darn you, Rob Praed,' she had said aloud. 'I didn't want my ... my ... stirred up.' Her maternal instinct was what she hadn't been able to say. But she got round to admitting that a maternal instinct was natural, and hers was growing stronger every day. She understood now why married women longed to have babies.

Evie let every word of Rob's hopes and promises sink into her mind. It was exciting and scary to think of going to eat out with him – or do anything at all with him, come to that – but if she went out with him once she didn't have to go again if she disliked the experience. At least she would have had one outing with a young man and it would still the tongues of Judy and Alison, who kept telling her to stop training herself to be an old maid. They and Mrs Coad said she would miss out on so much and when she had left it too late she would bitterly regret it.

'Rob likes you, really likes you, Evie. You know that,' Judy pestered her. 'It's why he keeps popping round your place when he's home. He was very attentive to you at Lily's tea party. Don't say you didn't notice, and don't say you found it altogether unwelcome. If he makes as good a husband as he is a brother you couldn't do any better. Don't be shy, snap him up. Don't lose him to someone else. If you do you'll find her living next door to you and you might not like that one bit.'

Evie didn't know if she'd hate that thought or not care at all – this romance thing was new to her. If she did go out with Rob, what would it be like if he took her hand, if he moved in for a kiss? What should a first kiss be like? A peck on the cheek, on the lips, surely not a full kiss on the first occasion. She pictured Rob in the house last weekend; he'd come round to borrow some gravy browning, saying Alison had forgotten to get any in and both his sisters were too busy to go to the shops.

'Oh, it's you again,' her father had muttered at Rob, clearly displeased, but he had allowed Rob to linger and mull over the week's pilchard hauls, the performance of their boats and sea conditions. Rob had smiled very pleasantly at Evie then eyed the teapot. She had poured a cup for him and her father, drinking her own as she got on with washing the dishes. She had not really minded Rob being there, or when he had enquired about the wandering Smoky and stroked the lazy Fluffy. His sisters had said he didn't like cats but it seemed he was warming to Evie's. After Rob left, her father had muttered, 'Thank goodness he's gone, jumped up big-head.' But Davey hadn't said any more so he didn't seem to really object to Rob's presence. And he probably wouldn't object to Rob taking her out for a meal, particularly a daytime meal.

Did she want to go out with Rob? To be at some time physically alone with him on a different footing to when he'd rescued Smoky? Rob was handsome and manly. His manliness was enticing, but it also unnerved her. Rob had sworn to be respectful, vowed that she had nothing to fear, so there was nothing really stopping her from taking the plunge. Evie's emotions were all over the place. She put her hands together. 'Dear Heavenly Father, tell me what to do.'

No peace came to her now, as had happened on other occasions. She had to make the decision herself. If only her mother was here to advise her. There was Judy and Alison but they would be biased in Rob's favour. Beth. It would be good to talk to Beth about this. She could give an impartial opinion. Evie had seen Beth twice this week. Beth had told Evie her friend had gone home.

'You'll miss her very much,' Evie had said.

'The house seems so quiet without her and her little dog. But I'm not leaving Portcowl,

Evie,' Beth smiled. 'I've got everything to stay for.'

'I'm so glad, Beth,' Evie had replied with meaning.

'I'm going to work at it so we can see each other when and wherever we like. Do you want that too, Evie? I think we have the right to be officially known as sisters, don't you?'

'Very much so, I think my mum would approve if she'd met you. But it still means winning my father over.' Evie had been a little worried.

'We can work on that together. Evie, there is one place where we could meet that's quiet nearly all the time, the churchyard. I'll take flowers for my brother and you could bring some for your mother. I'll have a picnic with me, enough for two. I'm sure you know some nice secluded places where we can chat in peace. What do you say?'

Evie was delighted with the notion, although it went against the grain to make plans so furtively while knowing her father would disapprove. They were to meet next Tuesday afternoon.

Her father and Rob would be home shortly from Newlyn and the moment Davey was in the door Evie would show him Rob's letter. Only regarding Beth would she hold anything back from him. Davey would quite likely say it was up to her if she wanted to accept Rob's invitation, but he would also make it plain he'd prefer it if she gave Rob a firm no. Mixed feelings and

323

longings caused chaos in her mind. Why shouldn't she step out with a young man? She would keep it innocent. Then again, why couldn't Rob have kept on virtually ignoring her? She had felt safe not having to consider romance and its furtherance. Yet Rob had numerous points of attraction, and as Judy had pointed out, it would be ideal if Evie only had to move in next door, from where she could still look after Davey, if things grew serious with him. Evie did not want in the slightest to end up like Muriel Oakley. And now she had been urged to think about it, she did not want to miss out on having children. Her mother had said a thousand times that she would never have missed out on having Evie, and that her child was a blessing to her. Evie wanted to know what that blessing was like. For the first time she saw Davey as being over-possessive with her. And she thought him a little selfish to want to deny her own sister.

After several days at sea during which the pilchard fleets had experienced mixed fortunes, Rob walked close beside Davey, whistling cheerfully as they made their way towards their respective back doors. The men wore smarter clothes for the journey to Newlyn and home again. Although Davey was speeding along trying to shake Rob off, he was no match for Rob's longer legs. 'I'll be dropping in later, Davey,' Rob drawled.

'Better if you just dropped dead!' And Davey

used foul language for the first time in his life, elbowing the brash younger man aside as he bulldozed through his back gate and went into his home.

Rob chuckled, halting to peer through the open top of the Vages' stable door. He saw Evie on her feet, facing her father with a pale blue envelope in her hand. Rob smirked at Davey's back and smiled over Evie's intention. It was Rob's letter she held and she was about to show it to Davey. Rob was confident that if she had wanted to shun him she would have destroyed the letter without ever intending to speak about it.

'Another cup of tea, Dad?' Evie asked, on edge. Ten minutes had passed since he had read Rob's letter and he had not spoken a word.

'Yes please, my handsome, and I'll have another slice of cake.'

He had replied so quietly and as if dreadfully hurt. Evie eyed him while getting the drink and food, wishing with all her heart she had burnt that wretched letter.

Davey spooned sugar into his tea and stirred it slowly. 'Sit down, Evie.'

Evie did so, full of guilt and wanting to blurt out that she was sorry and would forget Rob and other men for the rest of her life. She owed Davey too much to make him miserable.

'Do you want to go for this meal, Evie? Don't be afraid to tell me the truth.' Davey looked straight at her, his expression neutral.

'It doesn't matter,' she murmured forlornly, admonishing herself for sounding so self-pitying. That hadn't been her intention. 'I'll tell him not to come round any more.'

'You don't have to do that. You're a grown woman, twenty-five years old. If you want to walk out with someone that's natural and you have my blessing. I won't pretend I like Praed. I see him as a selfish so-and-so and I don't believe he'd stay faithful to a wife. He thinks he's the cat's whiskers. S'pose he's got one or two things going for him. Go out for this meal if you want to, Evie, but I implore you to be careful of him. Don't say nothing for now, I can see your chin wobbling. You're upset and un-settled. There's no need to be, I'll always be here to protect you. Now come and give your old dad a hug.'

Evie flung her arms round his neck and Davey kissed her. 'There's a good girl. Show me what you've been stitching this week, then I'll tell you what I've been up to. We having pasties for tea, eh? Can't wait. Oh, I got you a little present, my handsome. With all them painters around about Newlyn I took a look at some woman's work where she'd set up an easel, after all the boats were in and fish market was over. She does watercolours. She had *Morenwyn* in nicely and there's a white cat strolling along the quay. I thought 'twas done well but she said she was disappointed with it. Anyway I knew you'd really like it, so I asked her if I could buy it and she let me have it for ... well, never mind that.'

Evie loved the painting. Davey found a hook and hung it up on the picture rail. 'There,' he said proudly. 'You can think of me every day on the boat when I'm not here. Want to go a stroll round? I'll buy us some ice cream.'

With her father talking more than she had ever known him to and not intending to sit in his armchair and read the newspaper as he usually did when he arrived home from Newlyn, Evie knew he was trying to take her mind off Rob.

Suddenly Rob was there. He knocked briskly on the back door and came straight in. Evie saw her father's expression darken like thunderclouds. 'Hello, Evie.' Rob smiled deeply at her. 'Hello again, Davey.'

Evie was watching Davey and missed Rob mouthing something to him.

'There's *someone* on the way here.' Rob jerked his dark head towards the quay. 'Jack Mitchell's on his way here with your baccy, Davey.'

Evie was shocked at how ugly Davey's weathered features turned. Then he rearranged his cast. 'He is? I'll nip and get it. Let him in I'll never get rid of him, he's such a gasbag.' Davey was straight out the front door.

Evie thought her father had acted strangely, yet it seemed he had deliberately left her alone with Rob.

Beth had her head up, but was not really

looking at anything as she rehearsed her lines to Davey Vage. It was hard to know what to say at first for she didn't know who would open the front door to her. She thought the fisherman would take affront at her going round to the back of the cottage; that was for closer acquaintances. Then, with trepidation, she saw a short man tearing along the quay front, dodging past meandering holidaymakers and giving a mere grunt in response to a neighbour. Her heart sank, for this had to be Davey Vage, alerted somehow to her approach, and he was bearing down on her like a demon out of hell.

Rob had never felt so smug or amused. Thanks to Elizabeth Tresaile he could play Davey and Evie like a golden fiddle. Evie's darling little face was as red as a raspberry now she had been suddenly left alone with him. Now he would play his master card. 'Evie,' he said softly, his voice all concern. 'You may want to know this. I also saw Elizabeth Tresaile, and she was obviously on her way here. Davey's made it plain he doesn't want the two of you to mix. There might be some unpleasantness.'

'Beth's coming here now?' Evie wrung her hands. 'I'd better go out there.'

Round the quay, Ken Tresaile was watering the pub's window boxes. The flurry of Davey's charge made him look in that direction. Beth was heading the other way towards Davey, gradually faltering in her steps for she was aware of a coming clash. Now Evie was out of

328

the cottage and running after Davey, with Rob Praed a step behind her. News had filtered round the cove that Rob had designs on Evie. Evie was Ken's niece and he thought all in all that Rob would make her a good husband, but he knew Rob would have to get past Davey first. It went without saying that Davey would hate Evie becoming involved with Beth. Now everyone was about to be embroiled in a fierce wrangle. Davey rarely lost his temper but when he felt pushed to the limit he came down on others like a raging storm. Dropping the watering can, Ken hastened to join what would soon be an overwrought assemblage.

Most of the passers-by had gone on their way, but some were still lingering about the area, and Beth found herself for the first time facing Davey Vage full on. Even if she had met him before, she would hardly have recognized him thanks to the twisted, gargoyle-like expression on his face. Beth quaked with a flash of disquiet. There was something more than just hostility in the fisherman. 'You must be Mr Vage,' she said. 'You obviously know who I am.'

She thought he would interrupt or hurl harsh words at her but he remained silent, his hands taut at his sides while he glared at her. His expression was more malicious than a barrage of fury. He was making her plead and she resented it. 'I'm no threat to you, Mr Vage. I only want to see Evie once or twice a week. I won't enter your home. I won't encroach on

329

your time with Evie at all.'

Evie, and the tall, ruggedly good-looking man she knew to be Rob Praed from the photograph of him on Posy Praed's mantelpiece, had reached them. Evie was gazing at her father appealingly. Now their Uncle Ken was there, with a no-nonsense look on his face. Beth continued, firmly now, 'When Evie and I met we immediately connected, we're sisters and nothing can change that. Please, can't we put the past in the past?'

'Is this what you want, Evie?' Davey stared directly at his adopted daughter. His expression softened but there was accusation in his tone. 'Do you wish to see this woman?'

Mortified, Evie glanced at Beth. Beth was sorry that Evie, so reserved and private, had to endure this public confrontation.

Evie's pause allowed Ken to speak up. 'I don't really understand what objections you could have to letting these two young women meet, Davey. Beth is my niece and so is Evie and I've never shunned either of them. They were both innocent victims of my immoral brother, but they've had the opportunity to do well in life and that is exactly what they've done. They are decent, pleasant, intelligent young women. They want to be part of a family, and if you're set to deny them that then it'll be nothing but damned selfish of you.'

Davey seemed unmoved by Ken's speech. 'Evie, I asked you a question.'

Evie was heartened by her uncle's support but

330

she did not need it to determine her answer. 'Yes, Dad, I do want to see Beth, very much. Please say it will be all right with you.'

Rob pushed his hands into his pockets. He was enjoying this. If Evie got her way it meant Davey was losing his grip on her. Rob had no objection if Evie saw her half-sister, there was no good reason to stop it; family was important, and Beth Tresaile was a tasty piece. If Davey succeeded he would be pleased Rob had put him on to Beth Tresaile's presence here today. Rob planned to whisper later to Davey, 'Sorry, Evie was out the door like lightning after you.'

Davey knew he was in an impossible situation. If he banned Evie from seeing this blasted Tresaile woman it would drive a wedge between him and his daughter, but he wouldn't accept the Tresaile woman under his roof if he could help it. He was aware of Rob smirking. Davey's heart was wrapped in loathing. *But you, you bastard, there's no way I'll let you marry my Evie. You're not good enough for her.* Davey's determination was growing fiercer. He could never trust Rob not to blab one day about his sexuality in order to separate him from Evie, or just out of spite. He would have to still Rob Praed's mouth good and proper.

Davey cleared his throat and all eyes studied him more intently. 'I wouldn't dream of saying otherwise, Evie. Slip back inside and get changed. Why not meet Miss Tresaile in The Tea-shop?' Davey voiced the words but each one nearly choked him. At least this was a way of

331

getting Evie away from Praed for the moment.

A variety of thanks were sent Davey's way. 'I'll walk you to The Teashop, Beth,' Ken said. After exchanging happy smiles with Beth, Evie was preparing to walk home with her father. Rob was going to follow on, his hands still jauntily in his pockets.

But Beth had something to say to someone else, the man who was obviously hanging around Evie and obviously for his own ends. Rob Praed had too much of Phil Tresaile's character in him and Beth wasn't going to allow him to taint her sister's life. 'Mr Praed, I've heard a lot about you.' She pitched her voice at its most superior, ensuring she had an avid audience. 'You dallied with the feelings of my friend, Miss Copeland, then you cut her off as if she was so much rubbish, humiliating her in front of your family. Not the act of a decent man, don't you agree?'

The gasp escaping from Evie's throat told Rob his campaign was lost with her, good and proper. She wouldn't consider him now; she was too bloody righteous. Well, it was her loss. 'I've got no more time to waste,' he snarled in an effort to save face. Shrugging his shoulders as if he didn't care, but scowling at Beth because he hated being beaten and this would ensure he was on the wrong end of his companions' mockery for the first time in his life, he made a show at sauntering off.

'Good for you, Beth,' Ken said. 'Rob isn't totally bad really, but he's not for Evie. I hope you're not disappointed, Evie.'

'Not at all,' she said. All Evie cared about right now was establishing true sisterhood with Beth, and she would do everything to ensure her father was comfortable about it.

'Evie will be with you shortly,' Davey told Beth. Silently cursing Ken Tresaile for his untimely interruption, for Ken had said nothing that could be taken issue with, Davie took Evie away.

He damned Elizabeth Tresaile all the way to hell but he was grateful to her for getting rid of Praed so efficiently and condescendingly. But if she expected too much from Evie, or upset her in the slightest way, Davey would work on ways to turn Evie against her. He was still worried about Praed though. He had just been made a fool of in public. He would never be able to boast again that he always got what he wanted. He'd brood over the way his scheme to make Evie his wife had been cut off so quickly. He might decide to take revenge by spilling his knowledge about Davey and his lost love.

Praed had to be shut up for good.

'Thanks for coming to my rescue, Uncle Ken,' Beth said, having walked proudly on his arm to The Teashop. 'Would you like to join us?'

'Not this time, my dear. This is special between you and your sister, but I shall invite both my nieces to share a meal with me soon. You know, I'd like to see your mother some day. She and I never fell out.'

333

'I'm sure she'd like that. She always speaks well of you.'

Beth thought she would burst with joy. Everything had worked out better than she'd hoped. From where she stood and waited she could see the Vage front door. Seconds later Evie, in high heels, a pretty hat and cradling a clutch bag, was hurrying along, head up and smiling and waving to her.

Twenty-Six

'Beth! Kitty's on the phone for you!' Joe yelled up the stairs.

Beth bounded down to the hall and entered a playful tussle with Joe to claim the ivory-coloured handpiece, for he wanted to go on chatting to Kitty. Joe went off with Chaplin, chuckling.

Beth got comfy on the telephone seat. 'Hello Kitty, how are you? Tell me all your news. I must burst in first and tell you Evie will soon be arriving here to spend the entire day. Mark's bringing his little girl this afternoon and we're going to have a big picnic on the lawn. Mum and Mrs Reseigh are going overboard in the kitchen at the moment, so I'm on bed-making duties. Joe, Richard and Lily are going to provide us with some entertainment. I think Chaplin will be involved too. How's little Grace? Sorry, I'm babbling on. Over to you.'

'It's lovely to hear how happy you are. Thank you again for putting Rob Praed in his place. Mind you I bet he couldn't really give a fig and already has his sights set on someone else. The thing is,' Kitty sighed deeply down the line, 'I'm afraid there's some bad news from this quarter.'

'Oh Kitty, is it something to do with Grace?'

'No, she's chipper. It's poor Stuart,' and Kitty let out a watery sob. 'I can't believe this has happened to him. Not Stuart, he doesn't deserve it.'

'Tell me what's happened, Kitty!' Beth was plunged into turmoil, all the old feelings she'd had for the lover she had adored resurfacing.

'As soon as I got back I realized the second honeymoon had gone terribly wrong. Then Stuart told me things hadn't been good between him and Connie for a very long time. And last night Connie admitted she's been having an affair. It started just before she and Stuart went on the trip abroad. She told Stuart she'd been willing to give their marriage a second chance, but it didn't work out for her and she lied about wanting another baby. She said she'd fallen out of love with him soon after the children were born, and that although she loves the children she found motherhood stultifying and hated not being able to follow her own dreams. Poor Stuart, it seems he had barely got used to that announcement when she told him she was leaving him there and then, and going to join her lover in London. And from there they are going to travel round the world.

'Stuart said he didn't beg her to stay, he could see her mind was made up. He said he and Connie talked calmly together and then they told the children Mummy was going off on a trip with a friend. It wasn't unusual for her to do that so the children were quite happy about it. Stuart's got a full staff so it won't affect the children until they start to wonder when their mother's coming back. Connie is insisting she doesn't want maintenance. Well, she's always had more money than Stuart. I can't come to terms with all this, Beth. Poor Stu, he's so shocked and down.'

'I'm so sorry for you all,' Beth replied calmly, for she was in control of herself now; her former feelings of loving and longing for Stuart had faded away inside her within seconds. Stuart was in the past and now she had her new life here. 'All you can do is support Stuart and the children.'

'Beth, Stuart's asked me to ask you something.'

Beth closed her eyes and sighed inwardly. She had a good idea what was coming. 'Yes, Kitty.'

'Well, it's a lot to ask really, I know, but the autumn college term doesn't start for Stuart until a couple of weeks yet, and he was wondering if he might come down with the children and stay in a hotel close to you. I've told him how peaceful and glorious the cliffs and the sea are there and he thought it might help soothe him and help him accept his marriage is over. I'd come down as well and amuse the children to give him the chance to take some long walks and go out in the boats. Perhaps we could all drop in at Owles House, and the children can run wild with Joe and his little gang. Stuart says he'd really like to see you again and meet

337

Christina. What do you think, Beth? Would it be an imposition?'

Beth paused out of kindness to Kitty before she gave her answer, but she had it complete and ready. 'Oh Kitty, I'm afraid it wouldn't be a good time, even though it would be wonderful to have you here again, and to see Stuart and the children. Things have moved along here, you see. I was about to telephone you, actually, to tell you all about it. I finally had a confrontation with Davey Vage, and after some tricky moments he's agreed for Evie and me to meet, though we're taking things slowly to appease him. Evie will be here soon to spend the day, and this afternoon Mark is bringing his little girl for a picnic on the lawn. Mum has offered to do what she can to help the new curate bring the vicarage up to scratch to live in, and she's drummed up some help from the cove, even from among the non-Anglicans and non-churchgoers. The locals feel it's important that their parish church and the churchyard where their loved ones are buried are returned to good order. The Oakleys' things have been removed, but there's enough junk left for Mark to keep several bonfires going. Mrs Reseigh, Posy Praed and I, and Evie too, are going to give the house a good scrub through. So you can see there just wouldn't be any time for us to entertain. I do feel bad about it.'

The only thing Beth felt bad about was putting Kitty off. To Beth, Stuart's idea appeared to be that he would turn to her on the rebound, but she considered herself too good for that. She wasn't a woman to be picked up as second best. Besides, her life was here now. Stuart would not want to move here with his family and she certainly was not going to return to Wiltshire.

'There's no need to feel bad, Beth. I'm glad that you've said all you have. I think it's better for Stuart to face the desertion head on and spend lots of time with Louis and Martha. The children love Grace, by the way, she will be a good distraction for them, and I'm here to see them all through. Well, Beth, I'm so pleased to hear you can see Evie openly now. It sounds like you'll all have a lot of fun getting that murky old vicarage sorted out. I wish I were there with you really. I'll pop down to Cornwall in the near future.'

Dear Kitty, Beth thought as she went outside and walked down the drive to meet Evie at the entrance, *you're not a bit jealous of my new relationship with Evie. You're a true friend and no one deserves true happiness more than you.*

As for Kitty's brother, Stuart had to find his own way out of his emotional troubles.

With the fish berth of *Morenwyn* only half filled with shiny-bodied pilchards it would take only about an hour for the catch to be unloaded at the quayside of Newlyn fish market. Sadly the fleets had not even had a fair week, so the wages would be low. The fishermen thought nothing of it, they were used to it. The sea was their master.

All week the pilchard numbers had been far from Davey's priority. He had been biding his time for the opportunity to catch Rob Praed alone. *Our Lily* was next in line after *Morenwyn* to come alongside the quayside. From *Morenwyn* only six maunds – baskets – of pilchards were hoisted up and loaded on to a wagon, to be carted away for salting in the vats. The merchant had to be given back two hundred fish out of every ten thousand, and the night's work, in which Davey had earned salt-water boils thanks to the muscle-tugging exertion, had earned the crew six pounds, a quarter of what could be earned on a good night.

Later both luggers berthed across the quayside, *Morenwyn* the second and *Our Lily* the third boat in a row stretching across the harbour. It meant the crews of the outer boats had to cut across their neighbours to alight on the quay. After the night's hard graft the fishermen went through the rituals of washing down their boats and making any necessary repairs to wood and nets. Davey offered to stay behind today and scrub out the cabin while the others went off to fetch fuel, food and water, and to Davey's delight he saw that Rob was the last man on *Our Lily*. Good. Now he could still Praed's mouth for good.

Davey gave a prearranged signal to someone lingering on the quayside, someone who was making her presence known – although it wasn't necessary, she stood out like some

340

garish landmark.

Davey watched that someone clamber clumsily on to the *Pilgrim*, the lugger berthed alongside the stone wall, then chivalrously helped that someone on to his boat. 'Welcome aboard, Miss Hopley. Time couldn't be better. You met Rob Praed last night in the pub as I'd instructed. Here's your money. Do a good job on him.'

'Oh, Mr Anonymous,' the excessively made-up, young-looking bottle blonde simpered, adjusting her net stockings. 'I'll give him the time of his life. I can hardly wait. It'll be a treat to even go near that handsome hunk of manhood.'

'Don't forget I'm paying you handsomely to tell a white lie and then to keep your mouth shut. Right, I'll call him out of the cabin for you.' Hiding a smug sneer, Davey yelled, 'Rob! Rob Praed! There's someone here for you.' As Davey intended, the men in greasy overalls who'd eyed the tart on the quayside were staring his way.

Rob poked his dark head out of the neighbouring cabin, a cigarette between his lips. Puzzlement was quickly traded in for a saucy smile. 'Sabrina, isn't it? What are you doing here?'

'I thought I'd come and see your big boat, Robbie.' The blonde swivelled her hips and looked sultry in an imitation of Mae West. 'Aren't you going to invite me over there?'

Davey kept behind Sabrina Hopley, looking thoroughly disgusted. He knew that would

341

amuse Rob and he was equally sure the young braggart would invite the tart, in the area just for this job alone, on board *Our Lily* just to snigger at him. Sure enough Rob beckoned the girl on to his boat. Shortly afterwards Davey truly was disgusted at the noises coming from the next cabin. Davey had told Sabrina to make the proceedings last and she was going at it with gusto, but Davey was horrified at how quickly Rob Praed could bed another woman after losing out on Evie.

He can smirk for all he's worth and make all sorts of snipes at me, Davey thought with malicious glee, *but I'll have the last laugh.*

Twenty-five minutes later, Rob was shouting at his companion to 'Get out of here!' Sabrina appeared from the cabin and put her hands out for Davey to take her back across *Morenwyn.* She made a spectacle of straightening her skirt and checking her stocking seams, then she puckered her lips at Davey as if she was saucily mocking an appalled man. Instead she whispered, 'Mission accomplished, nice meeting you. Call on me anytime.'

Clambering over to *Our Lily*, Davey peeped into the cabin.

Rob was shoving a mop over the floor with angry force, his expression as dark as night. 'What do you want?' he growled.

'She seemed a bit shaken by your shouting, that's all. Fleece you, did she? You got to watch those tarts,' Davey chuckled. Of course she had fleeced the unsuspecting fool. Sabrina would

342

have demanded a great deal more than her normal charge from the young stud as payment for keeping silent that he'd just had sex with an under-age girl. Like any tart worth her trade she'd be a convincing liar. Even a rumour of the kind would put Rob in Lofty's bad books and he might be sacked from the boat. 'Bit young looking, wasn't she? Not much experience yet then?'

'It's none of your business, Vage. Clear off!'

'Fair enough. All I can say is thank God my Evie is safe from you.'

Davcy went back on board *Morenwyn* and got on with scrubbing it out. In a bit he would make a mug of tea and light his pipe. The rest of the crew would be back soon and they would all get their heads down for a well-deserved nap; Davey would fall asleep knowing that he had tied up Rob Praed's tongue from causing trouble against him for good, now that Praed too had committed an offence under the law.

Twenty-Seven

It's sad Kitty isn't here with us all now, Beth thought, as she sat at the picnic table. The weather was still warm enough for such an occasion. Kitty was so much a part of the family at Owles House it would have been lovely to see her, and quirky little Grace trotting on after Chaplin. When the dogs had sat side by side they had looked like a huge rock protecting its little sister rock a little way out from the shore.

Mark, Joe and Richard had carried out the long table and eight chairs on to the lawn. Beth was sitting between Christina and Evie, with Mrs Reseigh at one end of the table. On the other side were Joe, Lily and Richard, and down at the end was Mark, with Rowella on his lap. The white linen tablecloth was spread with sandwiches, scones, savoury and sweet tartlets, little dishes of jam and strawberries and clotted cream. There were brandy snaps and a magnificent iced sponge cake. Christina poured out tea in good china and Mrs Reseigh poured glasses of cordial for the children.

Beth was delighted that Evie was relaxed and enjoying the meal, not shy in helping herself to food and politely asking for more. After Kitty's telephone call, Beth had gone down to the end of the drive to meet Evie. Evie had been striding along in a new pink hat and a new dark pink panelled dress trimmed with piping, and sparkling with a pretty brooch. Her hair was cut a little shorter and nicely waved. She was slim and vibrant and her new confidence showed all her previously hidden beauty. The girls broke into a half run and met with a close hug.

'I can't believe I'm here,' Evie laughed a really happy laugh. 'Are you sure Mrs Vyvyan doesn't mind me coming to her house?'

'She couldn't be more delighted.' Beth put her arm through Evie's and they strolled along. 'We're going to have a wonderful day.'

Christina had walked on after Beth, using her walking stick more as a precaution than a necessity. 'It's good to meet you properly, Miss Vage. We've barely caught a glimpse of each other over the years, since both of us rarely go far. You're very welcome here. I'm so glad that your father has relented and you and Beth can be together whenever you like.'

'Thank you, Mrs Vyvyan.' Evie had soon lost her shyness with Christina. 'Your house is beautiful. I've glimpsed it on the bus but I've always wanted a closer look.'

'Well, Beth can show you over the house and gardens. The sun is gently bright and the breeze is our friend. We have nothing to do except enjoy ourselves.'

Beth felt she and Evie were growing closer by

345

the moment as they toured the house. Evie was fascinated with the size of the house and its elegant furnishings and paintings.

'I had a happier childhood than you did, Beth,' Evie said looking round Beth's former bedroom. 'I can sense the sorrow you felt in here. Is Mrs Vyvyan going to keep the room like this?'

'She has talked about putting all the toys in one corner and turning the room into a store for a charity. We've been talking about starting something to help neglected children and their families where the parents find it hard to cope. We'll make and collect things to raise funds. Mum's thinking of holding a winter bazaar and an annual summer fête here in the grounds. She's certain she can manage that. I shall be the coordinator. It will be a memorial fund in Francis Vyvyan's name. He was a very caring man. Did you know him?'

'Not really, but he always acknowledged me kindly, when because of my circumstances many others didn't. I'd like to be involved in your charity. I could make some soft toys.'

'See,' Beth had slipped her arm round Evie's waist and Evie had instantly done the same, 'we're all one big gang. Joe is very resourceful. He says he'll make up some typical games, coconut shies, races, and that sort of thing.' Beth had become serious. 'Evie, do you want to talk about our father?'

'Not really, unless you do. He means nothing to me. I've had the joy of a wonderful man bringing me up. He's my father. I know he's a little crotchety but hopefully he'll come round quite soon to the thought of us.'

'I won't do anything to make Mr Vage resent me. When he's home we'll meet away from there. Evie, you know about my twin Philip, and he was your brother too. I want Phil Tresaile left in the past, but now we've got plenty of time to talk I'm afraid I'm going to mention another child he fathered. It's a tragic story.'

When Beth had recounted the terrible trauma Muriel Oakley had undergone as a result of their father's abuse, Beth noticed Evie wasn't greatly surprised. Evie said gravely, 'That dreadful confession explains a lot. The day I took Miss Oakley home she said he was there in the churchyard tormenting her then he raped her. I thought she was rambling. I could hardly pass it on to you, Beth. Poor Miss Oakley. I hope she's found peace and comfort in the nursing home. I'd like to visit her.'

'I'm going there to see her next week. We can go together in the motor car. Isn't it great we can do things together?'

They had spent a good morning in which Evie had petted the lazy, sociable Charlie, and then shared a ham and salad lunch on the terrace with Joe and Christina. Evie had been a little worried about how Joe would judge her but he took her presence, and the fact of who she was, in his stride. As long as people respected his mother he was happy to accept them.

Now the larger group were tucking into the

delicious picnic. Rowella, her gorgeous dark looks partly concealed by a voluminous sun hat, was the star with her toddler chatter. She nibbled the food Mark chose for her and she pointed and chuckled and made cute faces and drew heaps of gushing praise, and lots of adoring kisses from Mark. Even Richard, the one person expected to be offhand about a little girl, was captivated with her.

After the feasting was over, the food was left covered in muslin so people could help themselves to more at their leisure. Joe organized a game of croquet for all except the two older ladies, who sat in padded garden chairs under parasols and watched Rowella, under another parasol, playing on a blanket with some of Beth's old toys and the bagful of things Mark had brought for her. Eventually Rowella became drowsy and snuggled up to sleep against a dozing Chaplin.

While Beth played croquet purely for the fun, she was surprised at how competitive Mark was over the game. He won the first round and conceded to Joe on the second. Evie was quite useless at it and laughed every time she missed a hoop. Richard and Lily bickered all the way through. 'Put a sock in it, both of you,' Joe ordered them, but neither took any notice of him. Mark and Evie hardly passed a word to each other.

Fresh drinks and a strawberry trifle, Joe's favourite, were served, and Joe and his gang took theirs, as well as plates piled high with other food, off to the tree house. Giving Beth a sneaky look, Mrs Reseigh passed a cup of tea to Evie. 'Here, dear, pass this to Mark for me, please, and this plate of sandwiches. He don't go in for much sweet stuff.'

Mark had dropped down on the rug and was stroking the still sleeping Rowella's shoulder, his eyes entirely on her. Beth and Mrs Reseigh and Christina all pretended not to watch, but they did so avidly.

Evie advanced slowly on Mark, who was half turned away from her. 'Excuse me, ahem, Mr Reseigh. Your mother asked me to give you these.'

Mark turned round to her. 'Oh, um, thank you, Miss Vage.'

Mrs Reseigh nudged Beth and Christina on either side of her. 'There now, wouldn't that be good, come a day...'

'They will need more than a little help in that direction,' Christina said, but her eyes were bright over the prospect of a possible romance.

'Well, one thing's for sure. If I could head Mark in the right direction, Davey Vage would not get in the way of me,' Mrs Reseigh promised stoutly.

Beth simply smiled. This summer she and Evie had made a new beginning as sisters. Anything else for them – well, what would be would be...

Her eyes drifted down over the garden and the cliff top and out into the bay. All indeed was a vision of enchantment. When she had arrived here just a few weeks ago she had thought the whole scene held an insidious magic. She knew differently now.

There was magic here, but it was pure and gentle.